I0565923

THE VIEW FROM CASTLE ALWAYS

THE VIEW FROM CASTLE ALWAYS

MELISSA MCSHANE

Night Harbor Publishing

Copyright © 2019 Melissa McShane

Published by Night Harbor Publishing

ISBN-13 9781949663068

ISBN-10 194966306X

All rights reserved.

No part of this book may be reproduced in any form or by any electronic or mechanical means, including information storage and retrieval systems, without written permission from the author, except for the use of brief quotations in a book review.

This book is a work of fiction. Names, characters, businesses, organizations, places, events, and incidents either are the product of the author's imagination or are used fictitiously. Any resemblance to actual persons living or dead, events, or locales is entirely coincidental.

Cover design by Adrian Păsărin (Adrian DSGNS)

Dedicated to Ivan,
in thanks for many years of snuggles and silent purrs

CHAPTER ONE

The world felt fractured, broken into jagged splinters that dug into Ailanthe's head and chest and legs. She gagged on the smell of sap filling the air like syrup, gagged and coughed and tried to sit up. Her body refused to obey. She felt as if the mother tree's roots had her tied to the ground, which, she now realized, was digging hard, cold knuckles into her back and hips. She couldn't even open her eyes.

An atonal thrumming sound that echoed in her bones resolved itself into the sound of a harp; it seemed to be coming from everywhere at once. With a great effort, she dragged her eyelids open and saw the branches of the mother tree's many trunks arching high above her head, unexpectedly blurry in the morning light. "Banazir, what—" she began, addressing the unseen player of the harp.

"You're alive," her mother said, and her face swam into view, as blurry as the branches. She put her arms around Ailanthe and lifted her, clutching at her so tightly it hurt. "We thought—Ailanthe, what happened?"

"I don't remember anything," Ailanthe said, but fragments of memory were beginning to piece themselves together. She'd risen early, crossed the bridge from one trunk to another to the stores where she could get a bite of cheese before breakfast, come back along the main branch, and then...the rest was gray nothing.

"I think you broke your back," Banazir said, still out of Ailanthe's line of sight. The *kerthor* continued to strum the harp, whose music was gradually becoming melodic as her magic wrapped around Ailanthe. It was making her whole again, she realized, easing the pounding headache and the stabbing agony in her legs and lower back, lifting away the other miscellaneous pains Ailanthe was only just becoming conscious of. "I had to use a song I barely knew to put you back together again. You must have fallen four flights."

Ailanthe went numb. "Fell?"

Her mother nodded. "Varden saw you. You...slipped."

"That's impossible." Ailanthe struggled away from her mother's embrace and sat upright, blinking to clear her vision. "Impossible. No one falls." But she could remember now. Two steps along the wide branch, and it had...*bucked*, rippling like the ocean waves in her father's stories, knocking her off balance, another impossible thing. She had taken her first steps on branches higher than that one. In the whole twenty-three years of her life she had never fallen. No Lindurian ever fell from a mother tree's embrace.

"It's all right," her mother said, her voice trembling beneath its soothing tones. "It doesn't mean anything."

Ailanthe pushed herself to her feet, closed her eyes against a momentary dizziness, then looked up at the branches of the mother tree again. From this perspective, here in one of the clearings between the trunks, the many rope bridges spanning the distance from branch to branch looked like black webs against the cloudless sky. A few people stood on those bridges, or on the thick branches wide enough for three of those people to walk with arms linked, and stared down at her. Backlit by the rising sun, their faces were impossible to read. She looked around at the few other people standing around the clearing; they all stared at her, expressionless, as if deferring judgment on whatever she had done to make the tree—*no, it wasn't me, it was an accident. It doesn't mean anything.*

She walked with slow steps toward the nearest trunk. The two women standing near it moved out of her way, stepping to either side of her as if showing her honor. *Or attending my funeral.* Ailanthe put her hand out to caress the silky bark of the mother tree. It tingled, but nothing more. She clambered up the rope ladder strung from the first flight to where it was tethered to the ground, moving more quickly as her confidence returned, and pulled herself onto the first broad branch—

—and sharp pain like icy needles stabbed at her hands and arms where they touched the living wood, and she screamed and slipped backward, flailing at the ladder. Her bare feet tangled in the ropes, her hands caught at a rung, and she hung there, upside down, panting. Tears pooled in her eyes and slipped down over her temples. Then there were hands, helping her disentangle herself, half-carrying her to the ground, and she tried to stand, but found she needed those hands' support if she didn't want to collapse. The pain was gone, but in its place was a terrible weakness, as if something had sapped her energy and left her wrung out and empty. She closed her eyes and focused on breathing.

"It's an accident," her mother was insisting, "you must be ill, sometimes that can make a person lose her balance...." Her voice trailed off.

Ailanthe opened her eyes and looked up at her; her mother, four inches taller than she, looked as drained as she felt. Ailanthe ran her fingers through her short brown hair, trying to smooth it. "I'm not ill," she said. "You know what this means. The trees have rejected me."

Her mother turned away. Banazir said, "That hasn't happened to anyone in the settlement since...it must be over one hundred years."

"Well, you won't be able to say that anymore," Ailanthe said, but the joke came out sounding flat and weak.

"I'll start searching the records," Banazir said. "You're just out of balance, that's all, and someone must have written down how to fix that."

"What if you...you could stay on the ladders," Ailanthe's mother said, "and we could cover the branches near our home..."

Ailanthe put her arms around her. She felt strangely empty, as if every emotion had been drained from her along with her energy. "I think," she said, "we should find me a tent."

THEY ATE on the ground that evening despite the chill in the early spring air, not only Ailanthe's family but the entire settlement, consuming what was almost the last of their winter stores in near silence. Once again Ailanthe was reminded of a funeral—but, then, for a Lindurian to be out of balance with the trees that sheltered and nurtured them was a little like death, wasn't it? She still felt numb inside. At some point her predicament would become real, and then...she had no idea what she'd do then. She couldn't live on the ground forever, tethered like the rope ladders.

"Ailanthe," Banazir said, and she looked at the young *kerthor,* who had just leaped down from a low branch and was advancing toward her. In the half-light of twilight, Ailanthe could see everyone else was looking at her, not at Banazir, and she laced her fingers together in her lap and wished she were not so conspicuous. The pale skin of her hands seemed to glow in the moonlight as if lit from within.

"I've read everything there is," Banazir went on, "which isn't much. But it's not hopeless. Just...unexpected."

"Tell me."

"You have to go to Castle Always," Banazir said.

It *was* unexpected, so unexpected Ailanthe at first didn't understand what she'd said. "Castle Always?" she said. "That's for people who want a destiny. I'm happy with who I am."

"It sets you on your true path. It reads your heart, gives you your destiny, and sends you where you're supposed to be. The records imply that means bringing you back into harmony with the trees."

"'Imply'?"

"The earliest records are over two hundred years old. I'm lucky I can read any of them."

"Castle Always," Ailanthe repeated.

4

Her father took her hand in his and squeezed it. "If that's what it takes," he said, "then I think you should do it."

"But—" her mother began.

"You're right," Ailanthe said. She stood and faced Banazir. "I don't suppose those records say where it is?"

Banazir shrugged. "It exists in all times and in all places," she said. "I think, if you're meant to find it, it doesn't matter in which direction you go."

"Then I'll leave in the morning." She took a deep breath. "I've always wanted to travel. Maybe not this way, but...it's not that bad, is it?"

"It's too soon," Morwenna cried out. "There are preparations...we have to give you a farewell...."

Ailanthe looked around at all those familiar faces. "This is as good a farewell as anyone could want," she said. "And I won't need much. Mor, I just...I want to get this over with." What no one was saying was that it might be years before she returned home, depending on where the Castle sent her. If she returned at all. Three people of the settlement had left for the Castle over the last ten years, and none of them had come home.

Ailanthe looked around again, this time at the massive trunks of the mother tree, and felt again the stinging pain of her rejection. If Castle Always could restore her balance.... "It will be an adventure," she said with a weak grin, and a murmur of amusement rippled through the crowd.

"Then let's make this a celebration," Morwenna said, and embraced her. "Clear the ground, everyone, and we'll dance and sing for Ailanthe and her destiny!"

Ailanthe laughed, but to herself, she thought, *What if my destiny never brings me home?*

FOUR DAYS LATER, Ailanthe trudged through the forest in the pale light of dawn, gnawing on one of the hard, dry, odorless trail biscuits that were all the food she had left. She hadn't thought the Castle would be so difficult to find, so she'd packed lightly, and now she was regretting it. The idea of delaying her journey to gather food or set snares made her impatient, but it seemed she might have no choice.

A flock of tiny white birds, eerily silent, circled her head, and she turned to watch them flutter away like dry leaves on the wind. When she turned back around, she nearly stumbled over a low-growing bush, took a few more steps, and found herself at the edge of a clearing so sharply delineated it could not be natural. Across the clearing, looming up before her like a gray, perfectly vertical mountain, was a building that could only be Castle Always.

She stood gaping up at it for a while, barely able to comprehend its size. Its stones, which might have been hewn out of the granite cliffs of Duathenin, fit together so tightly that from where she stood she could barely make out the outlines of each one. High above her head, glass windows winked at her in the early morning light, mirror-opaque against the brightness. Ahead, set into a stone arch too plain for the Castle's grandness, were two doors not much taller than Ailanthe herself that looked entirely out of place in the majestic gray wall. There was no movement in the clearing, which was covered in long green and yellow striped grass, not even the leaping and buzzing of insects.

Ailanthe wiped her suddenly sweaty palms on her tunic and crossed the clearing to the doors. She laid her palm against the cool dead wood, a stripe of sunlight across the back of her hand providing a warm contrast, then pressed down on the plain iron latch and pushed the door open. It squealed like a dying animal, making her jump. Well, if there were anyone inside, they knew she was coming now. She took a few steps inside, letting the door close behind her with another shriek.

Beyond the door lay a short hall carpeted in black and gold that ended in a wall covered by a tapestry. Ailanthe went to look at it: it depicted a man and a woman fighting a creature with the body of a lizard and the head of a snake and wings that belonged to no bird or bat she recognized.

There were openings on either side of the hall, and she looked into one and saw tables and chairs made of dead wood, their legs carved to look like animal feet, a plush carpet thicker than meadow grass, and a long, cushioned seat drawn up before a fireplace big enough for her to curl up in. Ailanthe had never seen anything like it outside of books. She ran her finger along the back of the...*sofa*, the word was, and marveled at how it was smooth in one direction and resisted her stroking in the other. Amazing.

She turned around to look into the other room and realized with surprise that the front door had no latch on this side. Ailanthe stood back and regarded it, hands on her hips. "Already playing games, Castle?" she said. "I'll just have to find another door."

Her words sounded strange in her ears, and she clapped a hand to her mouth. "What—what language am I speaking?" she whispered. It was not Lindurian, nothing she recognized. She couldn't even remember the Lindurian words for what she'd said. *It's not permanent*, she told herself, *Banazir would have said if the people who returned couldn't speak Lindurian.* She took a deep breath and moved into the next room.

This room had one wall that was nothing but windows; it looked out not on the grassy clearing, but on a dry and cracked desert landscape with one tree that looked as if it had been dried out by the sun for a thousand lifetimes. She walked closer and laid her palm flat against the glass, which was warm from the heat of a sun much hotter than the one that shone over Lindurien. So these were magic windows. Banazir had said the Castle existed in all times and places; it made sense that people within the Castle should be able to see those places.

A soft breeze blew past her ear, carrying with it the smell of peaches. She reached up to push her short hair back into place. That the Castle might have an orchard growing within its walls would not surprise her at all.

She crossed the room to a door on the far side and opened it to find a room packed full of books, neatly lined up on the shelves, all of them matching in height and color. Ailanthe had read the few books her family owned many times over; it would take her years to read this many. She counted, did a little calculating in her head—over three hundred books! A pity she wasn't here for reading, especially since the chairs in this room looked so very inviting. She cast one last glance at the shelves, then opened the next door.

She stepped from the comfortable, warm library into a vast stone chamber paved with slabs of dark gray rock four feet on a side that were set in pale mortar that crumbled in places. High above, curving arches of white stone supported the roof, like the ribs of some unimaginably large beast. The chamber smelled of dust and old stone and made Ailanthe, who had never felt intimidated by the size of her forest home, feel small and in danger of being crushed. She straightened her spine. If the Castle were alive, it might be watching her, and she wanted to look strong. Another peach-scented breeze blew past her face, and she filled her lungs with the tantalizing smell. She was starting to feel hungry again, but food could wait.

In the center of the cavernous chamber stood another room, this one of a coarser stone that looked like undressed granite, but pale yellow instead of gray. Window arches that came to a point at the top pierced the walls in several places, and light shone from those windows, brightening the dark stone floor.

Ailanthe advanced toward it and looked through one of the arches. The room beyond was empty, its glossy waxed floor reflecting the curving wooden beams of its ceiling high above. More window openings looked down on the room from the upper stories. The light came from dozens of glass hemispheres attached to the walls that glowed steadily instead of flickering with firelight; Ailanthe reached out to touch one and yanked her hand back when it burned her finger.

Around the far side of the room were three shallow stairs going down to the floor, which was made of thousands of pieces of dead wood set in an intricate, abstract pattern. She walked around to the stairs and looked down at the floor again. The pattern was fascinating. She went down the steps to look at it more closely—

—and the moment both her feet were on the floor, the room was no longer empty, but filled with tables and cabinets overflowing with objects. She gasped, leaped backward, and the room was once again empty. Cautiously, she put one toe on the floor, but nothing happened. She took another step, and the objects appeared between one blink and the next.

Stunned, Ailanthe moved forward along a narrow path that threaded between the tables and past a tall cabinet that bulged with so many things its doors were unable to close. It looked like a treasure room, with golden crowns and silver necklaces set with bright, faceted gems, but at a second glance Ailanthe saw more mundane items, like reels of thread and wooden boxes with chipped lids. None of it seemed magical at all.

She reached out to touch a beautifully embroidered handkerchief, and an urge to pick it up struck her so powerfully she jerked her hand back. She could feel, deep in her bones, that the Castle wanted her to choose something. If this was how it determined her destiny, she wasn't going to pick up the first random object she saw.

She made her way to the back of the room, where a squat cabinet with slim, curved legs stood, its top piled with coins of different metals and sizes in irregular stacks. Ailanthe wanted to pick them up to look more closely at them, see what distant foreign lands they came from, but she put her hands behind her back to resist the temptation and instead bent to get a closer look.

In leaning forward she saw, hanging from one of the lower doorknobs, a key on a short silver chain. It was made of gold and had silver tracings all down the shaft. It was so unusual, an ordinary object made from such precious material, that she reached out and took it in her hand.

Between one blink and the next, the room was empty. Ailanthe straightened and looked at the key in her hand. This definitely looked magical. The silver lines flowed across the golden shaft like trickles of argent water. It looked as if it might open something extraordinary, like a chest full of treasure or a box containing the breath of the North Wind. She looped the chain around her wrist—it was too short to go around her neck—and went back up the stairs. It was time to find the exit. Maybe she would be lucky, and the Castle would let her out where she'd entered.

A movement caught her eye, something furtive, and she tensed. Suppose she *wasn't* supposed to take anything, and the Castle had servants to enforce that? Whatever it was had been small, low to the ground—she looked across the flagstones and saw a black and white animal approaching from the direction she'd come from. A cat.

She moved cautiously toward it; it could still be dangerous. But it merely twined around her legs and rubbed its head against her shin. She scratched its head. "Are you the Castle's guardian, then?" she asked. "Because if you are meant to welcome guests, you're late." The cat's purr was inaudible, barely more than a vibration. Ailanthe scratched its head a little longer, then straightened. "I don't suppose you can show me the way out?"

The cat either didn't know the way out, or he didn't feel like helping, because he just followed Ailanthe down halls and through rooms as she looked for the exit. She wandered for a long time until the rooms blurred together, most of them so opulent and strange she felt out of place, like a bird trapped indoors. Several rooms seemed dedicated to foreign cultures; she'd read about Indrijan in one of her family's books, and here were robed mannequins dressed the way the Indrijanese had looked in the pictures, and one of their stone-bladed plows, and the *machines* that did everything from make their wheeled carts go to create books bound in leather and gold.

Finally she came to a corridor tiled in gently pitted red stone with a comfortably low ceiling. Leading off the corridor were store rooms, pantries, and a kitchen filled with more cabinets and drawers than she had ever seen. The cat leaped onto the big stone-topped counter in the center of the room and flopped over to lie on it, but Ailanthe didn't stay to investigate further. She passed through more store rooms until she came to an ancient wooden door bound with iron. Its knob was in the exact center of the door, and a small barred window at the top revealed only a dim glow.

The door opened easily on a short, low-ceilinged corridor, no more than ten feet long and half as wide, paved with the same large stones as the vaulted passageway. The mortar here was almost entirely missing, though she saw no dusty chips; it all looked much older than the rest of the Castle.

At the far end was another iron-bound door, though this one had a latch rather than a knob and its small window had glass instead of bars. Through the window, Ailanthe saw clear, bright daylight, not the cool light of the forest but a hot, blinding light that left her blinking and seeing its dark inverse when she closed her eyes. Ailanthe set her hand to the latch and pressed down on the thumb lever. It didn't move.

She laid both her palms on the lever and pushed down, hard. Still nothing, not even a minute shift that would tell her it was simply stiff with disuse. It might as well have been a decorative handle, fixed to a door that wasn't a door but one of those museum displays.

She searched the door with her eyes and her fingers, feeling for the real latch, or a keyhole, or anything that might open it. She pressed the whorls on the door, hard as iron itself, pushed every rivet and bolt she could find, tried to fit her fingers between the door and the jamb, thinking wildly that she might pull the door open with her fingertips alone. It didn't respond to anything she did.

She was trapped inside Castle Always.

CHAPTER TWO

*S*he leaned against the wall, panting not from exertion but from fear. She'd done something wrong, failed to perform some step, and now the Castle wouldn't let her go. Or she'd taken the wrong thing. She lifted her wrist to look at the key hanging there. Well, she could go back and return it, take something else. Maybe she was supposed to take the first thing her eye fell on. Maybe she was supposed to take something symbolic of what she sought.

Or maybe there's something wrong with me, maybe it's rejecting me the way the trees have, she thought, retracing her steps at a sedate pace; she wasn't afraid, this was a temporary problem, nothing to worry about. But her steps came more quickly despite her efforts, and when she reached the flagstone passageway she was almost running.

She trotted down the stairs and waited. Nothing happened. She backed up, tried again, but the room remained empty. She walked slowly across the patterned floor and removed the key from her wrist. "I'm sorry I took the wrong thing," she called out, and set the key on the floor a short distance from her feet. "I'm putting it back. I'm ready to choose again."

Nothing. The key glimmered on the floor and its reflection glowed dully. Ailanthe sat on the steps. The key lay there unmoving.

The room remained empty. Ailanthe clenched her hands and willed herself to breathe slowly, regularly, not to pant in rhythm with her racing heartbeat. She was *not* trapped in Castle Always. She just hadn't found the way out.

She left the key where it was and retraced her steps to what she'd thought was the outer door. *There must be another one I've overlooked. I'll just have to be more thorough.*

She began opening doors, feeling her way around the windows and walls; maybe the glass swung outward, leaving a gap she could crawl through, or maybe there were doors concealed in the panels of dead wood covering some of the walls. She searched for what felt like hours, went through dozens of rooms, and found nothing.

Eventually she ended up back in the vaulted stone passageway, where in despair she leaned against the wall, pressed her cheek against the cold stone, and stared blankly down its length; it gave her the momentary illusion that she was lying on the ground, looking out across the floor. The cat came trotting along the passage toward her, appearing from that perspective to be walking along the wall. She ignored him when he once again butted his head against her legs.

Banazir's lore was clear: go in, take your destiny, go out again. It said nothing about the possibility that the Castle wouldn't let you go. Ailanthe couldn't think what she'd done wrong. Was it the key? Why would the Castle present her with that object if no one was meant to take it? She didn't even have it anymore, so why couldn't she open the door?

She fought back panic. Someone else would eventually come to the Castle, and that person would open the door, and she would walk out with him. *Unless the Castle traps him too. Unless the Castle is broken.* The panic tried to turn into a scream, which she muffled with her hands. She'd lived all her life in the shelter of the wide forest, and these walls and doors of dead wood were starting to close in on her, trying to choke the life out of her—no, that was ridiculous, she was being ridiculous, and she needed to stop being a fool.

She stood erect and thought for a moment. There was food back there in the kitchen; there must be people here to eat it, or else what was the point? Maybe one of them would know a way out. Her stomach growled at the thought of food. She'd been searching all morning without rest, and the stone-hard biscuit she'd eaten just after dawn had not filled her. She would eat, and then she would find a place to sleep, and perhaps in the morning the Castle would have changed its mind.

She took a few steps, and hesitated, then descended the stairs once more and crossed the floor to where the gold key shone. "I chose you, so you might as well stay with me," she said, and looped the chain around her wrist. The key felt warm, as warm as her own skin, though the silver lines were a cool contrast and tickled her palm as they moved. Ailanthe examined it again. It would be interesting to see what lock it opened, though the size of the Castle made it unlikely she would ever find its hiding place. Assuming it opened something here.

She moved off in the direction of the kitchen, the cat at her heels, trying not to think about the possibility that she might have plenty of time in which to seek it out.

She took a different route this time, down a long hallway tiled entirely in tiny squares of blue of all possible shades, with curling borders of gold marking off sections of the walls and more gold tiles making circles and crosses at random along the floor. Windows looked out on a gray, depressing courtyard with a couple of spindly trees and thin grass trying to hold its own against the clayey mud it was growing in. Across the courtyard, Ailanthe could see the Idrijian room; her heart leaped to see human figures there before she remembered the mannequins.

She was almost at the back door before she realized she wasn't the only one making noise. Someone was in one of the kitchen rooms, someone who moved without attempting to be stealthy. The cat put its ears back—was that a good sign, or bad?—and bolted forward around the corner. She stayed where she was, trying to calm her heart. Now that she was nearly face to face with one of the Castle's inhabitants, her earlier eagerness deserted her. Suppose the person attacked her? She didn't belong here, after all, and the people who did might not like intruders.

She closed her eyes and breathed deeply, then quickly opened her eyes so whoever it was wouldn't come upon her unawares. She needed to get out. This could be the Castle's way of giving her an exit. She took another deep breath, then walked around the corner and into the kitchen.

The man had his back to her, busying himself in one of the giant store rooms nearly the size of the kitchen. He was tall and broad-shouldered, dressed plainly in loose trousers and a short-sleeved tunic with a sword belted to his waist, and his long brown hair was tied back at the base of his neck. The cat was trying to tangle itself around his legs, its purring now barely audible at the limit of her hearing.

Ailanthe was about to clear her throat to announce her presence when the man turned around and jumped in surprise, juggling his armload of food. "You're still here," he said.

It wasn't at all what she'd expected him to say, and it left her groping for a reply. "Was I supposed to be gone?" she finally said.

"Yes," the man said. He had a strong, angular face and brown eyes that were uncomfortably direct. "Didn't you take anything from the Honor Hall?"

Ailanthe held up her wrist with the key dangling on its chain. "But the door won't open."

He continued to gaze at her with that steady expression. "The door always opens after you've made your choice. Maybe it's stuck."

"You're stronger than I am," Ailanthe said, eyeing the well-defined muscles of his arms and his broad shoulders. "Will you open it for me?"

The man shook his head, making the hoop in his right ear quiver. "It won't open for me." He set his armful of food on the counter in the center of the room, then bent to pick up a fruit with a pebbly orange skin that had fallen to the floor and rolled a short distance away, chased by the cat. "Not even if I try to open it for someone else."

"But—if *you* can't get out, you must know why I can't!"

"It's not the same." He looked at the fruit in his hand, then set it on the pile. "I can't help you. The Castle must have some reason for keeping you here."

"But—" Ailanthe closed her mouth on the rest of the sentence, not sure what it might have been. "But I can't stay here! I was supposed to go on a journey so I could return home!"

"I'm sorry." The man began gathering food into a more stable pile. "You should eat something. The food won't hurt you."

She put her hands on the counter and heard the key go *clink* against the white stone top. She quickly raised her hand again. "Could this be what's keeping me here?"

The man shook his head. "None of those things are magical. The Castle gathers them up from all over itself and takes the rest back after a quester chooses something. I don't think it has anything to do with where it sends people."

Ailanthe looked at the key again. It had to be magical; how else could the silver streaks move like that? "I—no, wait!" she said, seeing the man was heading out the door with his pile of food. "What's your name?"

The man looked at her as if she'd asked him to give up some secret. "Coren," he said finally.

"I'm Ailanthe. Can I...can I come with you? The Castle is so quiet..." Her voice trailed off in the face of that level gaze. He seemed to be considering her, and she wondered how she looked, disheveled from sleeping rough in the forest for four nights. She wondered what he would do if she slapped him, or pinched him, anything to get a reaction out of that still, expressionless face. She felt as if she were beginning to go mad in the face of his silence.

Eventually, he shrugged. "Take what food you want," he said, and waited for her to gather bread and apples and a round of cheese, the only foods she recognized that didn't require cooking.

Clutching her food and a wax-sealed bluish glass bottle of what had turned out, when she picked at the seal, to be water and not alcohol, she followed Coren back down the blue-tiled hall and around the stone passageway to a flight of steps broad enough for ten people to climb at once, arms linked. They climbed and climbed until Ailanthe, who'd never seen more than ten stair-steps in one place before, was out of breath and felt the prickle of sweat start under her arms.

The stairs changed as they passed each landing, going from shallow carpeted steps to steep unvarnished wooden ones to stairs covered in a strange green material that gripped Ailanthe's shoes like a burr clinging to her shirt. Brightly lit hallways led off the stairs' landings. Some of them had long rows of windows through which she could see the ocean, or the scrubland desert, or a range of snow-blown mountain peaks. She longed to explore those corridors, but obediently followed Coren instead. If she wandered off, she might not be able to find him again.

Eventually the stairs ended, and Coren went down a hallway with white rough-textured walls that was lit by more of those glowing hemispheres, then through a door set into a carved wooden arch. Ailanthe followed him, her leg muscles burning, past a bedroom the size of the kitchen and into a spacious chamber with a ceiling twenty feet tall and floor-to-ceiling windows on three sides. She'd never seen so much glass in one place. Coren put his load on the floor, and Ailanthe did the same.

"I use those padded boxes as chairs," Coren said. "They might actually *be* chairs. The Castle has a lot of furnishings that make no sense."

He took a stiff white rectangle as wide as his outstretched arms off a stand in the center of the room and laid it face-first against the inside wall; Ailanthe had time to recognize something was painted on it before it was hidden. He next moved the stand over to the same wall, then removed his sword and laid it on one of the boxes. He dragged another box over to the eastern windows and settled there with the pebbly orange fruit.

Ailanthe selected her own box and pushed it over to the northern windows. Now that she was here, wherever here was, she felt awkward about intruding on this man's...well, it seemed to be his home. Had he lived here his whole life? Was that even possible? He sat peeling away the bright orange rind of the fruit, revealing a paler orange meat veined with white inside, and stared out the window as if he'd forgotten she was there.

Ailanthe bit into a crusty loaf of fresh bread and sighed at how soft and rich it tasted. The window looked out over sand dunes that stretched as far as she could see. Wind rippled the tops of the dunes, then a tiny creature, unrecognizable at this distance, came trotting over a crest. Ailanthe stared at it in fascination, turned to point it out to Coren, and realized his window had a very different view from hers. The eastern windows overlooked a narrow valley through which flowed a shallow stream. The walls of the valley were sheer granite cliffs that rose high above the Castle, the tops shrouded in fog.

Ailanthe went up to the glass and pressed her forehead against it, trying to see the base of the Castle far below. "Are we at the top of the Castle?" she asked.

Coren startled again. Maybe he really had forgotten she was there. "Yes," he said. "There's only one place taller, and the door is locked."

"If it's locked, how do you know it's taller?"

"I read about it in a book." He pulled the orange meat apart into neat sections and ate one, then glanced at her. "Where are you from?"

"Lindurien."

He offered a section of fruit to her. "You won't have had this before. Be careful, there's a lot of juice."

She took it from him and bit, carefully, and was surprised when juice spurted into her mouth and down her chin. It was sweet and tangy and delicious. She caught the drips in her other hand and pushed the rest of the fruit into her mouth, and was rewarded with another burst of juice she kept her lips carefully closed over. She swallowed, wiped her chin, and licked the last drops of juice from her palm. "What is it?" she asked.

"It's called an orange. Not very imaginative, I know."

"It's incredible. Where do they come from?"

"Much farther south than I'm sure your people ever go." He looked out the window again. "People grow them where I come from."

So he hadn't lived here forever. "Where is that?"

"Hespera."

"I've seen drawings of the olive groves. They were beautiful."

"Pretty enough, I suppose." He took out a belt knife and sliced cheese, then bread, and put the one on the other and took a large bite. He had a stillness about him that made Ailanthe feel uncomfortable about speaking, even though she was filled to bursting with questions. Was he really so emotionless as he seemed?

She busied herself with an apple, then bit off more of the delicious bread. She thought it was useful but strange that the bottle contained water—why bottle something that was freely available at any stream?—but then there probably wasn't a stream flowing through the Castle. She considered that thought, and wondered if it was a good idea to make such assumptions about a place that existed everywhere at once.

A long drink of water made her realize she had another pressing need. "Is there, um, a place to...relieve myself?" she asked, trying not to feel embarrassed.

"Oh. The bathroom," Coren said, setting his food aside.

"There's a room for baths?" At home, Ailanthe bathed in the pool her people had dammed up from the river, or in a tub in front of the *gyrsta* during winter.

"It took me a while to figure it all out."

He led her back toward the stairs and opened a door to reveal a mysterious red-tiled room holding shiny white basins of various sizes and with short pipes sticking out of the walls. "Chamber pot." He pulled a chain hanging above a round basin filled with water; with a whoosh, the water emptied itself into a hole at the bottom of the basin and then filled again. Ailanthe dropped to her knees to examine it.

"Why doesn't the water go all over the floor?" she asked.

"There's a pipe that must lead outside. Washbasin." He turned a handle attached to one of the pipes and water began pouring from it into a white basin somehow attached to the wall. "Try it."

Ailanthe gingerly rotated the handle, making the water flow more rapidly, then turned it the other way and saw the flow diminish to a trickle and then a single drop. "How does it do this?"

"Plumbing. Though I'll admit this is all a lot more sophisticated than anything we have back home. I don't even know what country might have this kind of thing. Indrijan, maybe, but...." He shook his head. "Then there's a bigger one of these you can sit in to bathe." He pointed.

"I've never seen anything like it. Is this room the only one?" A bath would be nice, after four days of traveling.

"There are dozens of them, usually near the bedrooms." Coren turned and left the room. Ailanthe played with the handle for a few moments, then used what he'd called a chamber pot, sitting gingerly on its edge and standing well away from it when she pulled the chain. She pulled the chain a few more times just to see the water swirl around before it disappeared. Amazing.

She glanced around the room at all the strange fixtures that seemed even more alien now that she knew what they did. There was nothing here at all like home, and the more she learned the more she didn't know why she'd had to come here in the first place. Was the Castle keeping her here to taunt her, show her how much greater the wide world was than Ailanthe had ever dreamed?

She clenched her teeth. Damn the Castle anyway. She was going to get out, she was going to go home, and she'd never think of the place again.

CHAPTER THREE

*W*hen she returned to the room with the windows, Coren had finished his bread and cheese and piled the rest of his food on another of the padded boxes. It looked as though he'd stocked up for a few days, which, given how far up these rooms were, was probably sensible. Or he might just be a big eater. She sat down across from Coren, who silently stared at her until her discomfort led her to blurt out, "How long have you been here?"

For answer, he turned his head and pointed at the wall. It was neither stone nor wood but some substance that crumbled easily, because gouged into it were the words 6 YRS 23 DAYS. Ailanthe blinked at it. "Are you...do other people live here?"

Coren shook his head. "People pass through. No one stays."

Ailanthe struggled to conceal her horror. Over six years alone? No wonder he was so silent; he'd probably nearly forgotten how to talk. It was astonishing that the man wasn't mad. *Or maybe he is mad, and he's good at hiding it. How certain are you that you could defend yourself against that knife of his?* "Why won't the door open for you?"

"Do all Lindurians ask as many questions as you do?" He smiled, a non-threatening, entirely sane expression that transformed his face.

It was so surprising she returned the smile, shrugging in self-deprecation. *So he's more than just a block of wood.*

"I want to leave," she said, "and you must know everything about the Castle if you've been here this long. I'm sorry if I'm prying."

He shook his head. "I'm not used to talking to the questers who come through here. It's easier for everyone if I stay out of the way."

"Then how did you know I was here?"

"The Castle bell rings." He made a motion with his hand. "It makes everything vibrate. You'll know it when you hear it."

"I don't intend to be here that long."

"There's no other door. And the Castle can be stubborn." He smiled again, but this was a private smile, one that said he was thinking of a joke he didn't intend to share with her.

"Then I'll have to out-stubborn it."

"Good luck. I hope you find it." He settled back to watching her, and Ailanthe fidgeted until she couldn't stand it any longer, and said, "Why are you looking at me that way?"

He scratched his chin. "I was trying to discover if you were an elf without asking outright."

Ailanthe sat up indignantly. "Because Lindurians live in the trees and enchant living wood, is that it? As well say all Hesperans are...are olive farmers with no time for elevated cultural pursuits."

Coren smiled, and his distant air faded a little more. "I'm sorry, I didn't mean to offend you," he said. "That will teach me to blindly trust the things I read in books."

"If I were an elf, you wouldn't be able to look at me so directly," Ailanthe said, less angrily. "You would feel as if something else was more interesting, and have trouble focusing your thoughts to even remember there was an elf there. And no, they don't interbreed with humans."

His lips quirked. "Another dream dashed," he murmured, and Ailanthe burst out laughing at the humor in his eyes. "I suppose they don't have metallic hair?"

"No, that's true, but it's not pretty metals like silver and gold, more like iron, or old bronze. Where did you learn all this?"

"The Library. I read a lot. Not much else to do, most days."

"I saw it downstairs across from the...did you call it the Honor Hall? I'd never seen so many books in my life."

Coren's smile went wicked. "That's just a book room," he said, and stood. "Let me show you the Library."

She followed him down one flight of stairs and down a twenty-foot-wide hallway lined with doors, some shining metal, others wood painted with flowers and fanciful creatures. "All locked," Coren said, which made Ailanthe wonder if the exit she needed lay behind one of them. They came out into a high-ceilinged, echoing hallway, this one of pale gray stone shot through with darker streaks. A smooth path was worn into the floor as if hundreds of people over hundreds of years had passed this way, and Ailanthe thought about who might have lived in the Castle centuries ago, and what had happened to them.

Coren turned a corner, then stepped back to allow Ailanthe to go first. "Just ahead," he said, "through that doorway." Ailanthe glanced at him; his voice was tense, and she wondered if he was trying to play a trick on her, but his smile looked more like that of someone antici-pating a pleasant surprise, so she went forward through the doorway, which was formed of two pillars supporting a stone slab for a lintel, and immediately had to grab hold of one of those pillars to avoid falling over in amazement.

The room beyond was bigger than the Honor Hall, and the shelves that lined it from floor to ceiling were entirely full of books, books lined up on shelves and books piled atop other books until Ailanthe didn't know where to look first. She didn't see a single straight line anywhere, except for the smooth-sanded boards the books sat on; the shelves curved like half-moons that doubled back on themselves and the walls of the room were rounded as if following some natural contour not visible elsewhere in the Castle.

She regained her composure and walked forward across a deep, leaf-green carpet so thick her steps were as soundless as the cat's. Short flights of stairs turned what was probably two stories worth of space into four levels, the stairs carpeted in the same lush green as the floor. High above, a skylight took up most of the ceiling, bright sun streaming through it in a cloudless blue sky. It was impossible to see what land those windows looked out over.

But what left her breathless were the trees. Whoever had built the Library had carved the large exposed beams to look like tree trunks and branches, and in places had made actual trees grow through the floor, their leaves brushing the skylight's circumference but never blocking the light. Without thinking, she went to lay her palm against one smooth trunk, then jerked her hand away when it stung her.

She pushed away her heartache and continued wandering the room, astonishment soon driving away sorrow. One giant tree took up most of the center of the floor, surrounded by shelves that encircled its trunk and a bench that practically begged her to sit on it. The books on those shelves were unusual. The other books in the Library were bound in leather dyed in jewel tones with their titles stamped in gold upon the spine. These books were more simply bound in white painted boards, their spines unmarked.

Ailanthe went to take one from the shelf and Coren's hand restrained her. "Not a good idea," he said. "The Castle keeps track of its questers, writes their stories in these books. Most of them don't end well."

"Oh," Ailanthe said. She turned in a slow circle, overwhelmed by the presence of so many volumes waiting to be read. "It's *incredible*."

"I think so," Coren said. He sounded smug, pleased with himself that he could astonish her, but it was a friendly kind of smugness and Ailanthe let it pass, relieved that his stiffness seemed to have evaporated. "I've only read a fraction of what's here. Makes it easier, knowing I'm not likely to run out of books no matter how long I stay here."

"Coren, why is it you won't say what's keeping you here?" She hadn't missed the fact that he'd evaded the question twice now. Part of her was embarrassed at invading the man's privacy, but if there was anything in his experience that might get her out of here, she wanted to know about it.

Coren took a seat in a high-backed chair, well-padded and with wide arms. "It won't let me out because I never took anything from the Honor Hall," he said, all traces of good humor gone.

"I don't understand."

"I just came in here to get out of the rain," Coren said, interlacing his fingers and staring at them. "I didn't want a destiny. I figured if I didn't touch anything, I could pass through and move on. I figured wrong."

Ailanthe sat on the bench opposite him. "So all you have to do is take something from the Honor Hall, and it will let you go?"

"I'm not going to let some heap of stone and glass that may or may not be alive force me to do something I don't want to do," Coren said. "I've read those books—" he jabbed a finger at the white-bound books—"and I know what happens to almost everyone who comes here for a destiny. I don't want to be cast out in some land a thousand miles from my home, trapped into some adventure that might well leave me dead, never to return again. I want my life to be my own. So I'll be damned if I take any of the rubbish the Castle hauls out."

He spoke with such vehemence Ailanthe was startled, but she said, "I understand."

"Do you? You *wanted* a destiny. What are you running from?"

"I'm not running from anything," said Ailanthe, stung. "And that's personal."

"More personal than me telling you I'm trapped here because I'm a stubborn bastard?"

Ailanthe looked away. "I can't climb trees," she said. "The trees don't want me. You know what it's like, being Lindurian and being tethered to the ground? Is that something your books tell you?" Her voice went suddenly shrill; her mother's tearful face rose up in memory, and she felt so homesick and resentful she could barely speak. "Sorry," she said after a moment. "Anyway, Lindurians are supposed to seek out the Castle when they need to be restored to... why does the Castle make us speak this language, anyway?"

"I think it's the language of its creator. Someone who wanted everyone inside it to be able to have uncomfortable conversations like this one."

She caught his eye; he was smiling again, and she managed to smile in return. "Well, this language doesn't have words for the concept, but it's like restoring our balance, being in tune with the trees, which is entirely the wrong image and I'm sure you're thinking about elves again."

"I wasn't. But I am now."

For someone who'd been isolated for six years, Coren had an excellent sense of the ridiculous. Ailanthe smiled despite herself. "And that's why I'm here. It wasn't that I wanted the adventure so much as that I wanted to find my true path."

"And you're sure the Castle knows what that is."

"Why wouldn't it? Isn't that what it's here for?"

Coren shrugged, the smile falling from his lips. "I don't know anymore. I used to talk to the questers until it became too depressing. All those bright faces, headed off toward their doom. I had to ask myself, if the Castle knows so much, why does it think sending people out to die is the best thing for them?"

"I thought the Castle could see into our hearts and choose the best path for us. Is it its fault if we don't make the best use of it? I mean, if I stay away from cliff edges I won't fall to my death—at some point we have to choose."

He shrugged again. "You may be right." His good humor was entirely gone now. "Anyway, now you know where the Library is. You should find a place to sleep—lots of bedrooms available. I'm going to get some exercise." He stood and crossed the room. Ailanthe said, "Wait!"

He stopped at the doorway, but didn't look back at her. "What?"

"Will I...I mean, do you mind if I...visit with you sometimes?"

"If you like. But I might not be very good company." She heard his footsteps fade away across the floor, and then he was gone.

Ailanthe sat staring at the chair he'd vacated. He'd been good company for a while, and then they'd started talking about the Castle, and he'd retreated into that silent shell again. She suddenly didn't feel like very good company herself. The idea of searching the first floor again for a door that probably didn't exist exhausted her.

Maybe she could chop the door down. There was an axe in the armory...an axe she probably couldn't lift. Coren wasn't likely to want to participate in that mad scheme, and he'd probably tried it at some point already. Maybe he was right, and she should find a place to sleep, assuming she couldn't get out before nightfall.

She felt awkward about taking a room near Coren, as if she were so desperate for human companionship she'd curl up on his doorstep like a whining puppy, but she didn't want to be so far away that she felt like the only living person in the Castle.

She left the Library, promising herself she'd return soon, and went back down the stairs. She'd start exploring the second floor, and if she miraculously found a way out, she might even tell Coren about it.

CHAPTER FOUR

S ix hours later Ailanthe pressed her face against the glass and looked down into the courtyard. It wasn't any more cheerful from this height than it had been at ground level, and the growing darkness made it even more depressing, though she saw a tangle of twigs that might be a bird's nest in the top of one of the spindly trees.

She turned her back on it and slid down to sit on the floor, pressing her palms flat against the reassuring solidity of the polished oak floor. The dead wood made no pulse of rejection against her hand; her mother would tell her to be horrified at how many trees had been sacrificed for this Castle's sake, but Ailanthe was more pragmatic. Trees died, and what a waste if their bodies went to rot.

She'd searched the second floor thoroughly that afternoon and now she was exhausted. Half the rooms she'd investigated had been so unfamiliar she couldn't even guess what they were for. She'd found several more of the bathrooms, some of them plain, others designed to look like a forest glade, or tide pools on a sandy beach. Dozens of bedrooms furnished so richly she was afraid to sleep in them. More book rooms, more museum rooms dedicated to cultures Ailanthe had never heard of. Rooms piled high with what she thought were castoffs; rooms with long tables set with dishes so fine she'd be afraid to eat off them. She rubbed her temples, and as if in response, her stomach growled.

She pushed herself up and headed for the kitchen. It was a strange room, white and shiny-hard and windowless, with drawers that slid as if greased and doors that opened on deep cabinets filled with spice jars whose scents mingled in the air like filmy ribbons. She hadn't recognized any of the tools, some of them white and some shining silver metal, most of them with moving parts that made her nervous. There was no fireplace, but she didn't mind eating cold food.

As she went down the stairs, something brushed past her legs— the cat again. He'd followed her on her investigation, vanishing at times, but always returning, as if his feline senses knew where she was at all times. Now he ran down the stairs, pausing to look back up at her. Clearly she was moving too slowly for him.

"You look like you want food," she said. For answer, he ran ahead of her into the kitchen and leaped onto the stone-topped counter in the center of the room. "Does Coren usually feed you? I suppose I could find you something, as long as I'm here."

A quick search turned up a tray of chicken livers, which she cut into morsels and set on the counter for the cat to eat. She put the rest back in the very cold room she'd found them in, so cold it had a bluish haze hovering inside it. It was full of all kinds of meat and fish, great slabs of beef hanging from hooks, smaller cuts laid out neatly on racks.

"Who eats all of this?" she asked the cat, poking one of the carcasses and watching it swing gently. She sniffed the air and smelled nothing rancid, just the faint aroma of fresh raw meat. She eyed a neatly sectioned chicken and wished there *were* a fireplace in here, with a spit, or a *gyrsta* she could fry meat on. She sighed and closed the door, and contented herself with more fruit, bread, cheese, and something brown that smelled deliciously sweet and melted on her fingers when she broke off a piece. She ate it, licked her fingers— rich and sweet and delicious. She took two thick slabs.

"This way, I can eat my breakfast without having to come back here in the morning," she told the cat, who sniffed at her round of cheese. She fed him a nibble of the soft yellow stuff. "I didn't realize cats liked cheese. I wonder what Coren calls you? I don't plan to be here much longer, but I can't just refer to you as 'cat'. That would be rude."

She arranged her stack of food, took another bite of the delicious brown stuff, and climbed all the way back to the Library level. There was a bedroom near Coren's stairs, close enough for an imagined companionship but not so close as to intrude. Ailanthe thought Coren might have been a fairly reserved man even before he was trapped for six years with no one to talk to, but those flashes of humor told her there was a real person inside the shell he'd built for himself, even if he did seem to like being alone. She, on the other hand, was already starting to feel anxious about not having anyone but the cat for conversation.

The bed was too soft; she felt as though it might swallow her up. She piled her food on a low table at the foot of the bed, took pillows and blankets and made a nest for herself on the floor. Then she went back to the Library.

Whatever magic had replaced her language with the Castle's own had made her literate in the new language too. There were so many books she didn't even know where to start. Finally she found a section of the Library devoted to books on all the countries of the world, and chose a volume titled *Hesperan Journeys*. Maybe this would give her and Coren some common ground for conversation. Or maybe he didn't want to talk about home when he had no way of getting there. *Well,* Ailanthe thought, *it doesn't hurt to be well-informed about his customs. And I do love reading about other places. When I get out of here, maybe I'll see some of them.*

The cat curled up in her lap as she sat in her nest, reading and eating, though she had to be careful not to get the sweet brown stuff on the book's pages. After only a few chapters, however, she found herself reading the same line over and over again, and the weariness of the day's activities settled into her bones with a dull ache that made her pillow look incredibly inviting. She closed the book and set it near her head, then stretched out, bumping the cat off her lap. It walked away without complaint, and Ailanthe realized she'd never heard it meow. *Strange cat,* she thought muzzily, *strange castle, strange world,* and sank into sleep.

Someone passed a peach-scented cloth across her face, and she batted at it, her fingers passing through what felt like cold fog that made the peach smell even stronger. She opened her eyes, but saw nothing. Something was digging into her back and hips. She rolled onto her side and discovered she was sleeping on bare floor, her face level with the underside of the bed. Her pillow was gone. Her blankets were gone.

She sat up quickly. A glance revealed her pile of food and her book were gone as well. She scrambled to her feet and patted herself; all her clothes were in place, and her small bag of gear was in the corner where she'd left it the night before. She heard her breath coming in quick, panicked pants.

She made herself take slow breaths, then clapped a hand over her mouth to stifle a shriek. The blankets and pillows were on the bed, neatly tucked in as if she'd never moved them. She reached out to touch the bed, then grabbed a handful of the top blanket and yanked it off, threw it as far from her as she could, and stared at it, willing it to do something mysterious. It lay there motionless. She kicked it, and it lifted an inch or so off the ground and settled back down.

Ailanthe turned and ran for the stairs, pounding up them and into Coren's chambers without thinking of what an intrusion it might be. He wasn't in any of the rooms. She turned around and ran back toward the stairs and shrieked when Coren stepped out of the bathroom. His hair was wet and he had a freshly-shaved look to him. He blinked at her in surprise. "Are you all right?"

"Something was in my room," Ailanthe panted. She knew she must look like a madwoman, her pale brown hair flying like an untidy halo around her face and into her eyes, but she was too overwhelmed to care. "It took my food and my blankets and made the bed. What kind of insane creature lives in this place, and why didn't you warn me about it?"

"It's not a creature, it's the Castle," Coren said. "I forgot you wouldn't know about it. I'm sorry." He did sound sorry, but even so, Ailanthe had to clench her fists to keep from yelling at him again. Probably he'd been here long enough he took all the strange things the Castle did for granted.

"So it takes things away from you?" she asked, more calmly.

Coren moved away from her toward the stairs. "It doesn't like things to be changed," he said. "Puts everything back the way it was around midnight. You can't even move a chair so much as an inch out of position without the Castle moving it back again. Fixes broken things, cleans up messes, all that."

Ailanthe followed him down the stairs, almost running to keep up with his longer strides. "But the food is all fresh. If it just keeps moving it back—"

"I don't know how that works. It doesn't reassemble the food we eat or we'd starve to death, what with it reclaiming loaves of bread and such from our bodies. Maybe it restores the food to its freshest state every night. All I know is there's always enough food to feed a Castle full of people, which is a mystery by itself."

Ailanthe remembered 6YRS 23 DAYS and asked, "Does that mean...your wall, the Castle repairs it every night?"

Coren nodded. "And every morning I carve a new number into it."

"But..." She couldn't think of anything to say that didn't sound like a criticism.

"Castle's going to keep me here, I'm not going to make it easy," he said. His tone was light, almost joking, but his eyes were serious. "I told you, if I take something from the Honor Hall, the Castle will send me out into the world far from my home to have 'adventures' that will probably get me killed. I figure, maybe if I make it uncomfortable enough, it will get the hint." He paused. "Now that I say it out loud, it sounds a little crazy," he said, and laughed. "I guess by now it's habit."

"No, I understand," Ailanthe said, and felt a rush of sympathy for him, though she had to admit if she were in his place, she'd have given in to the Castle before a month was up.

They crossed the blue hall to the kitchen annex. The counter where Ailanthe had fed the cat chicken livers was clean and glossy instead of stained with fluid—Ailanthe had figured out how to make water come from the pipe, but had found no cloths for cleaning.

"Coren," she said, "why do you take food all the way back to your rooms instead of eating here? That's a long trip."

Coren shrugged. "I like the view from upstairs," he said, "and it's another way I can...I don't know. Remind the Castle that I'm here and I'm not giving in to its rules. We can eat down here if you want."

"No, I'd rather the window room." It raised her spirits to know he assumed she'd eat with him. The cat jumped onto the counter, startling her. She stroked his sleek black and white fur and went to the cold room for some chicken. "What's the cat's name?" she asked.

"Don't know. Never gave him one."

"Why not?" She began cutting the chicken into small pieces, pushing the cat's nose out of the way of the knife.

"Just didn't think about it. He's lived here longer than I have; maybe he's got a name and he's not telling."

Ailanthe looked at Coren sideways. "Are you being serious?"

"No. I never thought about it, that's all." He grinned and scratched the cat under its chin briefly.

"Well, I'm going to call him Miriethiel."

Coren paused in selecting fruit from a basket. "Isn't that a girl's name?"

"It can be a boy's name too—and how do you know that story?"

"I read a lot, remember?" Coren surveyed her much smaller pile and added a few strangely-shaped yellow fruits to it. "That's a lot of chocolate you have there."

"Is that the brown stuff? I love it. How much is too much?"

"Why don't you eat it, and you tell me." He smiled at her, his eyes twinkling, and Ailanthe smiled back. It was so good to have someone to talk to who actually answered.

This time, Coren sat by the western windows, which looked out over an ocean whose shore stretched in both directions without sign of human habitation. It seemed as though the Castle's foundations went right up to the waterline. High, thin clouds obscured the pale light of dawn, making the waves below look gray under the white-caps as they plunged toward the shore. Ailanthe leaned against the windowpanes overlooking the desert and ate bread and cheese and let her mind wander. Today she'd have to search the third floor. Maybe a quester would arrive today. Coren had said the timing varied; there was no reason people might not arrive two days in a row.

"Here," Coren said, holding out one of the curved yellow fruits. She came over to take it, but he snapped the stem at one end and peeled the skin back, revealing the pale yellow insides, then offered it to her. She gingerly took a bite. It was dry on the outside, but smooth and sweet on the inside. "I suppose this is called a yellow?" she said between bites.

He grinned. "No, a banana. Comes from Rius-zara. I thought you might like it."

"I do. Thanks." Something else occurred to her. "I haven't seen any peaches, but I keep smelling them. Is there a tree in the Castle somewhere?"

"Those are sprites. They live in the Castle, doing...I don't know what they do. Float around, mostly. None of the books talk about them much. I think they might be loose magic. Sometimes they collect around me when I'm doing things, but not very often."

"Are they...alive, then? Creatures?"

Coren shrugged. "I think of them that way because it feels like they get interested, sometimes, in what I'm doing. But they're probably not."

Ailanthe surveyed the top of his head as he ate and stared out the window. *You're not as used to loneliness as you seem*, she thought. "I don't suppose there are any other useful things you didn't think to tell me?" she said.

Coren looked up at her. "It's hard to guess what I know that you wouldn't," he said. "The Castle moving things. Chocolate. Oranges and bananas. You'll probably come up with more questions," he said with a grin.

"Here's one. Who built this Castle, and why isn't that person around anymore? Why isn't this place filled with people?"

"I've never learned the answer to that. It's not in any of the books I've read—though with as many books as are in the Library, it's likely I haven't found the right one yet. Maybe you will." He stood and stretched. "I'm going to exercise now."

"Do you exercise every day?"

"It's something to do. Usually I exercise after breakfast, then I read for a while. Sometimes I go to the museum rooms or the galleries. There's not a lot to do here in the Castle."

Coren took the big sword from where it stood under one of the windows and removed the sheath with a metallic rasping sound. He laid it on one of the puffy cubes and removed his tunic. He was well-muscled, with brown skin a few shades paler than his hair, and he moved so gracefully he made even picking up the sword look like the first moves of a dance. Ailanthe realized she was staring.

"I, uh, I'll just take my food to my room," she said, and hurried away.

Back in her room, she put the food on the bed and sat next to it. The Castle put everything away at midnight? How demoralizing. It was fortunate she had no intention of making a life here. She tore off a hunk of bread and bit deeply into it. The smell of peaches floated past again, and she turned her head, trying to isolate it. There, to the left, something that reflected the light just enough to reveal something was there.

Ailanthe looked at it for a while and realized she saw it more clearly out of the corner of her eye. It didn't look like a person. It looked like a sheet of transparent fabric that contracted and stretched as it floated through the air, sometimes bunching up like a wad of dandelion fluff and sometimes spread flat like a leaf. Ailanthe reached out to touch it. It didn't avoid her touch; in fact, it curved around her hand and wrist before floating away in a different direction. It felt the way it had when one had woken her that morning, like dry fog she could pass her fingers through. In a moment it drifted into the wall, passed through it, and was gone.

Ailanthe lowered her hand. Sprites. They weren't even the strangest thing she'd seen all morning. She ate a little more until she was full, then stood. Third floor? Or the Library? She ran her hands through her hair, scratching her head, and felt the key bump gently against her cheek. She took it in her hand and turned it around, watching the silver streaks flow over the slender golden shaft. Or she could try a different approach.

CHAPTER FIVE

She ran back up to Coren's rooms, finding him in the middle of some complicated exercise involving the enormous sword. He didn't stop when she came in. "Yes?" he said. He was sweaty now, and Ailanthe had to make herself stop staring again.

"I was going to ask you if you know what this key fits," she said, waving it at him.

"Just a minute," he said. He continued through the movements of his exercise. Ailanthe shifted awkwardly from one foot to the other. He must be so tired of her questions and her interruptions. She was about to apologize and leave when he brought the sword around in what seemed to be a finishing move, laid it down, and crossed the room toward her. He held out his hand and Ailanthe removed the key from her wrist and handed it to him.

He examined it in silence, holding it up to better catch the light. "It looks magical," he said. "I didn't think the Castle handed out anything magical."

"You said it couldn't be keeping me here."

"Maybe I was wrong." He held it close to his eyes. "I can't think of any unusual lock it might go to. There are a lot of locked things in the

Castle, though, doors and chests and trinkets. You might have to try every lock until you find it." He handed the key back to her. "If you find out what it opens, I'd like to know. I've never seen anything like it before." He paused, then, with a wry smile, said, "Any other questions?"

Ailanthe flushed. "I'm sorry I keep intruding," she began, but he shook his head.

"It's nice to have someone else to talk to," he said. "But I've been alone a long time, so don't be offended if I forget you're there." He smiled. Ailanthe smiled back.

"I'm going to explore the third floor today," she said. "So I'll...see you later."

He nodded and turned away, picking up the sword again. Ailanthe made her escape. He wasn't as withdrawn as she'd first thought, and he certainly seemed welcoming enough now, but she still felt like an intruder on this strange, isolated life he'd made for himself. It was tempting to think in terms of doing him a favor by dragging him out of his isolation, but Ailanthe had never been good at deciding what was best for other people. She knew her interest in Coren was purely selfish: she disliked being alone, had always hated it, and she could admit to herself he was the only thing keeping her sane.

She tossed the key in her hand, once, twice, catching it by the chain and letting it swing free. *It must open something extraordinary,* she thought, and remembered something Coren had said the day before, about the tallest spot in the Castle. That door had to be on this level somewhere; suppose it was the lock the key opened? Key in hand, she set off down the hall.

Most of the rooms here at the top of the Castle were locked, but Ailanthe's key was clearly too big to fit any of the doors. The window-less halls were only dimly lit by more of the glowing hemispheres, which seemed to burn more weakly than their counterparts on the lower floors, or perhaps they were only dirty. A dinginess hung about the place, a griminess that didn't match the rest of the Castle. If the

Castle really were repairing itself every night, it had overlooked this area for years.

Shadows clung thickly in corners and seeped from beneath the locked doors. Ailanthe caught movement out of the corner of her eye and turned a little too quickly, thinking she saw the shadows move; it was only five or six sprites, drifting along as if the dimness and the increasing eeriness didn't affect them at all. If they were just pieces of loose magic, that was true. They floated in her direction and circled her head twice, brushing against her cheeks and hair, until she waved them away. Coren must have understated their interest in people; they certainly seemed to be attracted to her.

After several minutes of wandering, Ailanthe came to a long, straight hall, maybe thirty feet wide, that was floored in black and red tiles and lined with carnelian pillars larger than Ailanthe could put her arms around. It ended in a set of double doors paneled in wood painted to match the pillars, intricately banded in brass, with hinges shaped like aspen leaves. There was no latch, but the keyhole certainly seemed big enough to admit her key. Ailanthe pushed it into the lock; with a little resistance, it slid right in, and she turned it and heard the rasping clunk of the mechanism engaging.

The doors moved easily for their size, soundless and smooth. The space beyond, small by comparison to the spacious hall, was unfinished, the raw wood boards of the walls poorly aligned so tiny slits let bright sunlight through. It smelled of dust and peaches. Ailanthe stepped through and the floorboards creaked and shifted under her weight.

In the center of the room was an equally ill-built staircase spiraling beyond the range of her vision, and Ailanthe hesitated before it. It looked like it might fall apart under her weight, its handrail missing large sections and the nail heads protruding from the steps in places. *If the Castle repairs things,* she thought, *it's doing a poor job of it here.* She put her hand on the rail and her foot on the first step. It was going to be a long climb, but she had to know what lay at the top of it.

She meant to count the steps, but the first time one of the steps bowed under her weight, she lost track. She gripped the stair rail hard and gasped again when it too swayed. She released it and stood unmoving in the center of the staircase, trying not to do anything that might persuade it to drop her to the landing below, or all the way to its base.

When she'd regained control of her heart, she moved her foot cautiously to the next step and breathed more easily when it took her weight without complaining. It was unlikely she'd fall to her death, which was a terrifying thought; but if she broke her arm, or her leg, it was just as unlikely the Castle would heal her the way it did Coren's wall. She moved more cautiously after that, testing the steps as she came to them, so she was at the top before she realized it, her head rising through a round hole in the floor above.

How the floor of this room could be made of stone when the rest of the tower was wood puzzled her, but its rough, irregular cobs were reassuringly solid, and she sat down with her legs resting on one of the last steps and looked around. The ceiling was a miniature of the vaulted passageway surrounding the Honor Hall. Square windows with black-painted frames lined the walls, providing an unimpeded view of the pale, cloudless blue sky in all directions. Her legs still shaky from the climb, Ailanthe stood and went to look out the nearest window.

The forests of Lindurien lay spread out beneath her, as far as she could see.

It was so unexpected her breath caught and her heart pounded once, painfully hard. She threw herself at the window, not thinking about how dangerous that might be, that the window frames might be as rotted and unstable as the stairs, and pressed her face against it as if that might bring her closer to home.

Home.

A strong wind gusted across the tops of the trees, making them bend as wildly as if they were kites straining to fly free. Impossible to tell if they were *her* trees, *her* home, but at the moment she wanted so desperately to be back she felt she could endure any amount of rejection by the trees if only she could walk beneath them again.

The glass felt slick under her cheek. She reached up and realized she was crying. It was *so close* and all she could do was weep like a child and feel sorry for herself. She straightened, wiped her face and smeared the tears off the glass, and made a circuit of the room. She'd never seen Lindurien from this vantage point, but she recognized the heights of Duathenin, where the goats danced on the cliff side, and off to one side lay the blackened place where fire had taken some of the grandfather trees last year, and between those two locations she was able to determine where she was, and where home was.

Window seats lay at intervals beneath the windows, their dull green cushions rock-hard and dusty, but she knelt on one and stared out in the direction of her home, trying not to cry again. If she could get out of this tower, she could climb down and be back in Lindurien. If she could get out of this tower.

She could probably break the windows with little effort, but she would need a rope—a long rope—and some idea of what lay beneath her. But it could work. She pressed her hand against the glass, fingers spread, so her palm covered the place where her home might be. She could return. She just had to be smarter than the Castle.

She cautiously went back down the stairs and retraced her steps. The shadows seemed thicker in contrast to the bright sunlight, and her footsteps, strangely, seemed louder on the carpeted hall than they had on the bare wood of the stairs. She walked faster, feeling uneasy and not sure why. The hall was empty even of sprites.

Something moved in a doorway as she passed, and she whipped around, her heart pounding. Nothing but shadow. She broke into a run for a few steps before slowing down and laughing at herself. She'd been chased away from the tower by nothing more than an overwrought imagination. How fortunate for her Coren hadn't witnessed that; she must have looked so foolish.

Coren wasn't in his rooms; she found him in the Library, reading in the same deep armchair, his feet resting on a low stool. He raised his head from his book when she entered, waiting for her to speak. There was so much she had to tell him that it all tangled in her head, but what came out was, "Would you like to see Lindurien?"

"I've seen it—but that's not what you mean, is it?" Coren said, closing his book.

She held up the key. "This opens the tower. I took a chance—"

"Show me," Coren said.

They ran through the halls, Coren shortening his stride to a jog so Ailanthe could keep up with him, then ascended the rickety stairs more cautiously. Coren knelt on one of the dusty cushions just as Ailanthe had and gazed out over the forest. "Unbelievable," he said. "I've seen it from lower down, but this is…I had no idea the forest was this big."

"My home is that way, somewhere," Ailanthe said, pointing. "If I could get out of this tower—"

"You'd fall to your death," Coren pointed out. "How many feet higher than the roof are we? And who knows how much farther it is to the ground from there."

"There has to be a way." She gripped the key tightly, then exclaimed as its teeth bit into her hand. She looked at it more closely. "That's strange," she said.

"What is?"

She extended the key to him. "It didn't look like this before. It was thinner, and had three teeth instead of two."

"Why did it change?"

"I don't know." She closed her hand around it, more loosely this time, then made for the stairs. Back in the hallway, she trotted along until she reached a door, a white and glossy door with pink flowers painted around the keyhole. She rattled the knob, satisfied herself it was locked, then pressed the key into the keyhole. With hardly any resistance, it went in and turned easily. Ailanthe removed the key and stared at it again. A much thinner shaft, and several small teeth with deep notches.

"Did you unlock that door?" Coren said, coming up behind her.

Ailanthe nodded and pushed the door open. The room was empty except for a scattering of dust over the pale wood floor. "I admit it's's a little anticlimactic," she said, "but I think this is the master key to the Castle."

Coren held out his hand for it and examined it from all angles. "The Castle never gives out anything but junk," he said. "Why would it put this in the Honor Hall?"

"I don't know," Ailanthe said, "but I think it's going to regret it."

AILANTHE UNLOCKED the door and pushed it open, its shining lacquered metal surface cold under her palm. That made seven doors of metal, thirteen of unfinished wood, five of woven vines even more solid than the metal, and five of a gray, pitted material that echoed when she rapped on it. The Castle apparently could not make up its mind about the uniformity of its construction.

Three days of searching the top floor, and she and Coren hadn't found anything useful, like an exit or even a length of rope. Or, rather, they'd found any number of interesting things, like the palm-sized cylinder that emitted a beam of light when you squeezed it, but with the Castle returning everything to its place at midnight, there was nothing worth taking away. This would probably go no faster if Coren were here instead of in the middle of his daily exercise, but at least she would have company.

This room, like the other three she'd tried today, was a storage room about the size of the bedroom she'd claimed for herself; like the other rooms, it smelled of dust that hadn't been disturbed in, she guessed, centuries, with an unexpected hint of sweetness from flowers Ailanthe couldn't see. Furniture like no Lindurian had ever used cluttered every inch of space. What little she could see of the floor was scuffed and worn, gouged in some places from wooden legs being shoved more tightly into the available space.

She squeezed between an ornately carved armoire and a rosewood table with twelve chairs stacked atop it. Maybe it was pointless to search this room for anything but more furniture, but she couldn't take the chance that it might not contain the rope she needed.

To her left, something moved. She jumped, banged her hip against the table, then realized it was her own reflection in a mirror leaning at a sharp angle against the wall. She laughed at herself. All this stillness was making her jittery. She even imagined she'd seen the shadows moving, once or twice, in ways that couldn't be explained by the flickering, wan light of the decrepit glowing lamps.

She looked at her reflection. The mirror was cracked at one corner, covered with dust so her image was little more than a silhouette, her pale skin nearly white and her hazel eyes dull hollows. She waved at herself. The shadowy figure waved back at her, and she shivered; it looked like a ghost rather than a reflection.

She finished digging through the furniture, which was too tightly packed for her to reach the back of the room, and relocked the door. There was no reason to, but she felt, superstitiously, that the Castle would prefer her not to disturb it more than necessary. She tried to summon up outrage that she might give in to anything the Castle wanted, but succeeded only in feeling a mild worry that there was still a possibility it would let her out, if she only behaved herself. She pounded once on the door in irritation, then rubbed away the ache in her fist. She wasn't going to let a...a *thing* beat her.

She stretched, rolled her shoulders, and unlocked the next door. The room was full of trunks and dressers and wardrobes, all overflowing with clothing. There were a few mannequins dressed in Indrijanese caps and floor-length sleeveless tunics in jewel tones like the Library books, open over long-sleeved shirts and wide-legged pants that might be mistaken for skirts. She'd seen the same costumes in the Indrijan room on the first floor. Ailanthe lifted a filmy sleeve and let it fall, drifting, back to where it lay. Maybe there was something useful in one of these trunks. She began hauling clothing out and dumping it on the floor.

The light in here was dimmer than in the hall outside, the shadows thicker. Ailanthe couldn't see into the depths of the trunk; she used her hands to feel around inside, verifying there was nothing in it but clothing. She piled everything back into the trunk and moved to a dresser, opening each drawer and throwing its contents on the floor. Still nothing.

She turned, and once again caught movement out of the corner of her eye. She looked at the mirror and couldn't see her reflection from where she knelt on the floor. What...? Her eye was drawn toward the mannequin in the far corner, the one wearing the black cap and the red tunic.

It turned its head toward her, its blind, empty face tilted up as if sniffing the air. Ailanthe backed away until she bumped into the dresser, gaping, ignoring the pain in her hip where the corner of the dresser dug into it. The mannequin lifted its arm and pointed at her. It had no elbow joint, and its long arm rose like the hand of a clock sweeping out the minutes. Then it began to walk, stiff-legged, toward her.

Ailanthe turned to run and tripped over the open trunk. A jolt of pain went through her wrist as she caught herself on both hands. She scrambled to her feet, slid on a silky dress and went down on her knees. Behind her, footsteps and the occasional knock of cloth-covered wood against wood told her the thing was still advancing.

She pushed herself to her feet and looked behind her. Another mannequin had come to life and with both arms raised was trying to find a way around the chest of drawers that blocked its path.

Ailanthe clenched her teeth on a scream and bolted for the door, feeling the faintest tug of wooden fingers on her hair before she threw herself through the doorway and slammed and locked it. She leaned against it, her heart pounding, then shrieked as something struck the door from the other side, hard enough to make it bounce on its hinges. She backed up until she ran into the opposite wall and stared at the door. Something struck it again, not as hard this time, then a third time, and she could barely hear the thump. Then everything was silent.

Ailanthe realized she was clenching the key so hard the feeling had left her fingers. She opened her hand and let the key dangle from its chain, then massaged her sore wrist. What else might be locked up in these rooms? She looked around at the gathering shadows and told herself she didn't see them moving. Well, she wasn't going to give up just because the Castle had some eerie things lurking inside it. It was coincidence that it was time for lunch now.

Miriethiel was waiting in the kitchen when she arrived, just as he had the last three days. "I wish I knew how you always know when food is on the way," she said, scratching his throat and feeling the vibration of his purr through her fingertips. He leaned into her petting for a moment, then leaped onto the counter and paced, giving her his silent stare. "And you never meow. All the cats I've ever known were vocal about needing things. Maybe, with no other cats around, you've forgotten how to talk."

She cut up a small chicken breast and tossed a few little cubes his way; he snatched them out of the air and gulped them down almost without chewing. He always behaved as if he were two inches from starvation, though his fur was sleek and his flanks and belly lean but not emaciated. If there were other cats in the Castle, she'd never seen them. She guessed he was five or six years old, certainly not ancient or an adolescent, but it might be possible, given the Castle's abilities, that he was a good deal older than that. Miriethiel was just another one of the strangenesses of the Castle.

She swept half the cubes into a bowl and put it on a shelf in the cold room. "You'll get sick if you eat it all now," she scolded Miriethiel when he made imploring faces at her and butted his head against the counter. She took a cloth from the narrow, almost-hidden cupboard where they were stored and ran it under the faucet—amazing, all the new words she was learning—then washed off the counter.

Her own lunch was bread shaped like a ring with a hard, shiny crust, and a pot of blackberry jam that left her fingers sticky. It had turned out Coren didn't know how to light a fire either, so she only looked longingly at the enormous salmon laid out ready to be filleted and closed the cold room door.

She sat on the counter and ate her bread and jam and planned her next step. She ought to ask Coren about the mannequins. Surely if he'd seen anything like that, he would have mentioned it; the memory made her shudder, thinking of that light brush against the back of her head. Then she would go back to exploring the rooms. Whatever those things had been, they couldn't keep her from finding a way home.

A deep, low tone, almost too low to hear, rang through the still air. It sent vibrations all through Ailanthe's body and made her teeth buzz enough she clenched her jaw against it and closed her eyes. The sound grew in volume until she felt she was inside a giant bell, the clapper striking its bronze sides once and then hanging motionless. It had to be the Castle bell. A quester had arrived.

CHAPTER SIX

*a*ilanthe dropped her half-eaten bread and pot of jam on the floor. The pot shattered, and Ailanthe landed in the spreading puddle when she jumped down. She raced out of the kitchen annex and jumped over Miriethiel, who'd tried to rub up against her legs, bolted down the blue hallway leaving little footprints of jam, and raced across the flagstones surrounding the Honor Hall. If she could get there before the door closed....

There were so many little rooms between her and the entrance, all of them filled with unnecessary furniture she had to dodge or slide over, and she was panting when she emerged into the entry hall. But it was too late. The door was closed, the hall was dark except for the indirect light from the rooms on both sides, and a woman stood looking at her curiously, as if wondering what madwoman the Castle had produced for her.

She was very tall, probably six feet or more, and the way she carried her head made her look taller still. She wore the robes of a Rius-zaran nomad, the bright white fabric draped about her body to keep her cool in the hot desert sun, and more cloth was wound above and around her face so only her eyes were revealed. A belt strung with dozens of inch-wide silver rings surrounded her waist, and in her right hand she held a staff as long as she was tall, with a large knot at one end carved to look like something that was indistinct in that dim light. She wore rings on every finger of her left hand, and the edges of a gold bracelet peeped out below that sleeve.

"I am *so glad* to see you," Ailanthe panted. "I need your help. The Castle won't let me out. Will you open the door for me?" Somewhere in this torrent of words, she realized she was babbling, but she didn't care. This woman might mean her freedom.

The woman's eyes narrowed, and she pulled down the cloth covering her mouth to reveal copper-colored skin and firm lips set in a frown. "I do not understand how it is I speak your language," she said.

"The Castle makes everyone speak its language. It's nothing to worry about. It will pass when you leave. I'm Ailanthe. What's your name?"

The woman continued to frown at her. "Why cannot you leave?"

"I don't know. I think I took the wrong thing from the Honor Hall. But you won't have any trouble—"

"And you are sure of this why?"

"I…" There was no good answer to this question. "You came here for a destiny, right? So take your destiny, and we'll see what happens."

The woman nodded, slowly. "My use-name is Idantra," she said. "Where is this Honor Hall? I do not wish to linger in this Castle. It feels wrong, deep in my bones."

"I know," Ailanthe said, though aside from the mannequins and the shadows she hadn't felt anything particularly dangerous from it. "The Honor Hall is this way."

Despite what she'd said about leaving quickly, Idantra stared at the Hall for some time. "It seems impossible for man to have built something of this nature," she finally said.

"When you step into the Honor Hall, it will fill with things," Ailanthe said, wishing she could propel the woman down the steps and onto the shining floor. "When you take one, the rest of the things will disappear, and you'll be able to leave."

"So you say," Idantra said. "Suppose I am trapped here too?"

"There's no way to know unless you try." *Pick her up, carry her down the stairs, as if you could lift someone that size. And she'd probably brain you with that staff.* The knob at the top was carved to look like a snake's head, though so awkwardly it was barely recognizable as such.

Idantra took one last look around her, then strode without hesitation to the stairs. Ailanthe followed her. She almost went down the stairs before she realized the things—the Things, the Castle's strangeness made tangible—might not appear if she were in the Hall. So she stood at the top of the stairs and watched the Things flash into sight.

Idantra made no movement of surprise, simply began wandering the narrow paths made by the tables and cabinets. Ailanthe forced her fists to open and balanced on the balls of her feet at the top of the stairs, craning to see what the woman would choose. Was she really going to look at absolutely every item in the Hall? Ailanthe pressed her lips tightly together to avoid calling out advice. She was the one trapped in the Castle, probably by her choice of Things, and any advice she might give was probably wrong.

Idantra stopped to look at a pile of jewelry tangled together on a tabletop. "How strange," she said, and reached out to take a wide golden bracelet from the pile. Instantly the rest of the Things vanished, and Idantra twitched, surprised this time. She returned to the stairs, her attention on the bracelet.

"I believed mine to be unique," she said, passing the bracelet to her left hand and pushing up that sleeve with her right. A wide cuff of beaten gold encircled her wrist; she held up the bracelet she'd taken from the Honor Hall and displayed it to Ailanthe. It was identical to the first. "This seems a sign that I am on the correct path." She put the new bracelet on her right wrist, where it fit as snugly as if it had been made for her.

"The Castle is bigger than you can imagine, and there are rooms containing nothing but castoffs that don't have a home anywhere else," Ailanthe said. "Who knows what else it might hold?"

"Indeed," said Idantra. "Now show me the exit, and we will see if we can leave together."

Idantra's stride was longer than Ailanthe's, but she nearly outraced the woman to the door. "Through there," she said, opening the inner door and waiting for Idantra to walk through. The woman looked up at the small window, which today showed a night sky and part of a crescent moon.

"So Castle Always does exist in all places and all times," Idantra said, her voice subdued. "What place is that?"

"I don't know," Ailanthe said. "Somewhere far away, probably. If you open the door, you'll find out."

"How long have you been caught here?" Idantra said, her expression barely visible in the dimness of the chamber.

"Five days."

"And already so eager to be gone? This Castle does not feel hospitable, true, but five days does not seem so long."

"It is when you have somewhere else you want to be."

"True." Idantra put her hand on the latch. "Let us see, then, what will come of this."

She pressed down on the latch. It didn't move.

Ailanthe's stomach knotted. "Try harder," she said.

"I am putting all my strength into this, and it is not inconsiderable strength," Idantra said. "It is as if it was not made to move. Are you certain there are no other doors?"

Ailanthe nodded. She didn't think she could speak through her disappointment. "Then I suppose you're trapped here too," she said.

"Perhaps," Idantra said, again eyeing Ailanthe. "Or perhaps it is simply responding to your presence." In an instant, the hard knob of the staff was under Ailanthe's chin, pressing against her throat. "Back away now," Idantra said.

Ailanthe raised her hands. "Don't—" she began, and the staff pressed harder, cutting her off.

"There's no need for violence," Coren said. "She's no threat to you."

Idantra hissed and whipped her staff around toward Coren's head. He dodged it, stepped inside her guard and gripped the staff with both hands above hers. He twisted, and suddenly the staff was in his hands and Idantra was backing toward the outer door.

"Get out of the Vestibule, Ailanthe," he said, his eyes never leaving Idantra's. He had still been exercising when the bell rang; he was half-dressed and looked sweaty. Ailanthe dodged past him and through the inner door. "You, whoever you are, count five after this door closes and you should be able to leave. And for your sake I hope you're less willing to leap to the attack when something out there challenges you."

He threw the staff on the ground and had the door shut on Idantra before she could take it up again. "Back to the hall," he said, and took Ailanthe by the shoulder and steered her into the blue hall. Ailanthe was too surprised to resist.

They stood, waiting, until Coren said, "She must be gone now," and released her. Ailanthe rubbed her shoulder, though he hadn't hurt her, and stared back the way they'd come, half expecting Idantra to come leaping out of the kitchen annex with her snake-staff raised.

"I'm sorry," Coren said. "I thought, since you had your Thing, that maybe another quester could open the door for both of you. For me —it won't open if I'm in range to run through it, and if someone holds the door open, it slams shut when I approach." He hesitated, then laid a hand on her shoulder, gently. "If I'd known, I never would have given you hope like that."

Ailanthe turned and walked away down the blue hall, away from his touch that he probably meant to be comforting. Her mind was filled with the image of the door latch and Idantra's hand on it, trying to force it down, and then it was the image of her own hand doing the same thing, and Coren's, and when she came to herself she was at the top of the tower, looking out across Lindurien.

The cushion was hard beneath her knees, barely softer than the wooden bench it rested on, and without knowing why she brushed her fingertips against it and sniffed the dust that clung to them. It was dry and bitter and smelled of dead things. Maybe they were all dead, she and Coren and Miriethiel, and the Castle kept them moving out of some deranged need to have toys to play with.

"I really am sorry," Coren said from behind her. She nodded.

"I'm not angry," she said. "It's not your fault. I'm honestly surprised you're still sane after six years." She hadn't meant to say that, it seemed like such a personal comment, when what she really meant was *I'm not going to make it six years. I might not make it six months.*

"So am I," he said. He sat down beside her and looked out the window. "I did a lot of shouting, that first year. One week I had a sort of contest to see how many rooms I could smash before the Castle put them all back together. Then I got used to the silence. I've never minded being alone, and this was just more of it."

He traced the black window frame with his forefinger. "Sometimes I go to the Honor Hall and look at the empty floor, and think about walking down the stairs and taking something, just so I can make the door open. Then I remember being alone isn't the worst thing that could happen to me."

"Before I left home I'd never slept alone in my life," Ailanthe said. "My sister and I shared a room, and I didn't know what silence was until I curled up on that bedroom floor and didn't hear another person breathing."

"You're sleeping on the floor?" He was trying, and failing, not to sound shocked.

"The bed is too soft."

"You'll get used to it. The Castle won't make up the bedding if you're in it. It's more comfortable than waking to bare floorboards, or a carpet."

"I'll remember that." She didn't want to get used to it. She didn't want to get used to anything about this Castle. That reminded her of something else. "Do things in the Castle ever...come to life? Start moving on their own?"

Coren shook his head. "Have you seen something like that?"

She described her encounter with the mannequins, and added, "I was wondering if I should expect more of the same."

"I've never heard of anything like that."

"Well, I'm not giving up on getting out of here. Maybe I can at least ask one of these questers to send a message for me, tell my family I'm still alive. Though they probably aren't expecting to hear from me any time soon, since they think I'm off on a grand adventure."

"I wonder if the Castle would let a message through."

"It's worth trying."

"It is. I never thought about it. Though..." Coren paused for a moment, then said, "We'd be writing in the language of the Castle, so probably no one would understand anything we sent." He turned and sat with his back to the windows, laced his fingers together and rested them on his knee. "We could...no, that wouldn't work. Or...no. We'd have to wait for a Hesperan or Lindurian to come here, and that might take years. Damn it. That was a really good idea."

Ailanthe's heart sank again. She was going to be trapped here forever and everyone she loved would think she had died on her adventure. No. She was *not* going to be trapped here. There was a way out, and she would find it.

"You've decided not to give up," Coren said. He sounded amused.

"Can you tell that just by looking?"

"You have a very expressive face." He smiled at her, and she felt cheered by his presence.

"Thank you for stepping in with Idantra, back there," she said.

"Was that her name? She's not going to find much success, if she thinks she can get her way by threatening unarmed people smaller than she is." Coren stood, then seemed to realize for the first time his state of undress. "I'll go get cleaned up, and then I'll join you in searching. That Idantra must have thought I was some kind of Agranite savage." He grinned again and descended the stairs out of sight.

Ailanthe found her embarrassing desire to cry had passed. This Castle was not going to defeat her. It might be able to hold those doors closed, but she'd find a way out, and she'd take Coren and Miriethiel with her.

She and Coren spent the rest of the day exploring that hall. Coren, against Ailanthe's protest, insisted on investigating the mannequin room; nothing happened. The mannequins had returned to their original places. Ailanthe felt embarrassed, and wondered if Coren thought she had been imagining things, but he just shrugged and said, "Strange things happen in the Castle." They found nothing useful, though Ailanthe exclaimed in wonder at the long gallery filled with golden treasures that had to come from some Galendish queen's trove.

Finally, exhausted, she went back to her bathroom and luxuriated in a hot bath, then washed her clothes in the tub and hung them up to dry. Clad in her spare clothes, she went toward the stairs and met Coren coming up, laden with food. "Hungry?" he said.

"*Thank you*," she said so fervently he laughed.

The view from the window room at evening was extraordinary. The eastern windows showed the valley in twilight, the clouds at the tops of the cliffs turning pink and gold with the last of the sunlight. Sheep with matted grayish wool leaped from impossibly tiny ledges, unafraid of the hundreds of feet of open air beneath them. Through the western window, the ruddy disk of the sun was about to dip into the ocean, and the sky was molten gold and carnelian red above the white-capped waves throwing themselves against the shore. And through the northern windows, a blue-black sky burning with white stars hung over luminous sands stretching to the horizon. Ailanthe gazed out at the dunes and breathed, "It's so beautiful."

"The Castle may be our jailor, but it has some amazing views," Coren agreed. He offered her a leathery strip of something. "Dried meat," he said. "Not as good as the real thing, but better than nothing."

"I wonder why there's no fireplace," Ailanthe said. She bit into the meat and tore off a strip. It was juicy once she gnawed on it for a while.

"I can't imagine there isn't some way to cook food, unless the original inhabitants liked their meat raw, but I haven't been able to find it," Coren said. "And I don't want to risk setting myself on fire by experimenting. But sometimes I can't stop thinking about a nice, juicy steak, red in the middle and hot all the way through, or a leg of roast chicken—"

"Oh, don't start talking about that or I won't be able to eat this," Ailanthe said, waving the meat at him.

"I didn't realize Lindurians ate meat."

"Is this because we live in the trees, again?"

"No, it's because I didn't think you had anywhere to raise cattle, in the forest."

"Oh. Well, we don't raise cattle, but we keep chickens, and there are the goats out at Duathenin, and there are the plains where some of our people breed sheep. But what I really love is fish. Fresh salmon —you can't imagine what it's like, watching them thrash their way upstream to breed, roasting the filets over hot coals, and the salty roe...." Ailanthe looked at her meat and set it aside. "Now I've done it to myself."

"My family lives too far inland to have fish often. I've never cared for it. Too fishy a flavor."

"That means it's not fresh enough." Ailanthe took a small loaf of white bread and picked at it. "You know, raw salmon is pretty good, too."

Coren shuddered. "I'll stick to my leathery meat, thank you."

"Suit yourself." Ailanthe grinned at him. He smiled and took another bite of meat, then made a face. "Some days it's harder for me to accept my fate than others," he said.

Ailanthe couldn't think of anything to say to that. She looked at the wall—6 YRS 28 DAYS. And all he wanted was to go home. She looked back at him. He was staring out over the ocean and seemed not to notice her attention. He had a nice profile, all those sharp lines and planes—he was actually very good-looking, she thought, and flushed with embarrassment. She really must be lonely for human contact.

She walked over to the eastern windows and watched the last tinge of color fade from the mists until the sheep looked like faint clouds against the dark cliff. But he *was* remarkable, she told herself, and not because he was the only other human being, the only man, she had any contact with. He'd managed to stay sane all this time and he hadn't assaulted her, though he must be as starved for...female companionship...as any other kind of human interaction. And he still had a sense of humor.

"Ailanthe," he said, startling her. He beckoned to her, then pointed out the western window. At first, she saw nothing, then, far in the distance, water spouted from a sleek, dark back that crested the waves and then disappeared. She found she was holding her breath. There it was again, or maybe it was a different creature, but in either case it was so beautiful she was speechless.

"Whales," Coren said. "You don't see them very often. Makes me wish to be out there on the waves, close enough to really look at them."

"They must be enormous if we can see them from this far away."

"They are. I read a book that said some whales get to be almost one hundred feet long. But I don't think those are that big."

"That's amazing." He was close enough she could smell the fresh, clean scent of his soap, and it made her feel uncomfortable, as if she were intruding on his privacy yet again. They watched in silence until several minutes had passed with no more signs of the creatures, then Ailanthe went to look at the desert, conscious that she was moving out of Coren's reach and not sure how she felt about that, other than ashamed of herself. The desert was so still it might as well be a painting. The animal she'd seen the other day was probably still out there somewhere, free to travel as she was not. She suddenly felt tired all the way to her bones. "I'm ready for sleep, I think," she said. "Thank you for dinner."

"My pleasure," Coren said. He was still looking out the window. "I'll see you in the morning."

Ailanthe nodded, though he wouldn't see the gesture, and went back to her room, feeling dull of mind and body. It seemed darker than usual in the hall outside her room, and she was just able to think *I wonder what's wrong with the light* before the shadows engulfed her.

CHAPTER SEVEN

$\mathcal{I}$t was like being pulled under the forest pool in midwinter, cold so intense it burned through every part of her. She was drowning in spider's silk, sticky and cottony, surrounding her body and her mouth and eyes so she could hardly breathe, let alone scream. She tore at the shadows, but they barely gave way before more of them took the place of the ones she destroyed. Lights danced before her eyes, white and gold and copper and even, insanely, black. She needed more light to drive the shadows away. The lamp was in her bedroom, just beyond the closed door.

She clawed more shadows away from her face and tried to shout for Coren, but all that came out was a choked gasp. The dancing lights were brighter and larger now, and she felt herself becoming dizzy. She staggered backward into the wall, knocked her head hard against the doorframe, and the lights vanished. If she could only find the doorknob—she could see the lamp, feel its smooth casing under her fingers—then her hand closed on something hard, and white light filled the hallway, blinding her.

The shadows shriveled and fled, leaving her shivering with her back to the door and blinking away tears from the brightness. The hard thing was still in her hand, and she squinted at it until her eyes adjusted.

It was her lamp.

She fumbled and nearly dropped it in her surprise. There was no doubt it was the same lamp she'd been using all afternoon; there was a dent in the upper casing that she'd wondered at, since the Castle was so meticulous about mending everything in its domain.

She went to press the button that turned it off, then stopped herself. The shadows might come back. Instead she went into her bedroom and closed the door tight, locked it, then unlocked it. If the shadows were going to attack her again, they might be able to come through the cracks and under the door, and she might need to leave the room in a hurry.

All the lights were still burning in her room, and she set the lamp on a table near the door, then nearly knocked it over as she realized the lamp was already sitting, cold and dark, on the dresser across the room. She looked from one to the other, then took the burning lamp and set it next to the unlit one. They were identical. She turned the second lamp—the original lamp?—to its maximum brightness. There was not a speck of difference between them.

She began to shake again, but not from the cold. Too many shocks in too short a time. She gathered up the blanket, wrapped it around herself, and sat on the edge of the bed, her thoughts raging from one strange occurrence to another. Shadows attacking—the lamp—and the lamp again—she looked at her hands, both empty, the key dangling from one wrist. Was it the reason for the mystery?

She scanned the room, which with all the light from so many different sources was blessedly free of shadows. She'd needed light, and it had appeared. No—she'd needed light, and she'd *made* light for herself.

She lay down on her side and burrowed under the sheets, dragging the blanket like a cocoon with her, and stared sightlessly at the far wall. She had never shown the slightest aptitude for magic, or even for music, absolute prerequisite for becoming a *kerthor* and singing down the trees. But then, if this was magic—and what else could it be?—it was nothing like the magic of her home, where men and women with flute and voice bent the living wood to their will.

She clenched her hand into a fist and closed her body around it, as if that might seal in any other strange thing it might think to do. There had been the thought of a light, and then there had been the light, and the shadows had fled from it.

She threw off the bedding and was halfway to the door before she stopped herself. This was *definitely* something Coren would have mentioned if he had the same ability, if it were something triggered by living in the Castle. She had to tell him...but he was probably in bed by now, and the thought of knocking on his bedroom door made her cheeks burn. Who knew what he might think she was after? This would have to wait until morning.

She turned the disc on the wall that controlled the bedroom lights and set them at their maximum brightness, then carried the new lamp, her lamp, back to the table by the door. No shadows in her room tonight. She crawled back into bed and dragged the blanket over her eyes and waited for morning to come.

All night, she dozed, then woke to the reflections of the room in the dark windowpanes, then slept again to dream of spiders with frozen legs and peach-scented sprites wrapping them in their insubstantial bodies. When she finally woke to daylight beyond her window, it took her a moment to realize the light was natural.

She sat up and looked around. The bedroom lights glowed as brightly as ever. The lamp on the dresser was gone. The lamp on the table by the door, the one she'd made or summoned or imagined, still sat there, burning perhaps a little less brightly, though that could be in contrast with the sunrise. She rolled out of her tangle of sheets and approached the lamp slowly, picked it up and looked at the dent. It seemed far too solid a thing to have been created out of nothing, in response to her need.

She looked back and saw the Castle had made the bed for her. No, not for her, but to satisfy its need for control. She gripped the lamp's handle more tightly. The Castle hadn't taken it away in the night. Hadn't taken it, or couldn't take it? The Castle never showed the least bit of concern about the needs of the people trapped inside it, or their comfort, let alone their wishes. If it hadn't removed the lamp, it was probably because it couldn't.

She flexed her free hand. It didn't look any different in the light of morning than it had in lamplight the previous night. *The question is, can I do it again?*

She tried to remember the terror she'd felt and how desperate she had been, closed her eyes and waved her hand. Nothing. She had thought of the lamp—no, more than that, she'd almost felt the lamp in her hand, remembering how it had felt to carry it from room to room and how annoyed she'd been when she knocked her knee against it—

Her hand again closed on something smooth. This time, she hissed in surprise and dropped the lamp. It rolled a little way from her feet and she stared at it, then prodded it with her toe. It had a dent in the base now from hitting the floor. She looked from the lamp in her hand to the lamp on the floor and tried to calm her rapid breathing. The new lamp shed its light under the bed, dispelling the shadows there—she'd slept all night on that bed and never realized she'd forgotten there was one place that would always be dark.

She flattened herself on the floor and scanned the space, but nothing moved. She edged backwards, unable to take her eyes off what was left of the darkness, and grabbed the lamp and stumbled to her feet. The two lamps swung by their handles, their beams faded in the morning sunlight.

She remembered Idantra's Thing, the bracelet that matched the one she already had. Was it possible the Castle had *three* identical lamps and she was simply summoning them, one after another? That seemed unlikely, but how much more likely was it that she was creating them out of need or desire? She knew so little about magic; maybe this was perfectly normal, if you could call anything that twisted the basic nature of reality normal. It was past time to talk to Coren. He might know something, or know a book that would tell her what was happening to her.

She took the lamps with her, shining them behind her down

the dark corridor, but nothing moved. Even so, she was running when she reached the stairs and nearly bumped into Coren, laden with the day's supplies, his sword banging at his hip. "Good morning," he said. Then he looked concerned. "Did something happen to—"

"I made this lamp," she blurted out, holding both of them up. He winced at the brightness, and she lowered them away from his face. "I'm not mad."

"Mad was not the word I had in mind," he said. "Overwhelmed, maybe. I told you, strange things happen in the Castle."

"Strange like finding a lamp in my hand where there wasn't one before?"

"You weren't fumbling around in the dark and your hand landed on it?"

"Coren, something's happening to me and I need you to take me seriously."

He examined her more closely. "I am. You're whiter than usual and your lips are pale. Are you hungry?"

"Yes, damn it, but that's not what I'm talking about!"

He gave her that direct, considering gaze. "Come on," he said. "Food first. Then you can tell me about the lamp you made."

Ailanthe sat next to the desert window and ate strawberries as if they were shadows she could consume out of existence. A hand reached past her and took the bowl away. "You'll get sick," Coren said, and gave her half a loaf of bread. "There's milk if you want it." The milk tasted strange, not like the goat's milk she was accustomed to, but she gulped it down.

Now that the confusion and fear had passed, she found herself angry. She had done *nothing* to the Castle but what everyone else for centuries had done—enter the door and take what was freely offered. And now it had apparently decided she was an enemy to be eliminated. The moving mannequins and now tangible shadows—maybe she hadn't been imagining things when she'd thought the shadows were moving before. Why it wouldn't just let her go was a mystery, but she no longer cared about solving it. She was going to get out, and if she could destroy some part of the Castle in doing so, she'd enjoy that.

Coren dragged his seat next to hers and picked up the two lamps, comparing them side by side. "They're identical," he said. "Except for this dent."

"I made that lamp this morning and I was so surprised it worked I dropped it. The important thing is they're identical to the lamp I took from a storeroom yesterday while I was searching. Last night—" She paused to order her thoughts. "It felt as if the shadows took form. *Something* certainly tried to suffocate me outside my room. I needed light, and suddenly *that* was in my hand."

She pointed at the undented lamp. "And this morning I tried to do it again, and there was another lamp. I swear to you I'm not mad and I'm not making this up."

She closed her eyes and held out her hand. It was easier this time, as if she'd learned to flex a new muscle. The smooth casing of the lamp filled her palm, and she fumbled it a little before she found the handle. She opened her eyes. Coren was staring at the new lamp in astonishment. He looked down at the ones in his hands, then back at hers.

"It just appeared," he said. "Like when the Castle takes something."

"Is that what it looks like?"

"I've done everything I could think of to keep it from taking things at midnight." He set the lamps in his hands down, carefully, and held out his hand for the new one. "No dent."

"So it's like the original."

Coren nodded. "And the Castle didn't take the new one back."

"It's never taken the bag I brought with me. It doesn't take your sword."

"That's not my sword. I take it from the armory early every morning. If there were one thing I could keep the Castle from reclaiming at night, that would be it." He put his hands on his knees. "This can't be magic."

"It can't be anything else."

"Then it's magic like I've never read about. And I spent two months reading everything I could find about it."

"Tell me about magic, then."

"You know more about Lindurian magic than I do, probably. Your *kerthors* use music to build a framework for magic to cling to, and the shape of the framework tells the magic what to do. Most of the northern countries do it that way. Galendan and Enthalia, definitely."

"The *kerthors* tie their magic to the trees somehow—that's really as much as I know."

"It's different in the south and east," Coren said. "In Hespera, we talk to the spirits of those who refuse to pass on and ask them to perform magic for us. They're more or less made of the same substance, so it's no harder for them to touch magic than it is for me to take this chair and move it across the room. It's probably not as reliable as a *kerthor's* magic, but anyone can do it if they know the right way to get a spirit's attention. Most of the southern countries do it this way, though the ways people talk to the spirits vary. Like, in Rius-zara spirit-talking is part of their religion, so their priests are the only ones who are allowed to wield magic."

"What else?"

"There is no else. Those are the only two ways of using magic anyone's ever recorded."

"That doesn't explain the Castle."

"The Castle is made of magic. It acts on itself. Like you or me scratching an itch. You don't need some outside force to lift your hand for you." He set the third lamp down next to the first two and aligned them neatly into a row.

Ailanthe said, "But this had to be magic. I didn't imagine it."

"Maybe the Castle gave them to you."

"After trying to kill me? Why would it do that?"

Coren shrugged. "Who knows? Nothing it does ever makes sense. Or maybe...."

"Maybe what?"

"Maybe you made the Castle use its power for you. It's capable of instantly moving any item to any place it wants. And it's not impossible that the Castle has a room full of those things somewhere." He reached out and prodded a lamp on the floor with his toe.

"Why couldn't I have used the magic directly? Without music or spirits?"

Coren shook his head. "That's not possible."

"Are you sure about that?"

"Yes. It would be like trying...trying to touch time. We experience time passing, but it's not something we can alter, any more than a fish can make water flow upstream."

"But fish can fight the current."

"I'm not saying it's a perfect example."

Ailanthe scowled. "So I'm controlling the Castle. Why can't I make the door open?"

"I don't know. Have you tried since last night?"

Ailanthe gave him one startled look, then bounded out of her seat and ran out the door.

She flew down all the flights of stairs, arriving at the back door only a little winded, took hold of the latch and willed it to open. Nothing happened.

She gripped it more firmly and thought. She had pictured the lamp in her hand, had seen it clearly in her mind's eye. She closed her eyes and imagined her hand on the latch, pictured the motions it would take for the latch to depress and the door to swing open, and pressed again. Still nothing.

She imagined the Castle as a person, a tall, forbidding man with a face like a hatchet and long, bony fingers holding the latch in place, imagined those bones snapping one by one until his hand dropped away, and leaned on the thumb lever as hard as she could.

Nothing.

She sagged against the door, the solid unmoving iron of the latch the only thing keeping her upright. One more possibility gone. She said, without looking up, "It was a nice idea."

"It might still be true," Coren said. "So far all you've been able to summon are lamps. Why don't you try something else?"

She sighed. "Like what?"

"Another loaf of bread? I don't know about you, but this mystery has made me hungry."

She glanced up at him. In the few days she'd known him, he'd gone from being withdrawn to being the man she guessed he'd been before coming to Castle Always—not exactly outgoing, but easy to talk to and quick to laugh, and he seemed to enjoy her company. Now there was an unfamiliar light in his eyes, an alert look to his face that made her heart beat faster. She turned her head before he could see her blush.

"A loaf of bread," she repeated, and closed her eyes. She pictured a loaf of bread, crunchy-hard and brown, imagined its warm, faintly rough surface against her palm, the yeasty smell of it, and for a moment thought she felt something solid against her fingers, but closed her hand on nothing.

"Did you see anything?" she asked. Coren shook his head. "I thought I felt something, just for a moment."

"There wasn't even a trace of an image," Coren said. "I wonder what makes the difference."

"Well, I did know that lamp awfully well, after spending half a day clutching it," she said. "Maybe I need to try with something else I know well."

They both looked at the key dangling from her wrist. "I...think that might be a bad idea," Coren said. "It has its own kind of magic. It might even be what lets you summon things, if it's connected to the Castle in some way."

"But it could prove whether I'm summoning or creating," Ailanthe pointed out, "because I have trouble believing there's more than one of *these* lying around."

She closed her eyes and pictured the key, how the silver streaks moved under her hand, and a spike of pain went through her skull and into her spinal column so fast she couldn't even draw breath to scream. It drove the barely formed image out of her mind and made her knees buckle.

Dimly, she heard a keening noise coming from what she thought might be her own throat, and felt two hands supporting her, lowering her slowly to lie flat on the floor. Tears leaked from her eyes and slid down her cheeks into her ears. Now that the initial agony was past, her head ached and she could taste blood from where she'd bitten her tongue. She swallowed, tried not to gag on the copper-salty taste, and forced herself to breathe normally.

A hand brushed across her temple, wiping away a tear. "Does it help if I support your head?" Coren asked quietly.

Ailanthe started to nod, realized that was stupid, and said, "Yes," and he slid his hands under her head and lifted it to rest on his knee. The pain lessened dramatically. "You were right that that was a bad idea," she whispered.

"I wish I'd been wrong. That looked agonizing. Are you going to be all right?"

"I think so." The pain felt distant now, like the memory of pain, and she opened her eyes and looked at Coren, then had to blink to make his face come into focus. "This is far more powerful than just a key."

"If it's capable of opening all the locks in the Castle, it would have to have something of the Castle's own magic in it," Coren said, "and that's very powerful magic. Do you want to try to stand?"

This time, she was capable of nodding, and Coren helped her up from the floor, then kept a grip on her elbow just in case. A part of her registered again how good he smelled, but mostly she was preoccupied with not throwing up on herself or on him. "You keep saying the Castle has its own magic," she said, trying to distract herself, "but that it's different magic, and I don't see how that fits with there being only two kinds."

"There isn't a lot written about the Castle," Coren said. "Mostly theories. One is that a bunch of spirits came together to build themselves a new body using magic, and it took this shape. Another is that the Castle built itself and the quantity of magic that went into doing it made it sentient. And a few people believe it was created by a person who sacrificed his or her body and became the spirit of the Castle. Those are the less crazy theories."

"I don't see how that answers my question."

"The idea is that using magic on magic seems to alter it into something new. I don't know if anyone's ever proved it. Are you sure you're ready to walk?"

"I want to go to the Library and read some of these books. Will you show me where they are?"

"Of course, but I think you shouldn't walk so fast just yet. You're weaving a little."

"I'll be fine." Ailanthe leaned heavily on the stair rail and hoped Coren didn't notice.

They ascended in silence for a while, then Coren said, "There's two other bedrooms in my suite. I think you should move into one of them."

Ailanthe had to grip the stair rail harder. "Oh?" she managed.

"You producing things out of the air was a bit of a distraction, but I didn't miss the part where you said you were attacked outside your room. I think it would be safer for you if you weren't alone."

"Oh," she repeated. "I...think you're right." *And let's forget what I thought you were asking.*

She retrieved her bag from her room and left it in the bedroom across from Coren's. It was a pleasant room painted blue and white that looked out over a forest of broad-leaved trees populated by birds of every possible color; she wished she could push the window open and hear what their cries sounded like. Then they went to the Library, and Coren showed her the S-shaped curve of shelf where the books on magic were kept. There were more than a hundred of them, and Ailanthe's heart sank at the thought of searching every one.

"Don't worry," Coren said, taking in her despairing face. "Many of these are technical books for *kerthors*, though some are about convincing spirits to do your will. I suppose it's possible they might have something about the Castle in them, but I doubt it. At least, I never found anything like that in them." He pulled out two and handed them to her. "Try these. Good information on magic theory, and they talk a little bit about the Castle."

"How do you ever find anything in this place?" Ailanthe

exclaimed. She looked around her at the curving shelves. "Isn't everything just jumbled up?"

"I made a map." He went to a drawer under one of the lecterns scattered throughout the room and took out a sheet of cloth. "I tried to do this with some of the ink and paper here, sketch out where everything is, but of course the Castle isn't satisfied with returning the paper to the drawer, it has to put the ink back into the bottles. So this is what's left of one of my shirts and a stick of charcoal I brought with me."

It was smudged and hard to read, but Ailanthe saw how the contours of what Coren had drawn matched her guess as to how the Library looked from above. "Are you wearing the Castle's clothes, then?" she asked.

"Yes." He smiled and hitched up one of his trouser legs to draw attention to where the fabric ended about an inch above his anklebone. "It was one of the reasons I moved in here, that the man who had the suite before me was more or less my size, only a little shorter. I've gotten used to it, but sometimes I wish I had pants that fit."

Ailanthe looked at where the fabric of his tunic strained across those broad shoulders and felt a little guilty at thinking how good it looked on him. *So. Don't bother the man after midnight, unless...oh, do not start thinking like that.* "So these symbols, what do they mean?" she asked quickly.

"Different types of books. Histories. Natural philosophy. Stories. I'll write you a key."

"Thanks." She hefted the books. "I guess I'll start reading."

"And I'll try the histories, see if anyone mentions the Castle or its builder." He grasped her shoulder again and squeezed gently before turning toward another row of shelves.

Ailanthe nodded, though he had his back to her. He'd helped her explore all those rooms...well, she didn't think he was doing it just to humor her, but he certainly hadn't seemed this enthusiastic before. *He really was resigned to spending the rest of his life here,* she thought, *and now he...does he think this gives him, both of us, a chance at escaping?* Maybe he was right. Maybe her newfound, erratic ability would reveal a way for her to wrest control from the Castle and finally open that door.

She watched Coren more covertly now, because he'd taken a book from the shelf and turned around, already absorbed in its contents, to walk back in her direction. He moved like the young warriors of her mother tree, though without their self-aware swagger; he was graceful, completely unselfconscious. She lowered her head to her book before he passed. It was just that he was the only man around, that was all, and so different from the Lindurian men she'd grown up with, though he was an incredibly attractive man and now that she'd seen that light in his eyes she couldn't stop thinking about how to make it appear again.

She tried to focus on the first lines. What was she looking for again? Oh, yes, a better understanding of magic and possibly some information on how the Castle worked. She cast a furtive glance at Coren, who'd settled into his favorite chair and wasn't paying her any attention. Attractive or not, his presence reassured her. If she were trapped here alone...she shuddered.

A warm pressure against her legs told her Miriethiel wanted a lap, so she obliged him, then settled in to reading for real. It was possible one of these books could tell her about her strange new ability, and maybe how it could be used against their captor. She would not let this inanimate pile of stone defeat her.

CHAPTER EIGHT

*A*ilanthe waited, hovering behind Coren's shoulder as he reached inside the next door and felt around for the button that would turn on the lights. "I still think I should go first," she said.

Light flared. "You keep saying that," Coren said. "This way is safer. The shadows have never attacked me in all the time I've lived here." He pushed the door open fully and stepped inside. Ailanthe followed him, still nervous despite the circle of light her lamps made around her. A week of exploring together without being attacked hadn't freed her from the memory of those clinging, freezing strands.

"More storage," Coren said. The room had once been a salon like the ones off the entry hall, filled with couches and chairs arranged around a low central table. Its high ceiling and walls were painted white, and seascapes hung at intervals like windows on an ocean frozen in place. Stacked atop the couches and chairs were wooden crates labeled in a language that for some reason the Castle hadn't translated, or maybe they were the names of distant cities in Indrijan or Rius-zara or some country Ailanthe had never heard of.

More crates filled the spaces between the couches and the walls. Coren lifted a few out of the way so they would have room to move.

One of the lids fell off and landed upright between a crate and a chair.

"That will make it easier, if all the lids are loose," Ailanthe said, raising the lid of the nearest crate. Inside she saw bundles of fabric; she removed one and held it up. It unrolled, turning out to be a heavy, unnaturally puffy coat with a strange silvery toothed line up both edges of its open front. The hood was lined with soft fur. "This looks like it could keep someone very warm. I wonder how far north you'd have to be to need it."

"I don't know what half these things are for," Coren said, lifting a handful of metal spikes. "This box is full of them."

"This next one has nothing but coats, too." Ailanthe opened another box and saw stacks of flat packages wrapped in white, crinkling fabric and tied with string. She opened one and spread out the cloth. "Food, I think. Lots of dried meat, which I don't mind telling you I'm sick of looking at."

"It's good for you, if you don't have anything else. Ailanthe, I think this was all for some sort of northern exploration."

She nodded and removed another lid, and caught her breath. "It's for mountain climbing."

"How can you tell?"

She held up coils and coils of rope made of strange, slick fibers. "Because it's either that, or someone was founding a new mother tree."

A grin spread across Coren's face. "Now we just need a window."

They went up the unstable stairs to the tower as quickly as they dared. Ailanthe carried the coils of rope looped about her body. Coren carried a hammer they'd found in the box of spikes. At the top of the tower, he turned in a circle, surveying the windows. "I don't know if I can fit through any of these, even if we break out all the glass," he said.

"If I can get out, I can open another window lower down," Ailanthe said.

"Well, stand back, then," Coren said, and brought the hammer around in a powerful swing, his other arm covering his eyes. The hammer struck the glass and rebounded with equal force, causing Coren to lose his grip on the handle; it flew backward past Ailanthe's head, making her short hair lift in the wind of its passing. She gasped and ducked. It struck another window, bounced off and landed on one of the hard cushions, sending up a puff of gray dust.

"I didn't expect that," Coren said. "That could have killed you."

"I know." Ailanthe went to pick it up. "What kind of glass doesn't break?"

"The kind a magical Castle is made of, apparently."

"Didn't you ever try to break the windows before?"

"The glass is fairly thick. I tried with some of the furniture, but when that didn't work I assumed it was just too strong to be broken by anything I could lift. I didn't think it was completely unbreakable."

Ailanthe took a deep breath. Her heart rate was almost normal again. "There has to be a way out of here," she said.

"I don't think that's true."

"I can see my home from these windows, Coren. I am not giving up." She began feeling along the edges of the windows, which were well-sealed against the wind that must blow night and day around the top of this tower. Coren sighed and did the same. Almost immediately, he exclaimed, "This is a latch."

Ailanthe came to his side. "I don't see anything."

He took her hand, causing her heart to beat faster again, and pressed her fingers to a spot near the top of one of the windows. "It's set flush with the frame and painted over, but you can feel where it sticks out a little." He reached down to the bottom of the window, and added, "There's another one here. I don't see hinges. It must open outward."

Ailanthe took hold of the slim nub of the flange and pulled. "It's stuck."

"Let me try." But Coren's fingers were too large to grip the flange, and he stepped back and looked around the room. "I wonder if there are any more."

It turned out every third window was made to open. Ailanthe worried at the latches until her fingertips were sore, but they didn't move. Unlike the exit, this was probably because of the black paint thickly coating each one. "Someone didn't want these opened," Ailanthe said.

"I wonder how the Castle did it. Maybe the sprites, carrying a bucket of paint and tiny brushes?" Coren sat on one of the cushions and leaned back, his head against the window glass. "There's got to be a way to open them."

Ailanthe picked at the paint covering a latch. It came off in flakes. "This will take forever, but I don't have a better idea. And we might *have* forever to do it in."

"Stand back," Coren said. He stood, hefted the hammer and laid the flat of its head against the flange Ailanthe had been picking at. Ailanthe stepped well to one side, gauging where the hammer might fly if the latch was as recalcitrant as the glass. Probably into Coren's head, from the way he was holding it. "That could be a bad—" she began.

Coren swung, not as hard as he had before, barely more than a tap. The latch twitched. More flakes of paint fell. "Is it working?" Ailanthe said.

Coren shrugged and tapped the latch again. Nothing happened. He pulled back for a harder strike and missed entirely, causing the hammer to fly in an arc that barely missed hitting Ailanthe's nose. "Is there *anywhere* I can stand that I'll be safe?" she demanded.

"Probably not. Sorry. Do you want me to stop?"

Ailanthe looked at the latch. There was a fingernail's worth of brass shining where the sliding part of the latch had pulled free of the window frame a little. "It's working! Keep trying!"

Coren struck again and again, and finally the slider shot away from the window. "I don't understand why these are even here," he said. "Why bother, if you're just going to paint over them?"

"Just more of the Castle's weirdness, I expect," Ailanthe said. "Do the bottom one now. Please."

"I'm glad you can remember your manners at a time like this," Coren said with a grin, and took a swing at the lower latch. The flange bent and tore; the latch didn't move. "Damn," Coren said.

Ailanthe pressed her fingers against the flange and felt it bend a little more under pressure. "Try another window," she said.

But the other windows didn't yield so well to Coren's hammer; while none of the latches broke, none of them shifted at all either. Finally Coren put down the hammer and said, "We need another approach."

"I'm glad you didn't say we should give up."

"We're halfway to freedom. It's far too early to give up." He went to examine the broken flange, then the wood surrounding it. "I wonder," he said, and pulled out his belt knife and began hacking at the wood surrounding the latch. Ailanthe came closer to watch. "I'm glad the wood isn't as resistant to damage as the glass," she said.

"Me too." Splinters rained down onto Coren's knee where he knelt next to the window. "You realize we only have one chance at this? The Castle will repair any damage we do after midnight tonight."

"We can always come back and try again."

"I have a feeling the Castle will put this together more securely now it knows what we've done."

"Do you think it's that aware?"

"On some level, yes. Don't you think the way that outer door stays shut no matter what you try feels like there's a mind behind it?" He'd carved away enough wood that she could see the brass of the slider.

"I thought I was just imagining things."

"No, I—damn it," he said, as the knife slipped and skidded across the frame toward Ailanthe. "I swear I'm not trying to kill you."

"I'll just stand over here," Ailanthe said, backing away from the broad, sharp blade.

"It shouldn't be much longer."

Finally the entire length of the brass slider was exposed. Coren pushed hard on the window. It didn't move. "Help me," he said, and they both laid their shoulders against it and leaned with all their weight. The window remained closed.

Coren cursed and turned away. Ailanthe sank down onto the cushion beneath the window and stared at the latch. "You are *not* stopping me," she said, and took hold of the broken flange and wrenched it, hard, willing it to move. It jerked, held fast, and then flew out of the slot as if it were greased. The flange snapped off in Ailanthe's fingers. She sat for a moment, staring at it, then let it fall. Her fingers tingled from gripping the flange so hard.

"I can't believe that worked," Coren said.

"Neither can I," she said. It felt like a victory over the Castle, and she wanted to jump and shout, but she didn't want Coren to think she was crazy. She laid her hand on the window, gave it a gentle push, and it swung outward, letting in the wind. It was a strong gale that blew her hair into her mouth and made Coren's hair whip around his head like a real horse's tail blowing in the wind. Ailanthe leaned far out the window and felt Coren's hands clasp her about the waist. "I won't fall," she called out over the noise of the wind.

"That's right, because I'm hanging on to you," he replied. "What do you see?"

She looked down. "I think the tower is about a hundred feet above the nearest roof, but I can't tell how tall the Castle is. There's at least one hundred fifty feet of rope, which ought to be more than enough." She ducked back inside and told herself it was her imagination that he'd held on to her a trifle longer than was necessary. "I need something to tie this to." She trotted down a few steps, tugging on the stair rails until she found one thick and sturdy enough to support her weight.

"You're not trusting your life to that thing," Coren said.

Ailanthe looped the end of the rope around the stair rail in a neat knot. "This is the knot we use to connect the bridges to each other," she said. "It has to hold the weight of dozens of Lindurians. It's very secure."

"I was talking about the stairs," he said. "They barely support your weight."

"Then you can anchor me at the top. But I'm climbing out of here." She tested the rope, then ran it backwards up the stairs and into the tower room. "Loop this around your waist, and stand there."

"You ought to tie it around yourself, too," Coren said.

"I will, don't worry." She secured the rope around herself and stood on the cushion. "I'll find a window I can open or break, and then we can both climb out of here," she said. "I hope Lindurien isn't too far from your home."

"I don't care how far I have to walk, if I can get out on my own terms," Coren said. "Good luck."

She grinned at him and sat on the window sill, then turned to kneel on it, keeping one hand on the sill as she groped around for a foothold. The outside of the tower was the same granite she'd seen when she entered the Castle, but rougher, more worn, with slight projections where the stones met unevenly—nothing she could find purchase on. So she gave her whole weight to the rope, and slid out of the window.

The wind beat at her, making her twist as she dangled below the window. "You're going to have to lower me," she shouted at Coren, who was looking down at her in dismay. He nodded, and she began descending in little jerks, kicking at the tower to keep from being slammed into it by the wind. She'd never been this high up before, and she looked down once, saw the world spinning beneath her, and afterward kept her eyes resolutely forward.

It was a beautiful view. The roofs of the Castle were as varied as its rooms, tiled in crimson and gray and a blue stone that sparkled when the sun struck it. A storm was coming, she realized, and thought about urging Coren to lower her faster, but decided not to distract him. Far across the roofs, she saw the shining skylight of the Library, reflecting the sun, and she decided she would have to find a way across the roofs to look down through it at the shelves and the trees.

She came to an abrupt halt, the rope cutting into her waist. She looked up. She hadn't gotten very far, maybe fifteen feet. Coren was still looking down at her. "Why did you stop?" he shouted.

"I thought you stopped," she called back. He shook his head.

She yanked on the rope, thinking she might free it from whatever it was caught on, then realized it was probably caught on Coren. Suddenly she dropped, and for a few sickening moments she saw herself broken and bleeding on the Castle roof, then the rope caught and knocked the breath out of her. She clutched the rope in both hands and hugged it to her body. "What was that?" she screamed.

"I don't know! The rope flew away from me." It was hard to hear him over the wind, but Coren's voice sounded tight, as if he were exerting himself against a great weight. "It's trying to do it again," he said, confirming her suspicion.

"Can you let it out at all?" she shouted.

"I'm afraid it's going to—wait, it stopped pulling."

Ailanthe felt a tug as he began to haul her up. "Don't pull me back!"

"I'm not! The rope's doing it!"

Ailanthe pulled hard on the rope again, but she kept ascending. "No!" she shouted. "Push it down!"

"I can't! It's winding itself back around me!"

Ailanthe kicked again to keep herself away from the tower, and felt the tugging grow stronger, as if the rope was pulling her up faster. But a glance around showed her she was still ascending at the same speed. Something slid around her waist. She looked down, trying to focus on her body instead of the nightmarish drop, and saw the knot untying itself, the rope sliding free from her waist.

She clutched the rope with one hand and grabbed at its slithering end with the other. It slipped free of her grasp and unwound itself, inch by rapid inch, and she dropped farther as its support disappeared. She held on with both hands and felt it slide away from her fingers.

"Coren, *pull!*" she shrieked, trying to find purchase on the smooth stones with her toes and pulling herself up, hand over hand, the rope continuing to retract itself through the tower window. She climbed frantically, her arms aching, her palms burning from the strange fibers sliding across them, then made the mistake of looking down. Not only was the world swinging wildly beneath her, the end of the rope was coming at her fast.

She screamed and willed her burning muscles to move faster, and then the frayed end of the rope slipped through her fingers—

—and a hand closed around her wrist, stopping her fall and

jerking her shoulder painfully. "Don't move," Coren said in that same tight voice, and Ailanthe felt herself drawn slowly upward until she could grab the edge of the window and, kicking and scrambling, tumble through it. She landed on her face on one of the cushions and coughed at the cloud of dust she raised.

Eyes streaming, she looked across at Coren, who sat on the floor, breathing heavily. The rope was gone. "What was that you said about how secure your knots were?" he said.

"It untied itself," Ailanthe said, her voice shaking. She looked at her palms, which were red with rope burns, and saw her hands were shaking too. "It was so..."

"Terrifying?"

"Deliberate." The way the rope had moved, the knot sliding apart so smoothly, made Ailanthe think of invisible hands methodically unweaving her work and pulling the rope away from her. She rolled off the cushion to sit near Coren, hugged her knees, and tried to control her trembling. This had not been some kind of mindless response. The Castle had reached out and deliberately kept her from leaving—had nearly killed her in doing so. "Thank you," she said.

"I couldn't just let you fall," Coren replied. He rotated his arm and rubbed his shoulder, then hissed with pain. "We're both going to be sore for a while," he said, displaying his palms, which were marked with the same pattern of raw skin where the rope had burned his hands as well. Without thinking, Ailanthe gently touched his palm, then quickly removed her hand. "Sorry," she said.

"That's all right. It doesn't hurt much," he said, closing his fist and standing to take a few steps away from her. "I don't think we should try that again."

"Agreed." Ailanthe stood and looked out the window, not at the forest but across the roofs of the Castle. "At least not until we find a lower window."

CHAPTER NINE

One more, I think. Ailanthe stared at the round, orangey-peach cushion and remembered the faint roughness of its nap, then reached out with her left hand to catch the new pillow before it struck the floor. She arranged it next to the other three, then settled into the window seat and leaned her cheek against the glass. It was raining in Lindurien today, a fine mist that chilled the glass so Ailanthe's breath made patches of fog that faded almost instantly.

She'd been practicing her strange ability for over two weeks and it had only just occurred to her if she made her own cushions, the Castle wouldn't be able to haul them out of the tower every night. She dragged the old rock-hard cushion toward herself with her toe, reached down to pick it up, then concentrated briefly to make it vanish. She wasn't entirely sure where the cushions went when she sent them away, but it was easier than letting things pile up, and if it inconvenienced the Castle, so much the better.

She'd tried making her own rope, thinking at least it would belong to her and the Castle would not be able to play tricks with it. She'd only been able to create, or summon, six- or seven-foot lengths at a time, but to someone who'd been tying knots since she was barely able to walk, that was nothing. It took a week, but finally she and Coren stood at the tower window, Ailanthe lowered herself down the rope—and she hadn't descended ten feet when she felt a jerk like her stomach being yanked sideways, and she was standing next to an astonished Coren in the tower room. It took fifteen more attempts before Ailanthe could accept failure, and two days before she could bear to go back to the tower and look out over her forest home.

The smell of peaches barely preceded the soft brush of a sprite against her hand. Ailanthe saw them much more often these days, flickering past at the limit of her vision. If she didn't try to focus on them, she could see their edges were iridescent like broken rainbows. She twitched her hand and the sprite went through it, then floated away. Sometimes they massed in groups of seven or eight and followed her through the halls for a few dozen steps, swooping around her head until she felt choked by the cloying aroma of over-ripe peaches. Ailanthe had come to think of them as good luck, some-thing the Castle didn't control.

The sprite flowed through the window she'd tried to make her escape through and fluttered off across the lowering gray sky. Ailanthe looked at the still-splintered lower latch, its brass gleaming where Coren had hacked through the wood. Why the Castle hadn't repaired it, she had no idea. Possibly it was still taunting her with an escape she had no way of using. Or perhaps that tingle she'd felt meant she'd used her magic on the latch, taking it out of the Castle's control. Either way, she still never opened the window.

She picked up her book and settled in to read. It was a guilty plea-sure, reading the white-bound hero books, since Coren had strongly suggested it was a bad idea, and that was why she brought them up to the tower, away from his scrutiny. But the books of the still-living heroes glimmered with the same iridescence the sprites did, and she kept her reading limited to those. The idea of the horrible endings many of these heroes came to left her feeling sick. She hadn't sought out Idantra's book either.

This one was the story of a Rius-zaran named Usael whom the Castle had sent to Lindurien, which was Ailanthe's main reason for reading it. He'd come to the Castle some four months before Ailanthe had and was now traveling from mother tree to mother tree, trying to find someone who would teach him to be a *kerthor*. Ailanthe was a little embarrassed at how her people were so suspicious of Usael, who was never anything but respectful and who, she thought, might make a good *kerthor*. His story had the added benefit of teaching her things about Lindurian magic that weren't in the books in the Library, though nothing that applied to her peculiar situation.

Miriethiel leaped onto Ailanthe's lap, butting his head against the book for attention. Ailanthe scratched his head with one hand and held the book with the other. She was almost at the end of what the Library currently knew about Usael. Whatever magic scribed the actions of the questers into the books didn't do it continuously, as if someone were perched on their shoulders, watching every detail. Ailanthe would put the book back on the shelf, and in a day, or a week, there would be more of the story. It was a pity the magic didn't have some way to signal that there was new material.

Ailanthe turned the page. Usael was approaching a new settlement, hailing one of the sentries, now he was giving his name and the sentry—

It was Gilraen. Gilraen, her sister's betrothed, maybe her husband by now.

Usael had stumbled on her own home.

Ailanthe fumbled the book. She grabbed it with both hands and just read that line, unable to move on from *Stranger, I am Gilraen, what brings you here?* Then she shook her head as if she were coming up from a deep dive in the pool. There had to be other Lindurian men named Gilraen.

She scanned down the rest of the page, oh, there was Banazir and Morwenna and—it was *everyone*, it *was* her home, and she turned the page and nearly screamed when she found it blank. She slammed the book shut and clutched it to her chest. Could this be the Castle's new way to torture her? No, she couldn't believe it could determine which of the hero books she would pick up; it was just coincidence, horrible or beautiful coincidence, she couldn't decide.

She opened the book, hoping madly that the story might have

continued in those few moments, but of course the page remained blank. She closed it again and stared at its unmarked white cover, glittering with rainbow specks. Home. She'd almost let herself forget, between her fears of being attacked again and her need to understand the mystery of the magic she'd developed, or had taken hold of her.

She looked out the window again, in the direction of her home. It was too far for her to identify which of the vast spreading canopies was her mother tree, but Usael was there, right now, probably trying to convince Banazir to teach him to be a *kerthor*. Banazir was young for her responsibilities; maybe she'd be more flexible than the other men and women Usael had met.

The deep tone of the Castle bell startled her out of her reverie. Ailanthe sat up and swung her legs to one side, tipping Miriethiel to the floor, then hesitated. There was probably no point in asking this person to open the door for her, but suppose her magic had tipped the balance? Suppose her magic combined with the quester's destiny would allow her to make the door open? She left the book on the window seat and hurried down the stairs.

The quester had passed through the front door and the entry hall by the time Ailanthe reached the first floor. She searched the nearer rooms and concluded he'd already been through the Honor Hall as well. Decisive, this one. She took the long route through the museum rooms, her heart sinking as she passed from room to room without seeing anyone. It was unlikely this quester could help her, and it had been stupid for her to let that slim possibility raise her hopes.

Then she saw him, leaning over to look at something in a display case in the Enthalian room. He was short, with stringy blond hair, and was dressed in poorly-cut leathers and boots that were little more than animal skins laced with thongs over his feet and shins. He raised his hand, which held a thick, knobbly stick about three feet long, and prepared to smash the glass. "No!" Ailanthe exclaimed, then, with less vehemence, "It won't do any good. The Castle won't let you keep anything but the Thing you took from the Honor Hall."

The man had leaped backward at her first words, turning quickly to face her and dropping into a defensive crouch. Fear became confusion as he realized he was hearing her in the Castle's language. "I can show you the way out, if you like, and maybe you can help me," Ailanthe continued.

Confusion gave way to anger. "*Ruwari!*" he shouted. "You will not work your magic on me!" Raising his stick again, he ran at her, shouting incoherently.

Ailanthe screamed, turned and fled. She had just enough distance on the crazed man to slam the door shut in his face and keep going. Behind her, she heard the man or his stick thump into the solid oak of the door, then his shouts became louder as he tore it open and came after her.

She dashed through the maze of rooms leading to the Honor Hall, frantically trying to think of a way to escape. He sounded furious enough to care more about attacking her then taking the exit, so leading him to the kitchen annex was pointless. She made a sharp right turn and bolted up the stairs, her breathing already coming too rapidly, and paused on the third floor landing, listening.

For a long, long moment, she heard nothing but her own breathing and the rapid beating of her heart. Then, far too close, the man shouted that strange word again, and heavy footsteps sounded on the stairs below. Ailanthe turned and ran again. Weeks of treading these stairs daily combined with gut-clenching fear made her fleet-footed, and she reached the Library floor landing thinking *Coren, where is Coren?* when a large hand grabbed her ankle and she went down, hard.

Dizzy, she rolled onto her back and screamed again, kicking the man with her free foot and catching his knee hard enough he missed smashing his stick against her head. She struck out again, but he dodged, and raised his stick for another blow. Ailanthe rolled to one side and shouted Coren's name, then kicked at the hand gripping her ankle. He let go, but the blow from his stick grazed her temple, making tiny lights flash before her eyes.

I am not going to die here, she told herself, and a shape rose up in her mind moments before her hands closed on something long and dark. She brought the thing up two-handed in front of her and blocked the man's next blow, then shoved hard, pushing him backward.

The landing was too narrow for her to do anything but keep pushing, so she rocked forward, came to her feet, and when he raised his stick to strike again, caught him in the stomach and knocked him backward. He fell, rolled down the stairs and landed head-first against the wall of the next landing down.

"Ailanthe!" Coren ran around the corner. "I—who is that?" He took her by the shoulders and put her behind him, taking a defensive stance.

"A quester," Ailanthe said, still breathing somewhat heavily. "He was trying to kill me. I think he thought I was a monster." She looked at the object in her hands. It was a staff made of wood so dark it was nearly black, shod at both ends with silver woven into intricate caps.

Coren looked down at the quester. "That's an Agranite," he said. "They believe they die when they walk into the Castle and that their destiny lies in the afterlife. They're dangerous, Ailanthe. Why did you approach him?"

"I didn't know what he was. I was hoping maybe my new abilities would...never mind."

Coren went down the landing and checked the man's pulse. "He's not dead. Let's put him in the Vestibule and lock the inner door. Eventually he'll decide to leave."

With the man dangling over Coren's shoulder and Ailanthe still clutching the staff, they proceeded down the stairs to the kitchen annex. As they passed the fifth floor landing, Coren chuckled. "Is there something funny about this?" Ailanthe asked.

"It reminds me of the time I had to carry Senon—my younger brother—home from the harvest ball at the Catalins' home," he said, then laughed again. "This was...eight years ago, I think, and he and this other man, Matias, were courting the same woman. They were young and stupid and of course they decided they should have a drinking contest to see which of them would dance with her first."

"Didn't she get a choice in the matter?"

"Of course she did. Young and stupid, remember? Well, Senon was marginally less stupid than Matias, so he cheated, pretended to be drinking more than he was. Only Matias was cheating too. So Matias drank his weight in beer—and put some kind of sedative in Senon's. We couldn't get either of them to wake up, so Matias's father hauled him away and I carried Senon across three fields. Probably should have found a wagon, but I'd had a little too much to drink myself and it seemed like a good idea at the time."

Ailanthe snorted. "So they both lost."

"Sort of. Eldora married my brother anyway. They were expecting their first child when I left."

"Oh," Ailanthe said, then couldn't think of anything else to say. Her heart ached for him, for how much he'd left behind. At least she'd known, when she set out, that she might not see her family again for years.

"I hadn't thought of that night in years," Coren said, his voice sounding distant. "I wonder if they've had more children by now. I wonder—" He went silent. Ailanthe didn't feel so amused anymore.

They arrived at the Vestibule, where Ailanthe locked the door on the Agranite, then retreated to the hallway. Coren leaned against the wall, looking at the inner door for a long time, then said, "You should stay away from the questers."

Ailanthe bristled. "They can't all be murderous."

"Two in a row, Ailanthe—what are you going to do if one of them catches you alone where I can't hear you?"

"I defended myself perfectly well just now."

Coren flicked the silver end of the staff. "Because you had this, and even then I bet it was mostly luck. Why were you carrying it, anyway?"

Ailanthe looked at it, saw the knuckles of her left hand were white where her fist clutched the staff. "I didn't. I made it appear when I was afraid I was going to die. Coren, I've never seen it before now."

"It's from the armory. You must have noticed it in passing."

"But I have to know things well to make them appear." Ailanthe switched the staff to her right hand and flexed her fingers. "I don't think I summoned this." A sprite flowed past her face, and she batted at it.

"Let's find out," Coren said.

Ailanthe hadn't been in the armory since the first day, when she'd thoroughly explored the first floor. It was a large room that was more a museum than a store for arms and armor, with weapons in display cases and mounted on the walls, and armor made of everything from hardened hide to shining riveted metal on stands. Coren pointed at a corner of the room, where ten or twelve staves stood upright in a barrel. "There it is," he said.

Ailanthe pulled it out and compared the two. "They're identical. I swear I don't remember ever seeing this before."

"You must be improving, then." Coren studied her face. "It's getting harder to claim that you're summoning these from some-where in the Castle."

"I think I'm making them. But I don't see how."

Coren reached out and tapped the key, making it swing. "I was about to come looking for you when you shouted. I think I found something about the Castle that could explain what's happening."

Back in the Library, they sat side by side on the bench surrounding the hero books and Coren opened a book bound in purple-dyed leather. "Give me a moment," he said, "I dropped this when someone shouted my name like she was in mortal danger. Which she was." He mock-scowled at Ailanthe. "Here. This book is about summoning spirits to work magic, and there's a chapter—well, more like a section in a chapter—about how spirits work magic by shaping it and letting the shape fill with pure magic."

"The way *kerthors* do with music."

"Yes. And the book says creatures of magic are capable of the same thing. And the Castle is a creature of magic. Not exactly a crea-ture, but you see what I mean."

"But the Castle doesn't make new things."

"It has the capacity. I don't know why it doesn't. But that's not important. What matters is the key." He flicked it again. "I think the key is linked to the Castle's magic, and it's allowing you to use that magic as if you were the Castle."

Ailanthe eyed him skeptically. "I think that's a lot of guesses."

"It makes sense, though."

"Then you should try it." Ailanthe removed the key and held it out to him.

Coren shook his head. "I could try, but I don't think it would work for me. It's your Thing."

"Oh." Ailanthe put it back around her wrist. "Thanks for coming to my rescue even though it turned out I didn't need it."

"I see. And you were going to do what? Roll that man all the way down the stairs and across the Castle to the exit?" Coren shook his head, then gripped her hand. "Please promise me you won't approach any more questers."

"I...all right." *He cares what happens to me.* His skin was warmer than hers, his hands dry and striped with calluses from his sword exercises. She couldn't meet his eyes. Not meeting his eyes was something she did frequently these days.

Coren glanced over his shoulder at the empty space where Usael's book had been. "Bad enough you're reading these books now. Didn't I warn you most of them don't end well?"

"I think I can cope with an unhappy ending or two. But don't worry, I'm only reading the books that haven't ended yet." She remembered she'd left Usael's book in the tower, then decided she'd let the Castle put it away for her. Her impatience to know what happened next returned full force.

Coren raised his eyebrows and let go of her hand. "You are? How are you managing that?"

"The glimmering, of course. It's not *that* hard to see."

"Glimmering?"

They looked at each other for a moment. "You don't see it," Ailanthe said.

"No."

"And I suppose you don't see the sprites' rainbows either."

Coren shook his head. "The only rainbows I see are when I happen to be at the right window after a storm."

Ailanthe looked over her shoulder at the white-bound books, some of which glittered with faint but unmistakable iridescence. "I think I may have been taking some things for granted," she said.

"I think we need to look around the Castle and see what else you see that I don't," Coren said.

CHAPTER TEN

"*H*is eyes are definitely greenish-yellow," Coren said, holding Miriethiel's chin between his fingers. The cat stared back at him, unconcerned. "Not blue."

"Well, I see them as blue, and that makes me nervous," Ailanthe said. "If he's a creature of magic, or has some sort of magic on him... he's slept on my *bed*, Coren."

"Mine too." He released the cat, who sauntered away with no sign of interest in either of them. "But the eye color is all you see about him that's different from what I see?"

"Yes. And the sprites are getting clearer, and sometimes the stones of the walls have this sort of clear jellylike coating, just out of the corner of my eye. I don't like it."

"I don't blame you. That sounds unnerving."

"Yes. Like I'm turning into something I don't recognize. Back home I was the least magical person you could imagine."

"You still are, if it's the key that's doing it."

Ailanthe shook her head. "I've tried leaving it behind in the morning, but it doesn't make a difference. Whatever it does, it's altered me somehow." Her voice shook, but Coren didn't seem to notice, his attention back on Miriethiel.

She looked at him, at the tall solidity of him, and wished she dared put her arms around his neck and take comfort in his embrace. It was increasingly difficult for her to behave normally around him, to maintain a calm and friendly demeanor to match his and not stare at him when he ate or read or, God forbid, while he exercised. It was also increasingly difficult for her to continue to lie to herself that she only felt this way because she was lonely and he was, in theory, available.

He was intelligent and had a dry sense of humor, he was fiercely committed to finding a way out of the Castle, he loved telling stories about his family and encouraged Ailanthe to do the same, he'd saved her life, and the better Ailanthe knew him, the more she was convinced he was the most remarkable man she'd ever met. Now his glance threw her into confusion, which she covered with laughter, and she tried not to stand too near him, because that made her heart race in a way she was certain he could hear.

She was mostly sure he had no idea she'd fallen in love with him, but if he did, he was good at pretending otherwise. She hoped he didn't know. How humiliating that would be if he didn't feel the same.

"Maybe it's keeping him young," Coren mused. "Miriethiel. He was here when I arrived, but he doesn't look any older than he did six years ago."

"I hope it's something that innocent."

Coren turned to look at her. "So. The cat's eyes, the Castle stones. The haze you say is inside the cold room. The floor of the Honor Hall, which to me looks dull. The hero books. And the sprites are becoming more visible. That doesn't seem like much."

"There could be a million other things we don't know about because we don't think to compare our perceptions of them. And I really don't want to go through the whole Castle playing that game."

"Neither do I." He stretched. "I think it would be interesting to know if any of the other Things the Castle brings out for questers are magic like your key."

"We could find out. You could step into the Honor Hall and I could look at the Things when they appear."

"I'm not going to do that," Coren said. "I don't want the Castle tricking me into taking anything."

"That's probably wise. Well, we can intercept the next quester and find out."

"Just don't try it without me."

"I promised, didn't I?" Ailanthe looked over at Miriethiel, who was washing himself, so she wouldn't have to see Coren's intent gaze. To distract herself, she stretched out her hand, concentrated briefly, and caught a long, skinny loaf of bread out of the air. She tore it in half and offered one to Coren, then bit into hers. It was warm and soft as if it had just come out of an oven somewhere.

"I still feel strange eating food you've created," Coren said, though since he said it through a mouthful of bread his objection was blunted. "As if I'm eating the same loaf over and over again."

"You're probably doing that with the Castle food," Ailanthe pointed out. "And it hasn't killed you yet."

"Nevertheless, I'd like something more than bread for dinner, and it's that time. Want to help me carry?"

Raw salmon wasn't nearly as good as broiled, but it was so much more delicious than dried meat, and Ailanthe had no trouble finishing her filet, though she had to chase Miriethiel away from the plate with its pile of tiny, needlelike bones. The full moon painted the desert sands silver and cast pale shadows across the dunes.

She leaned forward, hoping to see movement far below; sometimes the furry inhabitants of the desert made an appearance when the cold of night descended. Instead, she saw her own reflection, the pale circle of her face and the halo of her brown hair she wished she'd thought to have trimmed before leaving her mother tree. She was a ghost hovering above the desert, crouched over on that strange cube of a chair. The notion made her smile; the ghost smiled back.

She saw Coren behind her, moving past toward the door, then the lights went out and her ghost disappeared.

"Sorry, I should have warned you," Coren said when she jerked around. "I thought I saw a whale out there and the lights were a distraction."

"Did you see one?"

"No, it was just waves." He brought a chair next to hers and sat facing the window. "I don't understand why this place fascinates you so much."

"It's about as far opposite to my home as it's possible to be, I think," Ailanthe said. "I think…it's hard to explain, but when I'm in the tower, it hurts to be so close, and looking out here, it's peaceful because there's nothing about it that reminds me of home."

"I think I understand. I never look out the windows on Hespera anymore. Too painful."

The moon cast its silvery light over them both, and Ailanthe could see, without turning her head, Coren's foot and leg and his hand where it rested on his thigh. "What did you do, back home?" she asked.

"I didn't do anything. Or, rather, I used to work on my father's farm, but it wasn't what I wanted my life to be. I was traveling when I ended up here, looking for something new. Though this isn't what I had in mind."

"*Did* you have something in mind?"

He shifted his weight and moved his hand from his thigh to the chair so it rested next to hers. "Not really. I suppose, if I had, I wouldn't have needed to wander. Now I just want to go home again. Though I still don't want to grow olives."

It would be so easy for her to put her hand over his, curl her fingers around his palm. "If you were a farmer, where did you learn to use a sword?"

Coren grinned. "Taught myself out of books. If I ever came up against a real swordsman, I wouldn't last a minute, probably. But that sword…I saw it on the stand in the armory, and it was so beautiful I couldn't help picking it up. It makes for good exercise, at least."

His nearness was making it difficult for her to concentrate on their conversation. She focused on the horizon and saw lights far too steady to be stars. "Do you see that? Or is it just me, again?"

"Where?" She pointed, and he leaned forward until his forehead nearly touched the glass. "I...that could be a city. I've never seen anything manmade out of these windows."

"What city could it be?"

"I have no idea. I'm not even sure what desert that is." He turned to face her, and this time she had no excuse for not meeting his eyes. They were filled with that light again, that alert, interested light, and she wished she were the cause of it. "I'll look it up in the morning. Not that it matters."

"It's nice to know what we're looking at," Ailanthe agreed. She turned to look out the window again and the room moved with her, just a little. She had enough time to gasp before the pale shadow of her chair flowed up her legs and wrapped itself around her head.

She tore at it, trying to free her nose and mouth, and overbalanced and landed on the floor, cracking her elbow painfully against the boards. Colored lights swayed in front of her eyes, and she felt herself become dizzy from lack of air and the intense cold wherever it touched her. Then bright light flared, and the shadow shrank to nothing, and she lay on the floor staring at the high ceiling and sucking deep breaths of warm air into her starved lungs.

"Did it hurt you?" Coren demanded. He knelt at her side and lifted her to sit against him, his arms going around her. She clutched at the front of his tunic, too grateful at being alive to be self-conscious. "You never said they were that aggressive. It wasn't even very dark in here."

"They come out of shadows, not darkness. Darkness against light." She was still light-headed and wasn't sure she was making sense, but the way only the shadow of her chair had moved while the darker corners of the room remained empty had given her an insight. "Damn it, if I have to see the Castle's magic, why can't I see those things?"

Coren released her and offered her a hand. "Maybe you will, eventually. Are you sure it didn't hurt you? I got to the light as quickly as I could."

"It was smart of you not to attack it directly. Thank you." Ailanthe rubbed her elbow. "I was going to read some more, but now I think I just want sleep. Don't worry, I sleep with all the lights on."

"Lights make shadows."

"Not if you use enough of them. I'll be fine. I'll scream if they attack again." She tried not to remember that it hadn't given her any chance to scream just now.

Coren still looked unconvinced, but he followed her to her bedroom door, checked all the corners and under the bed, and said, "Sleep well." When he was gone, Ailanthe laid down on the bed and stared at the ceiling, which was much lower than the one in the window room and painted dark blue. A storm was rising in the forest outside her window, the wind battering at the glass, though with the curtains closed she couldn't see how the trees were faring against it.

She could have asked him to stay, said something about fearing further attacks. Now she remembered his arms around her and her cheeks burned to think of how she'd clung to him. She curled on her side, closed her eyes and imagined him next to her, neither of them moving, just lying together, his arm around her shoulders and her with her head on his chest listening to his heartbeat. She was a fool.

She stripped down to her underwear and crawled under the thick blue and white blanket. This bed wasn't as soft as the first, but it was still far softer than anything she'd had at home. If the creatures came out of shadows, it would be more sensible to turn out all the lights and sleep in total darkness, but she couldn't bring herself to do it, remembering the furtive hunched movements of the shadows and their terrible clutching at her body. She shuddered and pulled the blanket over her face, then pushed it back again. It took her hours to finally fall asleep.

CHAPTER ELEVEN

*A*ilanthe sat cross-legged on her bed and clutched Usael's white-bound book in both hands. A week had passed with no new attacks and no strange new manifestations of magical power. All that had changed was that Ailanthe now saw the sprites clearly, their bodies tinted red or blue or violet along with the coruscating rainbow specks outlining their edges. Two fluttered past now, giving off brighter sparkles when they brushed against each other. They circled her head, then dropped through the bed and out of sight.

The clock above the dresser told her it was about fifteen minutes to midnight. She wiped first one palm, then the other on her trousers, never entirely letting go of the book. Coren had said the Castle didn't retrieve things exactly at midnight, and that the actual time varied, so she wasn't taking any chances.

He'd also said, "I should be there, in case the Castle strikes out at you."

Ailanthe had responded, trying to sound casual, "Wouldn't you, um, lose your clothes when it happens?"

He'd opened his mouth, closed it again, and said, "I'll be right across the hall."

Now she opened the book and re-read the most recent section.

Usael had convinced Banazir to teach him to be a *kerthor*. Most of the story was now about his training, which didn't much interest Ailanthe, but in between learning to play the flute and the harp, and practicing the language, he did his best to become part of the community. She'd wept when he met her father, who'd asked Usael so many questions about the Castle and told him proudly about his daughter and offered him every hospitality, saying he hoped Ailanthe might find the same reception wherever she ended up.

The tears threatened to well up again, and she scrubbed at her eyes and told herself to focus. If she was going to stop the Castle reclaiming this book, she needed no distractions. 11:56. She'd sat up once to watch the Castle take back a pottery bowl with a glossy green finish, and it was just as Coren described—one moment it was there, the next it wasn't. She should have done it again when her vision started to change, but it hadn't occurred to her, and now she didn't know what to expect.

She shifted, uncrossed her legs and stretched, crossed them again, and closed the book. The hero books' iridescence had gone from being a glitter to something more like the rainbows that spread across an oily surface, still faint but easy for her to detect. Idantra's book wasn't among the active ones; she felt guilty that she didn't feel more sorrow over that. She had no idea which book belonged to the Agranite and didn't really care.

12:04. Her hands were starting to ache from gripping the book so tightly. Would she feel a pull? Or would it hurt? She scowled at another sprite that drifted through the door and floated toward her as if it were interested in the book. If she didn't succeed tonight, she'd keep trying until she did.

12:19. Her eyes were sore from staring at the book's oil-slick cover; it had started to look blurry, as if she were seeing it through a piece of fine gauze. She blinked. The effect didn't disappear. She hugged the book to her chest, thinking *You can't have it, I won't let you take it.* A vibration very much like Miriethiel's silent purr shook her hands and chest and forced her to clench her teeth to keep them from chattering.

Ailanthe closed her eyes and concentrated on the angular hardness of the book's wooden covers, the faint grain overlaid with the smoothness of white paint, and willed that feeling to continue. The vibration increased until her whole body shook and she had to tighten all her muscles to keep from falling over. Her fingers had gone numb, but she could still feel the book clutched to her chest. *I am* not *giving up, damn you,* she thought, hoping the Castle could hear her furious thought.

The door slammed open. "Did it work?" Coren said, sounding a little out of breath. Ailanthe didn't respond; she was afraid if she tried to speak she would lose her concentration. She hoped he wouldn't touch her, because that would *really* distract her. She hunched her body around the book and willed it to stay with her. For the first time, she felt as if the Castle was paying attention to her, as if whatever it had for a consciousness was completely focused on dragging the book out of her hands. Ailanthe half expected to open her eyes and find herself in the Library, crammed onto a shelf.

The vibrations ceased. Ailanthe felt numb all over. She felt Coren's hands gently prying her fingers loose from the book and opened her eyes. He was dressed haphazardly and his long hair hung loose around his face. "It worked," she said.

"It worked," Coren confirmed, and set the book on her lap to take both her hands in his, rubbing them gently. She winced as the blood began circulating again. She ached everywhere and could feel a headache developing behind her eyes.

"I think I've proved my point to the damn thing," she said, closing her eyes so she wouldn't have to see how close Coren was, "and I'm not doing that again unless it's essential. Though I'm sure it would get easier with practice." He'd stopped massaging her palms and was holding her hands now, loosely, and she realized she was holding her breath and let it out slowly. Did it mean he felt—?

"No reason for it," Coren said, and let go her hands. He sounded casual, just as he always did, and the hope that had begun rising in her heart vanished, leaving her feeling empty. She heard him stand and take a few steps away, so she opened her eyes and picked up the book. "I'm curious," he added, "to see if the Castle is able to reclaim that book later."

"So am I. But mostly I'm exhausted. I think I'm going to try sleeping with all the lights off and the curtains closed tonight."

"Is that safe?"

"I don't know. I'm too tired to care. I just know if I sleep with the lights on, this headache is going to get worse."

Coren looked as if he were coming up with more objections, but only said, "I'm across the hall if you need me."

"Good night, then." *I do need you. I wish I dared say it.*

The dark felt blessedly cool, and her head stopped aching almost immediately. She lay wide-awake watching sprites cross the room. There seemed to be more of them around lately, or maybe she was just more aware of them now she could see them clearly.

She took the key in her right hand and ran her finger across the cool silver streaks. It was possible whatever changes it had made to her would persist after she left the Castle. The world would be a very different place if she could see magic wherever she went. Those spirits Coren talked about, for one, and suppose she was able to see the shape of the magic the *kerthors* summoned? The idea made Ailanthe a little afraid.

She let go of the key and ran her fingers across her body, over her legs and her narrow hips and her breasts and up across her face, her round cheeks and her too-straight nose and the hard ridge of her eyebrows. She didn't think her body had changed, she didn't look any different in the mirror, but how likely was it that it was a change she would notice? "I'm not afraid of you," she said to the darkness, but she thought she might be lying.

She woke the next morning as sore as if she'd spent the night trying to lift her bed instead of sleeping on it. Coren was already gone when she left her room, but rather than go downstairs to help him carry breakfast, she went into the window room and sat heavily on a chair facing the high cloud-capped cliffs. The clouds were moving rapidly today, blown by a wind that didn't touch the lowlands.

Far below, the stream rushed past the base of the Castle. It was wider today, swollen with ice-melt from the mountains, probably. It looked cold and made Ailanthe feel cold. She wrapped her arms around herself and tried to think warm thoughts.

Coren's hand came into view, holding an apple. "You look cold," he said, and returned moments later with the blanket from her bed, which he draped over her shoulders. "Go look out the desert window. That should warm you up."

She nodded, and took her apple and blanket across the room, leaning against the glass to feel the heat of the sun. Something skittered across the dunes, far below; it looked like some kind of lizard, and it had to be fairly large for her to be able to see it clearly at this distance. She took a bite of her apple, which was juicy and tart, and let her mind go blank.

She felt the vibration in her cheek before she heard the sonorous tone of the Castle bell. She sat up and turned to look at Coren, who had his mouth full of cheese and looked as startled as she felt. He chewed and swallowed, and said, "We watch the Honor Hall from above, Ailanthe. No rushing out to greet this quester."

Ailanthe grimaced, but nodded. Coren was taking this far too seriously, but he'd been here a lot longer than she had and his seriousness might be justified. She waited for him to strap the sword on —maybe the quester needed to be afraid of *them*—then followed him down the stairs to the second floor and the windows overlooking the Honor Hall.

Soon, they heard the faint, distant thud of the Castle door closing. Ailanthe looked over at Coren, who was intent on the empty hall below, his hand on the hilt of his sword. It was several minutes before they heard footsteps, and, strangely, a tuneful whistling. The quester was moving slowly, which combined with the whistling gave Ailanthe the impression of someone out for a casual stroll. The steps drew closer. Ailanthe focused on the Honor Hall, waiting for the moment when the quester would descend and the Things would appear.

She almost missed it. The air within the Honor Hall filled briefly with a cloud of glittering particles, then the Things were there. And, yes, a few of them gleamed with the iridescence of magic, though most of those were so small she couldn't tell what they were. Rings, possibly, or pendants. One of the crowns was magic, and the turnip that spun without stopping—she could have guessed that—and a scarf and the cherry wood armoire, which surprised her since it wasn't a Thing.

The quester wandered along the narrow aisles between Things, still whistling. He had short blond hair and wore ankle boots and hose and a particolored tunic with long, baggy sleeves. He was armed with a short sword and a knife and moved as if he knew how to use them. He never looked up. Ailanthe looked at Coren and saw his mouth was set in a grim line, which she guessed meant trouble. He beckoned her far away from the windows and whispered, "He's Galendish."

"I don't know what that means. I mean, yes, I understand he's from Galendan, but why is that bad?"

"*Spirit of the Castle*," the quester called out, startling her. "I come to you—but my words are strange in my ears! Truly, a most wondrous thing." He cleared his throat loudly. "Spirit of the Castle, I come to you as a supplicant, seeking my future. Guide my hand and the glory of my deeds will be entirely yours."

"That's what's bad," Coren said. "The Galendish have strange ideas about how the Castle works, and they have a tendency to wander. It might be most of the day before he leaves."

Ailanthe looked back toward the Honor Hall. "Is he dangerous?"

"Not really. Not the way that Agranite was. But it means we can't move freely until he's gone."

"Then I don't see why we can't approach him." Ailanthe started toward the stairs and was pulled up short by Coren grasping her upper arm.

"There's no point in approaching him," he said. "The door still won't open."

"I just won my first battle with the Castle. I want to see if that changes things."

"Ailanthe—"

"You don't have to come."

He made an exasperated grunt and released her. "As if I'd let you go alone."

They went down the stairs and around the stone passage toward the Honor Hall. The Things were still present and the Galendishman was still wandering around, looking at them. Ailanthe trotted across the passageway and called out, "Hello there!" Behind her, she heard Coren make another exasperated noise and hurry to catch up.

The man's head snapped up, and he gaped at Ailanthe for a moment before coming up the stairs to meet her. He was almost absurdly handsome, with a strong chin and firm lips and warm hazel eyes that looked as if they smiled a lot. "Spirits of the Castle!" he exclaimed, going down on one knee before Ailanthe. "I am blessed indeed by your presence. Tell me, spirit, which of these many items should I choose?"

"We're not spirits, we're people," Ailanthe said. "I'm Ailanthe and this is Coren, and the Castle won't let us out."

The man raised his head, glanced once at Coren, then focused on Ailanthe. "Surely such loveliness is not condemned to stay within the Castle's bounds?" he said, rising to his feet. Ailanthe thought he might be even taller than Coren, who wasn't short. He put his hand on the pommel of his sword and said, "Tell me, fair lady, what I may do to release you?"

Ailanthe didn't dare look to see Coren's reaction to this. "You can try to help me open the door," she said. "But you'll need to choose a Thing first. It won't let you go until you do."

The man looked back over his shoulder. "By my faith, where did they all vanish to?" he exclaimed. "I have not yet made my choice."

Ailanthe said, "That's perfectly normal. Go back down and they will appear again." She wondered why Coren wasn't saying anything, but still didn't dare to look at him for fear she might laugh. The quester's enthusiasm was almost comical.

"Then come with me, my lady, and let your fair hand guide my choice." The man held out his hand to her. Ailanthe shook her head.

"They won't appear while I'm there," she said, "and the choice is supposed to be your own. Just...take whatever draws your eye most."

The man bowed over his extended hand, then bounded back down the stairs. Coren said, "I hate the Galendish. Overly dramatic and foppish, every one."

"He seems perfectly nice, if a bit...all right, 'dramatic' is a good word. Why did he ignore you? For that matter, why didn't you say anything?"

"You were handling the conversation just fine. And he ignored me because any Galendish male would far rather speak to a beautiful woman than a man who might be a threat."

For a moment, Ailanthe couldn't speak. He thought— "So he might challenge you to a fight?" she said once she'd regained her composure.

"If he thought I was a danger to you, probably. Or if I got in his way. Better all around if you do the talking for both of us."

The Things vanished. The Galendishman bounded up the steps and approached them, holding out a palm-sized mirror. "Is this, then, my destiny?"

"Probably," Ailanthe said, not sure if that was a lie or not. "Can I show you the door now? And with luck, you'll be able to open it for us."

For the first time, the man looked at Coren, and a brief frown crossed his face. "With a surety, my lady, I will be happy to help you and your...friend." He extended his hand to take hers again, and to Ailanthe's surprise brought it to his lips and grazed her knuckles with a kiss. She felt her face go red and could almost hear Coren bristle. The man dropped her hand and said, "My name is Tristram, my lady, and now I hope I may free you from your captivity."

Ailanthe led the way down the blue hall to the kitchen annex, Tristram following her closely and Coren bringing up the rear. She was certain Coren was poised to attack the man if he so much as stepped wrong around her, and the thought made her heart beat faster. *He thinks I'm beautiful.* She opened the inner door and gestured for Tristram to precede her. "Just—it's just an ordinary latch," she said. He looked at her quizzically, then set his hand to the latch. It didn't move.

"Let me help," she said, and laid her hand atop Tristram's.

"My lady, surely you have not the strength," Tristram said.

"Just let me try." She couldn't think how to explain her magic quickly to this Galendishman when she was so impatient to see the door open. She let the memory of clutching the book to her chest well up inside her, tried to feel again the vibration and let that feeling travel down her arm into her hand. It didn't work. The latch was as solid and unmoving as ever. Ailanthe clenched her jaw to keep from crying. It had been a foolish hope, anyway.

"Will it not open?" Tristram asked. He didn't seem frightened by the idea that he might be stuck in the Castle with them.

Ailanthe shook her head. "It will open after we leave," she said. "Count to five after I close this inner door. And good luck to you."

Coren was leaning against the wall opposite the inner door when she emerged and closed it behind her. "You may be the most optimistic person I've ever met," he said. "And almost as stubborn as I am."

Ailanthe smiled and followed him around the corner to the blue hall. "I think I've given up on asking the questers for help. If the door is going to open, it will either be because I've grown strong enough to make it open or the Castle gets tired of keeping us here."

Coren nodded, then cleared his throat. "Ailanthe," he began, and Tristram came around the corner behind them. His smile was white and perfect, and his hazel eyes twinkled at Ailanthe.

"I find I cannot bear to leave you in such distress, my lady," he said. "I looked out upon my destiny and realized there can be no greater quest than to free you from your peril. Therefore, I refuse to leave until you are able to walk out by my side."

CHAPTER TWELVE

*A*ilanthe gaped at him. Coren said, "The door opened for you, and you didn't leave?"

"Even so, good sir." Tristram swept them both a bow.

"You—really, you ought to leave," Ailanthe said, her voice trembling. "There's no sense you being trapped here with us."

"Nevertheless, I choose to stay." Tristram smiled another of those dazzling smiles. "There must be another way out of this place, and I will not rest until I find it."

"You're going to go a long time without rest," Coren muttered under his breath.

"No, Tristram, I've already looked—"

"What can it hurt, having another pair of eyes? My lady, do not deny me my opportunity to serve you."

"I—" She looked at Coren, who'd gone impassive. "I suppose I can't stop you."

"Excellent decision, my lady!" Tristram captured her hand and once again brought it to his lips. "I shall begin immediately. Will you join me?"

"Ah...perhaps I should show you through the Castle first. You'll need a place to sleep, if you insist on staying here. And there are things you ought to know about the Castle itself." Ailanthe glanced at Coren again, who remained silent, but the closed-off look on his face told her everything he wasn't saying.

They ascended the stairs slowly, Ailanthe explaining about the Castle reclaiming things at midnight and how the windows looked out on different places. "I've tried breaking the windows, and climbing down from the tower, and of course going out with one of the questers, but none of that worked," she said.

"Then we shall simply try harder," Tristram said. "I have never yet failed at a challenge, my lady."

Coren muttered something Ailanthe couldn't make out. "And there's the bathrooms," she said quickly. "Do you have bathrooms where you come from?"

She had to demonstrate the fixtures because Coren remained silent and somewhat menacing in the bathroom door. Tristram was even more vocally impressed than she had been, working all the faucets three times and pulling the chain on the cistern even more. She left him to actually use the facilities and leaned against the wall next to Coren. "You could make an effort to be polite," she said.

"He's the one not being polite. Doesn't it bother you that he's dismissed everything we've tried as evidence that we're not trying hard enough?"

"He's a little too certain of himself, yes, but he's enthusiastic and I don't see a way of getting rid of him."

"I could knock him unconscious and lock him in the Vestibule. He'd eventually give up."

"You're the master of stubbornness; don't you know a fellow practitioner when you see one?" Ailanthe let out a breath. "You don't have to stay if he bothers you so much."

Coren glared at her. "I'm not leaving you alone with him. For all you know, the only reason he hasn't attacked you yet is my presence."

"You don't actually think he'd attack me, do you?"

Coren looked away. "No."

"Then—"

"Fine. I'll be in the Library. And don't bring him back to our rooms. I can be polite, but there's a limit." His walk as he left came close to being a stomp.

"Truly remarkable, my lady. Where is your large friend?" Tristram asked, shutting the bathroom door behind himself.

"He...has other things to do. Are you hungry? There's food in the kitchen."

"I would prefer to begin my investigation. Will you join me?"

Ailanthe remembered Coren's warning, but Tristram didn't look as if he were about to leap on her, so she said, "I can show you the places I haven't thoroughly searched yet."

"Then let us begin." He bowed low again, and Ailanthe stifled a sigh. His enthusiasm would quickly become tedious.

How quickly, Ailanthe wouldn't have guessed. Tristram felt the need to make comments on her beauty so frequently she finally told him to stop, only to be met with a look of incomprehension. "My lady, you should not be so modest," he said. "I say only what is evident to anyone who sees you. Now, if you would direct the light this way?"

They were searching the third floor, which was brightly lit, but Ailanthe never went anywhere without her lamp these days. There had been no more attacks in the last week, but the memory of freezing cold suffocation still frightened her enough that she wasn't willing to risk stepping into any shadows. Tristram made a great show of testing all the windows in this room, which held a variety of musical instruments, lifting the curtains and knocking on the walls, and Ailanthe suppressed a sigh. She could make her excuses and leave him to his search—she probably ought to do that—but he *was* being gallant on her behalf, and she felt guilty at the idea of letting him roam the Castle unsupervised.

So she held the light as he directed and tried not to think of Coren, who was probably having more fun than she was even if he was reading some of the driest of the Castle histories. Just how unhappy was he that she had chosen to stay with Tristram? She couldn't think of a reason for Tristram not to eat with them, and she was certain Coren wouldn't like that.

She was only giving Tristram part of her attention when he said, "Where are you from, my lady?"

"What? Oh. Lindurien."

"Ah, that accounts for your extraordinary beauty. I did not realize elves resembled humans so closely."

Ailanthe ground her teeth. "I'm not an elf, Tristram. You'd know an elf if you saw one."

"I beg your pardon, my lady."

"And please stop calling me beautiful. You're exaggerating and I dislike insincerity."

Tristram turned to look at her fully. "I am never insincere when speaking to a lady. You must hear such praise infrequently, to dismiss my words with such certainty. I wonder that your...companion...does not tell you such things himself."

Ailanthe blushed. "Coren is my friend. We don't have that kind of relationship." *But he thinks I'm beautiful.*

Tristram raised his eyebrows. "My mistake." He finished his search of the room and bowed to indicate she should precede him out the door. "Have you both been here long?"

"I've been here over a month. Coren's been here six years."

"Six years?" Tristram stopped in the middle of the hall. "I wonder he has not gone mad."

"He's the sanest person I know."

"He seems unwelcoming."

"He's just very private," Ailanthe lied. "Let's try this room."

Tristram continued to ask her questions until lunchtime, then again all afternoon until Ailanthe was thoroughly sick of him. Coren's proposal that they lock him in the Vestibule started to sound more appealing. By dinnertime her responses were short and unwelcoming, but Tristram either didn't notice or chose to ignore it.

When she took him to the kitchen, she couldn't tell if Coren had been there yet or not, so she gathered a large armful of food and said, "All that work has made me very tired. I'm going to eat in my room. Do you remember the way back to your bedroom?" She'd found him a place on the Library floor despite the nagging, guilty feeling that she ought to offer him something closer to Coren's suite.

"Yes, but may I not eat with you, my lady?" Tristram sounded concerned and a little hurt, which made Ailanthe feel even more guilty, but not guilty enough to change her mind.

"Tomorrow, perhaps," she said, "but tonight I wouldn't be very good company." She walked with him as far as the Library, then ran quickly up the stairs, fearing he might try to follow her after all.

Coren was in the window room, looking out over the ocean. He had a piece of dried meat in his hand and looked as if he'd forgotten it was there. "You started eating without me?" Ailanthe said.

He turned around to look at her, surprised. "I thought you'd be with your gallant defender."

"I told my 'gallant defender' I was too tired for company." She peeled the wax off a small round of cheese and bit into it. "He's nice enough, but his enthusiasm is exhausting."

Coren gave her a wry smile. "Not too tired for *my* company, I see."

"You're not exhausting. Quite the opposite." She pulled a chair next to him and settled in to watch the sunset. He handed her a strip of the dried meat, and she made a face, but started chewing it anyway. His presence both comforted and disturbed her. She'd chosen to sit near him, so her acute awareness of his proximity was entirely her fault, but she loved being near him even though she had to kill the impulse to put her head on his shoulder.

She risked a glance in his direction; he was gnawing on his meat and staring out across the ocean. "We, um, seem to have a lot of food," she said.

Coren shrugged. "The Castle can put it away for us." He chewed silently for a while. "It occurs to me if I ever get out of here, I'll have a lot of bad habits to break. I never tidy up anymore. Just drop my clothes on the floor, or leave books piled any old way."

Ailanthe tried not to picture Coren without his clothes on. "I've already fallen into those habits," she confessed. "Though I still have to put my clothes away because they don't belong to the Castle."

"I hope we get out of here before those habits become ingrained in you."

"Do you really think we'll get out of here?"

Coren looked over at her. His face was half in shadow, and Ailanthe had to struggle not to flinch at the image of that shadow detaching itself and leaping on her. "I think whatever magic you're developing will eventually become strong enough to overcome the Castle's restraint," he said. "Especially if you're taking that magic from the Castle itself."

"I hope you're right."

He shrugged and turned away. "Your optimism is infectious."

"After a day with Tristram, I don't feel so optimistic."

"Is he that tiresome?"

"It's not that. We're going through room after room and not finding anything useful, like a longer rope. Or a broken window closer to the ground than the tower."

"I'm guessing your gallant defender—"

"Just call him Tristram, Coren."

"All right. Tristram tried to break a window, didn't he?"

"He did. Several of them. The Castle will be mending a lot of broken chairs tonight. Though I almost thought he'd have success with the floor lamp."

Coren laughed. "I don't like him much, but he does seem to be trying."

"I wish he'd stop complimenting me. The words have lost their meaning."

"That's the Galendish for you. Empty compliments wrapped in protestations of eternal loyalty."

"I don't think they're empty. Just repetitive. And he hasn't pledged me any kind of loyalty."

"He'll get around to it. Just don't—"

Ailanthe hissed as Miriethiel leaped onto her lap, digging his claws in and kneading at her legs. "I think this cat presumes too much," she said, unhooking him and setting him on the ground.

"He likes the meat more than we do," Coren said, "though I don't know how he chews it with those fangs of his." He stood and walked to the window, where the sun had fully set and the clouds over the ocean made it hard to see where the waves ended and the sky began. Ailanthe watched him, admiring the way his tunic stretched across his broad shoulders, straining a little at the seams. "Just don't assume," he continued, "that because he's using pretty words he won't follow them up with an attack."

"Coren, you're too suspicious."

"I don't carry that sword for show, Ailanthe. I've had to fight more than a few questers who thought I was a threat."

"Tristram didn't challenge you. And I don't think it was because you intimidated him. I think he means what he says—he wants to help us find a way out."

"He wants to help *you* find a way out. He's certainly not concerned about my welfare."

"But you'll leave when I do. So what he thinks of you is irrelevant."

Coren sighed. "You're right. I'm just in a bad mood because I don't like him and I hate the idea of being indebted to him if he's the one who finds the exit."

"But we'd be free. And he'd go his way and we'd go ours."

"Ours together?"

Ailanthe stammered, "I—if we're both far from home, I'd prefer to travel back with you. No sense separating if we're going the same way, mostly."

Coren turned to look at her with that wry smile that made her heart beat faster. "I suppose you wouldn't get very far without me to protect you," he said.

"I can take care of myself."

"Two questers. The shadow. And you might have died on the tower if I hadn't been there."

Ailanthe flushed. "Coincidence."

"You're too reckless for your own safety. I suppose I shouldn't abandon you just because we're free."

"If protecting me makes you feel more confident about your masculinity, I suppose I shouldn't abandon *you*."

"Then we're agreed. And all we have to do is find the way out." He'd gone from smiling to serious in the space of two breaths. Ailanthe's heart beat even faster. Tristram's declaration of his desire to free her meant nothing compared to how often Coren had been there when she needed him. But to him, she was...not an obligation exactly, and she was sure he didn't resent having to defend her and he didn't think less of her for needing his help, but she wasn't anything more to him than a friend, and that thought made her chest ache.

"Are you sure you won't join us in the search tomorrow?" she said, adopting a casual, friendly manner and hoping her heart would take the hint. "I really don't want to be alone with him, and we *are* searching rooms I haven't given much attention to. It would help."

Coren had been about to say something else, but now he scowled. "I'm not above begging," Ailanthe said with a smile.

He snorted, but said, "All right. But don't expect me to be very polite to him."

"Just don't start a fight and I'm sure everything will be fine. Now I'm going to bed with a book."

"Usael's book?"

"No, one of the ones about magic. It talks a lot about what magic is and where it comes from. I think it applies to the Castle. Maybe, if I can work out how it was built, I can work out how to take it apart."

"Don't take it apart around us."

"I'll do my best."

CHAPTER THIRTEEN

*S*he read until the Castle retrieved the book, late that night. She didn't try to hang onto it, but sat in her bed for a while after it had gone, thinking. Coren was right that the Castle acted on itself, manipulating the magic it was made of, or that had made it, but that didn't explain how it had gotten the magic in the first place.

The author wrote of the limitations of spirits and their inability to work together, which meant even hundreds of spirits wouldn't have been able to build something the size of the Castle. And she knew *kerthors*, while capable of working together well, needed to be able to visualize their goal in its entirety, and she didn't think anyone could encompass the entire Castle in their mind. But she was only halfway through the book, and it was still possible the answer was in it somewhere.

She looked around at the lights burning around the room. She'd turned on all three of her lamps, as well as the wall lights, and any shadows cast by one light were eliminated by the others. The problem was she couldn't turn them all off at once, and every night she dashed around the room to put out every light before the remaining ones could cast too many shadows. Some nights she just left them burning. Tonight, the thought of having to race the shadows made her angry.

She clutched the key in her right hand and imagined her hand on the switch of every light in the room at once, then twitched the fingers of her left hand.

The lights flickered, but didn't go out. Ailanthe was so startled she lost the image. She glanced at the lamp next to her bed. She took a deep breath and tried again, laying her fingers on the lamp's switch and pretending to feel its smooth texture with every imaginary hand. "The Castle could do this," she said, "and so can I," and pressed down on the real switch.

The lights went out. She felt a pounding ache begin behind her eyes, but she didn't care. She'd made the Castle do as she wanted. She slipped out of bed and fumbled in the dark for her clothes. The door would open for her this time, she was certain of it.

She went carefully down the stairs in the blackness, afraid her lamp would do no more than cast a hundred vicious shadows. She had run up and down them so many times she had no trouble navigating the landings and the steps until her foot touched the cold tile of the ground floor. Trailing her fingers along the wall, she made her slow, groping way to the flagstones surrounding the Honor Hall, then over the tiny squares of the blue hall's mosaic floor, and finally to the inner door of the Vestibule.

It was dark outside the little window, and she patted the door until she found the latch. "The Castle can open this," she said again, "and that means I can too," and pressed down on the latch.

She felt it quiver, the tiniest bit, before resisting her again. She leaned on it with all her weight, but nothing happened. "*Open, damn you!*" she screamed, and pounded on the latch with her fist until it hurt too badly for her to continue. She sank down to sit on the floor, her hand still gripping the latch, and cried herself into a fitful sleep.

When she woke, cold and aching, she wasn't sure how much time had passed, but the Vestibule was still dark and her hand still hurt. She retraced her halting steps in the blackness until, safely in her room, she crawled into her bed and stared at nothing until a lightening behind the navy-blue curtains told her dawn had come. She rubbed her painfully sore hand and hoped she hadn't done it any permanent damage.

She used the bathroom, then went to the window room hoping Coren had already brought breakfast. "My lady!" Tristram exclaimed. "I thought we might share a morning meal, the three of us. Please, sit, allow me to bring you something." He sat next to several chairs holding fruits and bread, plates, glasses, and a tall metal pitcher.

Ailanthe blinked at him, then looked around for Coren. He was not going to be happy about this. Tristram ushered her to a chair, then brought her a plate of carefully arranged fruits and a glass of some pinkish-yellow drink that was surprisingly bitter and sweet at the same time. She and Coren had never bothered with dishes, and this touch of civilization made her both uncomfortable and grateful to Tristram for the courtesy. It seemed he really did mean all the gracious things he'd been saying.

"What's this?" Coren said from the doorway. He definitely did not sound happy.

"Tristram has been kind enough to bring breakfast for all of us," she said, fixing him with a stare she hoped he would interpret correctly as *You promised to be polite.* He stared back at her impassively, then helped himself to a half-loaf of bread and a pot of jam, not bothering with a plate.

"This is a most peculiar room," Tristram said. "You did tell me, my lady, of the wonders this Castle shows through its windows, but I did not expect to see such disparate views in a single room."

"It's the only one of its kind," Coren said through a mouthful of food. Ailanthe glared at him. She didn't know why he was being deliberately uncouth, but she guessed he intended to annoy Tristram, though how talking with his mouth full would do anything but make him look like a rustic bumpkin eluded her.

"Sit with me, Tristram," she said, ignoring Coren and indicating a chair near hers. Tristram joined her and offered her a loaf, still warm despite its trip up twenty flights of stairs. He smiled that dazzling smile again before tearing off a small piece of his own loaf and putting it delicately into his mouth. Ailanthe smiled to cover her confusion. He clearly wanted to underline the contrast between himself and Coren, and the look in his eyes told her he was doing it to impress her. She couldn't decide whether she hoped Coren was watching or that his attention was still on the valley cliffs.

"I have never seen such a place before," Tristram said, indicating the desert. The sky was dusky tan; a sandstorm was coming, something Ailanthe had seen once before and had to turn away from because it felt as though it was trying to engulf her. "Where is it?"

"The southern end of Rius-zara," Coren said. So he was paying attention after all. "It's all desert until you reach the ocean, where there's a fertile border along the coast."

"I once visited Rius-zara," Tristram said. "It is a marvelous place. Perhaps, when the door opens, it will take us there. I should like to show it to you."

"Thank you, Tristram, that would be...pleasant," Ailanthe said, almost meaning it. He was more considerate than she'd guessed yesterday, and he hadn't paid her any extravagant compliments, and he was very nice to look at, though not, to her eyes, as handsome as Coren; he was leaner, and taller, and his hazel eyes twinkled, but he didn't have broad shoulders or an angular face or those well-shaped, powerful hands that were equally comfortable wielding a sword and turning the pages of a book. "And thank you for bringing the food. It's delicious."

"I fear I could not find means to build a fire, or I would have cooked for you," Tristram said. He opened a pot of jam and spread some on a round of bread, which he offered to her with a smile. She accepted it graciously, though she was becoming nervous. Maybe Coren was right, and Tristram was working his way toward pledging her his undying loyalty. That would be uncomfortable. She'd have to stay alert to fend off any such protestations.

"Shall we begin our search on the next floor, my lady?" Tristram asked, sipping his pinkish-orange drink as if he enjoyed the bitterness.

"I suppose so. What do you think, Coren?" Coren shrugged.

"Then it's settled. Tristram, you don't need to clear away the plates. The Castle will take care of them later."

"I think perhaps this extraordinary room does not deserve to be cluttered with dirty things," Tristram said, taking her empty plate and glass and leaving the room.

Coren said, "I really don't like him."

"Why not? It's true, he's a little high-handed, but I think he genuinely wants us to be friends. And he worked very hard yesterday."

Coren shrugged again. "Maybe it's more accurate to say I don't like the Galendish. They have pretty manners and dress up their words like they're taking them to a party, but they've also got this code of conduct they hold to no matter the circumstances. God forbid they come up against a situation that requires subtlety."

"Tristram hasn't behaved like that."

"You've known him for a day. Just...keep it in mind, all right?"

Ailanthe sighed. "Let's meet him downstairs. I think there are some locked doors."

With Coren toting the lamp, they descended the stairs and met Tristram on his way up. "Ah, friends!" he said. "Let us begin our search, and perhaps we will have more luck today."

IT DIDN'T TAKE LONG for Ailanthe to become discouraged. She was tired, her hand hurt and was bruised badly—it took some doing to conceal it from her companions, because she didn't want to explain how it had gotten that way—and although Tristram's compliments were less frequent, probably because of Coren's presence, they now had a serious undertone that flustered her.

They went from room to room with no success other than finding some beautiful galleries filled with paintings and sculptures that had all three of them exclaiming in wonder. What they needed were more storage rooms, preferably ones with axes or rope or something useful.

The thirteenth room was draped in forest green velvet, not just the windows but the walls as well, the heavy curtains giving the chamber a somber feel not dispelled by the plush carpet of so deep a green it looked black. "This looks much as I imagine it would feel to be interred," Tristram said, his voice flattened, the sound absorbed by the drapes. The light came from a lamp set into the ceiling and only dimly illuminated the room.

"Turn the lamp off," Ailanthe said, moving closer to Coren. The shadows it cast seemed to move. Coren switched it off and put his hand on her shoulder. "Warn me if you see anything," he murmured. They hadn't told Tristram about the shadows, and Ailanthe wasn't sure why, except that it would give him one more thing he might feel he should protect her from, and his offers of protection, unlike Coren's, made her feel awkward.

"We need more light," Tristram said, and pulled one of the drapes to the side, letting in bright sunlight. Ailanthe quickly moved to uncover the other windows, staying well within the light they admitted, and tied the drapes back with thick black ropes hanging to each side of the windows.

Coren came to stand beside Ailanthe, but made no move to help her. "You could open those drapes over there," Ailanthe said, a little annoyed, but he stayed where he was, gazing out the window. "Coren," she said.

"It's Hespera," he said quietly, and reached out to touch the pane of glass before him.

Dusty green hills spread out before them to the horizon, scattered with small groves of trees that sprawled instead of reaching for the sky as they did in Lindurien. A wide river flowed lazily from right to left in the near distance, white rocks rising from it at intervals as if some giant hand had placed them there to change the way the river flowed. A cloud of birds swirled and dipped against the bright blue cloudless sky. "Oh, Coren," Ailanthe said in a quiet voice to match his.

"It's been almost four years since I saw it," he said. "But that landscape is unmistakable."

"My lady, good sir, I think you should look at this," Tristram said.

He was holding back one of the drapes along the wall, revealing a door. "It's locked."

Coren and Ailanthe looked at each other. "Go ahead," Coren said. Ailanthe turned the key in the lock, then pushed the door open. Cool air rushed in, smelling of green things and sunshine. She went through the door and found herself on a balcony that looked out on the same vista as the windows. It was about five feet wide and just as deep, with a stone railing. And it was open to the outdoors.

Ailanthe gripped the railing and inhaled her first breath of fresh air in weeks. It tasted like spring. They were in the lee of the Castle, shaded from the sun, but it was hard to believe in evil shadows when she could feel the wind on her face and see the sun's rays turning the river to bright flowing glass. She felt Coren and Tristram come to stand on either side of her. "Most beautiful," Tristram said.

"I'm getting the rope," Coren said.

CHAPTER FOURTEEN

*A*ilanthe tied the rope securely to the railing and said, "Coren, pull on this." He took hold of it and leaned away from the railing, putting his full weight on it. Tristram said, "Perhaps it would be better if I tied the rope, my lady. I have some experience—"

"Tristram," Ailanthe said, unable to fully contain her impatience, "I have been tying knots since I was three years old. My people trust their lives to rope bridges that run two or three of the Castle's stories in the air. *I* have experience. Now move aside and let me climb down."

"No, my lady, I cannot allow you to do that. It might be unsafe."

"*I* am going first," Coren said, "because I weigh more and someone should anchor the rope at the bottom to make climbing easier. And it's my country. So *both* of you get out of my way."

Ailanthe moved aside. So did Tristram, after a long moment in which he and Coren faced each other in fierce silence. Ailanthe wasn't sure if Coren had won that battle, or if Tristram had given in to make himself look gracious in front of her.

Coren climbed over the railing and gripped the rope in both hands. He met Ailanthe's eyes briefly, and she knew what he was thinking: there was a very good chance the Castle would pull him back up, or snatch him off the rope, the way it had done Ailanthe at the tower. She gave him a nod, and he lowered himself over the balcony and down the wall.

She and Tristram watched his progress, Ailanthe with her uninjured fist clenched tight. He was moving far too slowly, inching along as if waiting for the Castle to snatch him back. Halfway there, and Ailanthe discovered she was dizzy from holding her breath and made herself breathe in the fresh, beautiful air. He was almost to the ground when the rope began to tremble.

"Coren, *jump!*" Ailanthe shouted, and he looked up at her—

—and then he was standing next to her, his hands still curled as if around the rope, looking up at the overhanging roof of the balcony, his mouth hanging open as if he were about to speak. He stood that way for a single frozen moment, then his hands fell to his side and his mouth closed.

He continued to stare at the roof, unblinking, until Ailanthe said, "Coren." She was afraid to touch him, but not because his closeness always cast her into confusion; now she was afraid of what he might do if she did.

He lowered his head until he was staring at the stone floor of the balcony. He closed his eyes, and a shudder ran through him. Then he opened his eyes, pushed past her like a blind man feeling his way through a crowd, and went through the room and out the door.

"Should we follow?" Tristram said. His voice lacked the half-teasing note she was now familiar with. She shook her head fiercely.

"We are going to lock this door," she said, "and we are going to close the drapes, and then I am going to lock the door to the room and we're going to pretend it doesn't exist, understand?"

"I think I do, my lady," Tristram said. "I did not realize what a cruel mistress this Castle is until now. I am truly sorry for both of you."

"You think of the Castle as a woman, then?" Ailanthe untied draperies and settled them so they completely covered the windows.

"Do you not? She is careless and cruel, yet she provides for the needs of everyone dependent on her and grants blessings beyond the wisdom of men. Is that not female?"

Ailanthe now understood why Coren had such a dislike of the Galendish. "Are you suggesting careless cruelty is a universal female trait?" she said, feeling her fear and sorrow for Coren turn into anger inside her.

"I mean no disrespect, my lady. I have great regard for all women." Tristram looked puzzled at her response.

"Well, Tristram, do you know what I think? I think of the Castle as a man—stubborn, haughty, and unwilling to bend in his rigid attention to rules set down by God only knows who. Keep looking if you want. I'm done for the day." She strode down the hall in the direction of the stairs.

She didn't know if she wanted to find Coren or not. She didn't want to intrude on his pain, didn't have a right to comfort him, though she felt comfort was something he might need right now. What she wanted was to put her arms around his neck and hold him, and she wasn't going to do that. So she went to the tower.

Staring out over Lindurien, she understood a little of how he must have felt to be so close to escaping. It wasn't the same—when she'd dangled outside the tower, buffeted by that wind, she hadn't been locked up for six years, given up hope, and had it waved in front of her face only to be snatched away again. But to be so close to the place you loved most and to be unable to touch it—that, she understood.

She wished she had Usael's book now. It had been a few days since she'd read it last, and she was eager to see what happened next, because Usael had developed an attachment to Elara, one of her sister's friends. The thought that he might choose to settle at the mother tree, that she might have the chance to meet him someday, thrilled her. She leaned back and laid her head against the chilly glass of the window. She really wanted a book to read. But Coren might have gone to ground in the Library, and she didn't want to disturb him.

But...just suppose... She closed her eyes and thought of Usael's book, not just the binding and the grooves of the board, but the pattern of oil-slick rainbows that she'd discovered were unique to each of the hero books. She'd put the book back in its place in the Library, but whenever she chose to keep it in her room, it was still there the next morning. It was her book now, she was certain, not the Castle's, and if she had some of the Castle's power she ought to have some of its skills. She held out her hands, palm up, and said, "Come to me."

And the heavy weight of the book settled into her hands.

She opened her eyes and flipped through it. It might be a copy—no, it couldn't be a copy, because when she tried to work that type of magic on something magical, such as the key and the ring she'd found at the back of a dresser drawer, that yellow-black spike of agony went through her head and her vision went blurry and she had to lie down until it went away.

She turned it over in her hands, marveling, then sent it back where it had come from. It vanished with barely a trace of sparkling dust, just as she'd seen in the Honor Hall when Tristram's Things appeared. She summoned it again; it was easier this time, far easier than learning to create things had been.

She hugged the book to her chest, then opened it and turned to where she'd left off. She blushed, and flipped ahead a few pages. The book's magic didn't believe in giving people privacy, though at least she now knew Usael and Elara were definitely a couple. Everyone was celebrating their union, and Usael was showing off his growing *kerthor* abilities.

Ailanthe wiped away a tear. She reminded herself if she were home, she still would be rejected by the trees and her personal misery would have made it impossible for her to truly celebrate with her people.

Loud footsteps sounded on the stairs, and Coren emerged from the hole in the floor at a run. "You did it," he said, breathing heavily. He pointed at the book. "I saw it vanish. Then I saw it appear again, and vanish again. I knew it was you."

"So I did summon it?" Ailanthe exclaimed. "I hoped I hadn't just made a copy."

"No, you summoned it." Coren sat with his legs dangling down the stairwell. "It's another step."

"I don't know what use it will be."

"I don't give a damn about usefulness. Right now all I care about is tearing this Castle apart from the roots up. Summon something else. Summon my sword."

"I don't know if I'm familiar enough with it."

"Try, Ailanthe. *Please.*"

He'd been so excited about her summoning Ailanthe had assumed he'd overcome his grief at losing his home yet again. Now she realized he'd just turned it inward, and her heart ached for him. His jaw was set and there was a tightness around the corners of his eyes and mouth that told her how much tension he was still under.

So she closed her eyes and pictured the sword, with its strangely angled guard and leather-wrapped hilt, the silver pommel like a giant etched marble, the groove that ran half the length of the blade, and heard a clatter as something metal and heavy struck the stones of the tower.

She opened her eyes to see Coren pulling the sword toward himself across the floor with a loud scraping sound. He examined it carefully, and said, "It could still be a copy."

"But you don't think it is."

"No." He stood up. "Let's go find out."

It wasn't a copy. Coren had left the sword on one of the chairs in the window room that morning in response to Ailanthe's frown; Tristram wasn't carrying his own sword, and Ailanthe was a little impatient with Coren's antagonism toward the Galendishman. The chair was empty.

Coren hefted the sword in his hand and sighted along the blade. "It doesn't look like summoning damaged it," he said.

"Why should it? Nothing is ever damaged when the Castle does it."

"I know. I just expect things to go wrong, now." He turned away and walked toward the desert window. Ailanthe followed him.

"Are you all right?" she asked, knowing it was an inadequate question and not sure what she would do with his answer.

"No," Coren said. "But I will be. It was just so...why did it let me get so close, Ailanthe? It felt like the Castle was taunting me."

"I don't know. The more I learn, the less I understand. I'm so sorry, Coren."

He waved that aside. "It was my choice, and I knew what was likely to happen. I won't go back there again."

"That's good, because I locked the doors. And removed the rope."

He laughed, and Ailanthe relaxed because it was a normal-sounding laugh. "Afraid I might try something mad?"

"Afraid you might spend all your time staring out the window and mope around and be boring."

"I promise I won't do that. I—" He focused on her hand. "What is that?"

Ailanthe hid her hand behind her back. "It's nothing. An accident."

He grabbed her arm, then her wrist, and raised her hand so the light struck it clearly. "An accident with what? A hammer?"

Ailanthe tried to wrench away from his grip. "I tried to open the door again last night. I just lost my temper, that's all."

"And tried to break your hand?" He felt along the worst bruises, making her gasp in pain. "I don't think anything's broken, but— Ailanthe, what were you thinking?"

"I wasn't thinking!" she shouted. "It moved, Coren, a little bit, and then it stopped and I couldn't bear it any longer! I'm so tired of this place, and worrying about being attacked, and this magic is growing inside me and I don't know where that will end—what if it turns me into something neither of us recognizes? I just want to go home. I don't care if I never see the tops of the trees again. I want to go home."

They stood glaring at each other for a long moment. Coren cursed, let go of her hand and wheeled away to stare out the window. Ailanthe sagged onto a chair and covered her face with her hands, then hissed with pain and dropped her injured hand to her lap. She hurt, she was overwhelmed, and she wanted so badly to be held by him it was an almost physical pain in her chest.

She'd kept herself from thinking about the implications of the magic she was learning to use, or that was growing inside her, focused only on how it might help them escape. Now she was forced to admit there was a possibility she was being changed into something else. A magical being, not a human woman who could somehow tap into the Castle's magic. Suppose she did become powerful enough to defeat the Castle, but at the cost of her humanity? What would be left for her then?

"I don't know how to help you," Coren said quietly, and she raised her head to look at him. He was facing the window, and she could see by his faint reflection in the glass that he was looking down at the base of the Castle, far below. "You shouldn't be trapped here. You don't deserve it. And there's nothing I can do about it."

"It's not your fault," Ailanthe began, but he shook his head and overrode her.

"It's not about fault," he said. "I know what it's like to be trapped here for years. I chose that. I don't want that for you. But I'm tired of being alone and I feel guilty at how glad I am you're here with me. It's selfish and stupid and I hate myself for it. So if I could free you—if anything I could do would free you, I'd do it."

The unvarnished honesty of his words left Ailanthe with nothing to say. "Coren," she began, hoping his name might spark a train of thought that would let her answer him with some honesty of her own.

He turned toward her, an unfamiliar expression on his face, and opened his mouth and said, "Ailanthe, I—"

"My lady, good sir," Tristram said from the doorway. "I have discovered something I believe you must see."

CHAPTER FIFTEEN

"$\mathscr{I}$t was a chance discovery," Tristram said. They stood in one of the book rooms on the fourth floor, an interior room with no windows and all four of its walls covered by bookshelves. "There is a gap here where there is none elsewhere. Then I saw the marks on the carpet."

He pointed. There was a half-inch gap between two bookshelves, and barely visible on the carpet was a quarter circle arc with one of its endpoints lining up with the gap. "I guessed at the room's existence, and sought out the mechanism that would open it."

He'd wrecked the room in doing so. Most of the books had been removed from the shelves and piled haphazardly on the floor and on the round table at the center of the room and on the three leather-upholstered chairs surrounding it. Tristram had also moved the bookends, which were horseheads made of scratched and chipped ebony, and scuff marks showed that he'd climbed some of the shelves to feel along their tops.

"This is the device," he said, indicating one lone horsehead remaining on the shelf. He tipped it forward as if it were bowing to them, and there was a click and one of the shelves swung open a fraction of an inch. Tristram took hold of its edge and pulled it open the rest of the way. "I have yet to enter," he said. "I thought the honor should be yours, my lady." Ailanthe nodded at him, too distracted to register his bow, and slipped through the gap.

The hidden room was far too big to fit between the book room and the chamber with the mounted animal heads Ailanthe knew was next door to it. A dull golden haze of magic hung in the air, and she held her breath until she couldn't bear it, but nothing happened when she inhaled the particles except a series of sneezes.

Like the book room, it was windowless and filled with furniture. Shelves lined two adjacent walls, packed full of books with fraying leather bindings and embossed print worn away into illegibility. A glass-topped cabinet next to the door held an odd display of curios, with no theme Ailanthe could detect. There was a chair deeply upholstered in old gold velvet in the corner where the bookshelves met and another behind an oak desk stained dark walnut. The surface of the desk was bare except for a lamp and a sheet of some smooth green material nearly the size of the desk's top.

She moved around behind the desk and looked at the dozens of drawers of all sizes. "Don't touch anything," she told Coren and Tristram, who'd entered behind her. "This room is full of magic. Whoever it belonged to might have left traps for people like us."

"What magic do you see?" Coren asked.

Ailanthe looked around the room more carefully. "Most of the items in that collection," she said. "Some of the books. There's a haze around the lock on the bottom of the cabinet, and another on these locked drawers here."

"I see no haze, my lady," Tristram said.

"I...have some magic," Ailanthe said. "I can see which things are magical, and make things—" She raised her left hand and called another lamp into being. Tristan's eyes went wide, and he jerked as if he wanted to take a step away from her.

"Yet you are no *kerthor*," he said. "How can this be?"

"I don't know, Tristram. I think this key may give me some of the power of the Castle. You really shouldn't touch that."

"Most miraculous," Tristram said, despite Ailanthe's warning reaching out to touch the binding of one of the books. Nothing happened. He removed the book and opened it. "There is a book plate," he said. "This book is the property of one Gweron. Have either of you heard aught of the name?"

"No," Ailanthe said. She gingerly opened a drawer with the tips of the fingers of her left hand; her right hand had begun to ache more severely, probably because of how roughly Coren had handled it in checking for broken bones. Inside lay pens, a penknife, and brass inkwells. None of them were magical. She shut the drawer and exclaimed, "Not that one, Coren."

Coren removed his hand from the book he'd been about to take. "Magic?"

"Yes. I really don't think we should touch the books."

"I agree. This entire room makes me nervous."

Ailanthe opened another drawer. It was full of blank white paper, crisp and neat like the pages of the books in the Library. "It might be important. We're looking for a better understanding of magic, and this room is saturated with it."

"I didn't say we shouldn't investigate it. I said it makes me nervous."

"Me too." A third drawer yielded several devices Ailanthe didn't recognize, none of which were magical. She lifted one out and set it on the desk; it was a series of circles mounted on a base, each bearing a marble-sized orb, the circles centered on a much larger orb. The circles and orbs were made of brass, and its base was made of oak. Ailanthe prodded one of the circles, which wobbled.

"An orrery," Tristram said. "A model of the world and the other three planets. And of very fine workmanship."

"And yet it was stuck in a drawer," Ailanthe said. She opened a few more drawers, but found nothing interesting and nothing magical. Coren slid the glass top of the cabinet open and examined the curios without touching them.

"You said most of these were magical?" he asked.

"Everything except the disgusting shriveled mouse corpse. I

wonder if that was really part of the display, or if it just got trapped in there. Don't touch anything."

"I'm not stupid, Ailanthe. I'm trying to work out whether there's a pattern to this collection."

Ailanthe went to stand next to Coren. The shallow top of the cabinet was lined with white silk, upon which were arranged a metal butterfly made of colored wire, a red rose that looked as if it had been plucked that morning, a model house made of tiny bricks and slate roofing tiles, a square of roughly woven fabric with a bluebird and a rose painted on it, a handful of padlocks ranging in size from the size of Ailanthe's palm to one no bigger than her thumbnail, and, strangest of all, a motionless sprite in its contracted ball-shaped phase. She pointed at it. "Do you see that?"

"It looks like a dandelion clock. What is it, my lady?"

"That's what a sprite looks like to me. I don't know how it's visible to you."

"It looks dead," Coren said. "If the sprites are even alive in the first place."

"Maybe they are," Ailanthe said. She slid the cover closed. "I have no idea what it is, except that each of these objects has magic on it."

"Or was made by magic," Coren said.

"Or that."

"Dare you open that, my lady?" Tristram said. He pointed at the locked doors beneath the curio collection.

"I think it's a bad idea, Ailanthe."

"Anything locked in there might be what we're looking for, Coren."

She fumbled with the key, her injured hand throbbing, and Coren carefully removed it from her wrist and handed it to her. She crouched and, left-handed, inserted the key into the lock and felt the familiar resistance as it reshaped itself to fit. A tingle ran up her arm, a pleasant feeling and not at all what she'd expected.

She turned the key and the lock clicked open. She glanced up at the men; Tristram had taken two steps back, and Coren hovered over her left shoulder as if he were prepared to haul her bodily away from danger. She grinned at him and opened the door.

A hot wind that smelled strongly of roses blew through the room, making Ailanthe rock on her heels. Coren took an involuntary step back, then his hand closed on her shoulder. Tristram said, "That is a lovely smell." Ailanthe thought it was rather cloying and waved her hand in front of her nose to dispel it. Coren sneezed. "We're all going to stink of roses now," he said.

"There are worse things to stink of, good sir."

"True," Coren said, surprising Ailanthe. She'd thought he would disagree with Tristram if he said water was wet. She leaned forward, pulling away from Coren's hand, and peered into the cupboard. There were two shelves inside, and lined up on those shelves were sixteen glass spheres, each resting on a cradle of ash carved with symbols Ailanthe couldn't read. All of them shone faintly with magic.

Ailanthe reached in and removed one with its base. The sphere was bigger than her cupped hands could surround and seemed to be filled with water. "This is amazing," she said, holding it out for Coren to see. Tristram stepped closer.

Within the globe was a perfect replica of a grandfather tree, set in a base of green grass rumpled by its roots rising out of the ground. Ailanthe peered closely at it, but it quickly became blurry. She discovered the farther she was from the globe, the clearer the image became, and set the globe on the desk and took several steps back. At that distance, she could make out individual leaves on the branches. Another step, and she could see the veins on those leaves. She stepped forward and picked the globe up out of its base, and shook it. The leaves moved as if wind had ruffled them.

"Is that a good idea?" Coren asked.

"It hasn't hurt me yet."

Coren snorted. "You have just summed up your entire approach to life."

"I never learn anything if I don't take chances." She placed the globe in his hands; he juggled it in surprise, but didn't drop it. She turned her attention to the base. "How strange. We can read everything else in the Castle, so why not this?"

It was a row of symbols Ailanthe was certain was a name, or a title, but was pure gibberish. She set it down and held out her hand for the globe, but it was intercepted by Tristram, who turned it upside down and exclaimed when a tiny smudge that was probably a leaf detached from the grandfather and floated down to rest on what was now the bottom of the globe.

"These are all models," Coren said, his head halfway inside the cupboard. He brought out one containing a miniature farmhouse and held it at arm's length. "There are even tiny hens in the yard."

"Here's a snow-covered mountain. I wonder that the snow doesn't dissolve in the water," Ailanthe said. "And—oh, it's the Castle!" She put that one on the desk and all three of them stepped as far back as they could. It looked crisper and more finished than the real Castle. The tower looked unstable, as if it might blow over in a brisk wind, and Ailanthe felt uncomfortable looking at it. In fact, the whole model made her uncomfortable. It was so perfect she felt if she could step back far enough, she would be able to look through the windows and see herself looking out.

She went back to the cupboard and continued pulling globes out, handing them to the men to line them up on the green surface of the desk. All were models either of buildings or some distinctive natural feature. None of the buildings were duplicated, but there were several mountains and cliffs and trees, and all were executed in the finest, most accurate detail Ailanthe could imagine. One contained a beautiful red rose, half-open and perfect, identical to the one in the cabinet, and Ailanthe gazed at that for some time before giving it to Coren.

"Every base has something different carved into it," she said. "I really think those are descriptions of what's in the globe, or names possibly."

"I think you are correct," Tristram said. "So what magic is upon them, my lady?"

Ailanthe looked inside the empty cupboard, then at the lock.

"The magic that was on the cupboard is gone," she said, "but the globes are still glowing a little. I don't know what it does. I don't know what any of it does. It could be what makes the image become so clear at a distance instead of close up. It could mean they're made of magic. I just don't know."

"I am confident you will figure it out, my lady," Tristram said with a bow. Ailanthe acknowledged his compliment with a smile, but inside she was burning with frustration. She'd learned so much and now she had a new mystery to solve. She was tired of mysteries. It felt as if the day had already gone on forever.

"Maybe you ought to open these other locks," Coren said. He'd gone around behind the desk and was sitting in the chair.

"Did you just suggest I do something potentially dangerous?"

"You made a good point, about finding something we might need in here," he said, tilting back so the chair rocked on two legs. "And I think that key—" he pointed for emphasis— "may be absorbing the magic on the locks, or dispersing it, or something. I doubt the original purpose of the magic was to shower people with rose attar."

Ailanthe looked at the key. It was small now, with a single notched tooth, a simple key for a simple lock. "All right, but you need to move out of the way and stop playing with the furniture." She waited for Coren to sidle out from behind the desk, then leaned over and, after a moment's hesitation, slid the key into the first lock.

The lock gave almost no resistance to the key, and again she felt the pleasant tingle run up her arm and into her shoulder. The lock clicked; she slid the drawer open, and said, "It's empty."

The men crowded around to look inside. Tristram reached past her and put his hand into the deep drawer and felt around. "Possibly a false bottom?" he said, but his search turned up nothing else. Ailanthe shut the drawer and locked it again, superstitiously thinking the owner of the desk would want her to leave everything as she'd found it. Maybe she should have paid more attention to the order of the globes before they removed them. Then, impatient with her cowardice, she unlocked it.

"One more," she said, then, on a whim, took the key in her right hand, grasped it as firmly as her sore fingers would let her, and inserted it into the lock of the other drawer and turned it. The tingle that ran up her arm was stronger this time, and her hand immediately felt better. Even the bruising seemed diminished.

She pulled the drawer open, reached inside, and withdrew a book. It was bound in yellow cloth over stiff boards and the tip of a feather poked out of the pages, like a bookmark. She opened it there and touched the feather, which came from a red eagle. "It looks like a diary," she said. "It's written in the same symbols as the globe bases. And it's positively dripping with magic. Here's the name Gweron again, inside the front cover. I wonder why we can read that when we can't read anything else."

Tristram took it from her hands a little abruptly and flipped through the pages. "Indeed, my lady," he said, with a hint of condescension that made Ailanthe bristle. "You are perceptive. I wonder that we cannot read it."

"We said that already," Coren said, taking the book out of Tristram's hands and giving it back to Ailanthe. "I don't suppose you have any ideas on how we might read it?"

"Not really." She stared at the page, willing the symbols to make sense. She looked up at Coren, and something flickered at the edge of her vision. She gasped and slammed the book shut. "Did you see that?"

"Danger?" Coren said, stepping closer to her.

"I stand ready to protect you, my lady," Tristram said, closing in on her other side.

Ailanthe scanned the room, peering closely at the shadows, but nothing moved. "I...don't know what I saw. Just movement." She opened the book again. Still meaningless symbols.

"I regret that I did not bring my sword," Tristram said, pacing the room. "I allowed myself to be drawn into, no, lulled into complacency. This Castle has too many hidden dangers. I do not believe you are safe."

Ailanthe glanced at him, her mouth open to remind him she already had a protector, not that she needed one, and saw the flicker of movement again, right under her chin. She snapped her gaze downward and realized the flickering happened every time she passed her eyes quickly over the diary's pages. "I found it," she said. "But I don't know what I'm seeing." She handed the diary to Coren. "Face the pages and turn your head quickly."

He complied, but said, "I don't see anything but blurry lines."

"May I?" Tristram asked, and took the diary from Coren without waiting for permission. He repeated the experiment several times, muttering to himself, before finally saying, "Alas, I fear I see nothing as well. It seems this magic must be left to your divination." He handed her the book with a flourish.

"But I'm not *seeing* anything," Ailanthe complained. "It's as if the letters, the symbols, become clearer for a moment. That's all."

"But it suggests there's something more to be seen. What if the symbols cover up the real writing?" Coren said. "I think it's worth your studying further."

"I agree." Ailanthe closed the book with a snap and tucked it under her right arm. "Whatever it is, I'm taking it with me."

They left the hidden door to the study open and filed out into the hall, Tristram leading the way. Ailanthe saw Coren bristle at the Galendishman's presumption, and couldn't quite blame him for his reaction; Tristram did tend to behave as if he were in charge. "Shall we explore further, my lady?" he said, bowing to her.

"I don't think so. Right now I'm hungry and tired and I don't care that it's not quite time for dinner."

"Then I shall fetch food for us, my lady," Tristram said.

"That's my job," Coren growled.

Tristram stepped back and made one of his sweeping bows at Coren. "Then I shall leave you to it, and escort the lady back to her chamber," he said. Coren looked startled, then annoyed. By the gleam in his eye, Tristram had clearly planned to outmaneuver him. Ailanthe wanted to laugh at Coren's consternation at leaving her alone with Tristram, but that would embarrass him, so she only said, "There's a salmon filet in the cold room, if you wouldn't mind bringing that?"

Tristram offered Ailanthe his arm when they reached the stairs, which she wanted to refuse, but he *had* found the secret study, and he took such pleasure in his courtly game that she accepted it. He insisted on keeping the pace slow, exclaimed over her injured hand, and paid her so many extravagant compliments she wished she'd gone to the kitchen with Coren.

In between compliments, Tristram talked about Galendan, how he was the youngest of three brothers and had dreamed of coming to Castle Always his whole life. "In our country, the quest is a sacred rite for men in my position. Younger sons, I mean. Our families do not always have much to give us, so we come to the Castle seeking our fortune. When I return home, I expect to be greeted with much good cheer and acclaim. I will bring treasure and tales of adventure and be wooed by beautiful women—though in truth I think none will compare to you, my lady," he said with a dazzling smile.

Ailanthe's smile was not so dazzling. Being repeatedly reminded of her beauty was wearing on her, especially since she didn't think she was as beautiful as Tristram said. *But Coren thinks I'm beautiful.*

"Couldn't you make your fortune closer to home?" she asked.

"Where would be the adventure in that?" Tristram sounded surprised she would even suggest it. "Besides, the Castle knows better than we do where our destiny lies. It is far better to leave that choice to its wisdom."

"You mean the wisdom that has me locked up here for no reason?"

They reached the top floor and Tristram released her arm to take her left hand with his right. "Perhaps the Castle has some reason behind its seeming madness," he said. "Who can say but that your destiny lies here?"

"I don't think anyone has the right to make that decision for me."

"Is that not what you wanted, when you came here? To let the Castle decide?"

"Only because it was the only way to fix myself. Not because I wanted someone else to decide how my life was going to run." She tried to pull her hand free, but Tristram had a firm grip on it.

"The Castle sees further than we do. Is it not better to be guided by another's wisdom, if that wisdom is greater than our own?"

"I just want to go home. I'm not interested in philosophy."

"You deserve to go home, my lady. I intend to make that door open for you and restore you to your home, however far a journey that is. I swear it on my life." He raised her hand to his lips, which were warm but unpleasantly moist. His eyes remained fixed on hers.

She tried to pull away again, with no success. "I appreciate your offer, Tristram, but I wouldn't want you to give up on your own quest for me. Please let me go."

"You misunderstand, my lady. I am convinced that *you* are my quest. It is no coincidence that I should come to Castle Always when you are in such need of rescue." He stepped closer. "I have always believed a lovely maiden such as yourself waited in my future. Now that you are here, I realize my imaginings fell far short of the truth." He finally let go of her hand, only to put his arm around her neck and pull her close for a kiss.

Ailanthe was so shocked she couldn't move. His kiss wasn't unpleasant, but it was definitely unwelcome. She tried to back away, but he tightened his grip on her neck and kissed her again. "No—" she said, her words muffled, but he ignored her. She slapped him with her right hand and pain flashed through it. He didn't seem even to notice. So she raised her foot and stomped hard on his with the heel of her shoe. He broke away, uncharacteristic anger on his face.

"I do not understand," he said, "why you reject my embrace. We are clearly meant for one another."

"I don't think we are, Tristram," Ailanthe said, her heart pounding. "I appreciate everything you're doing for me, but I barely know you." She was aware of how much taller and stronger he was than her, and was also aware they were alone because Coren was taking far too long about collecting dinner. So she quashed her first impulse, which was to scream *Who the hell are you, kissing an unwilling woman and telling her she ought to want it?* and push him down the stairs. "And I don't enjoy kissing near-strangers."

"I see how it is," Tristram said, the anger dissipating. "You have a fondness for that oafish friend of yours. You are doomed to disappointment, my lady. He is one of those who prefers the company of men to women."

Ailanthe flushed. "You're wrong," she said.

"Am I? Perhaps. But I think not. I am not unfamiliar with men of his stripe. Remember, my lady, that I will wait for your affections to change. And I am a very patient man." He turned and walked ahead of her to the window room. Ailanthe didn't follow. Not only didn't she want to be alone with him, she didn't know if she could face Coren either.

She went to her room and shut the door behind her. Was Tristram right? She'd been stupid not to at least consider the possibility that Coren wasn't attracted to women. And it would account for how he could so casually call her beautiful without following that with a single admiring glance. But she hadn't gotten that impression from him...Tristram had to be wrong, that's all.

She sat down on her bed and looked at her right hand. The bruises had gone from purple-black to yellow-green, though hitting Tristram hadn't done them any good. She rested it in her lap and stared at the door. She couldn't exactly come out and ask Coren about his sexual preferences. She'd behave as she always had, pretending she thought of him only as a friend; nothing about her situation had changed, except that it might now be hopeless rather than improbable that he might eventually feel the same way about her.

A knock sounded at the door. "Ailanthe, I brought your smelly fish. Come on out and eat it before Miriethiel does."

"Coming," she said, but it took her another minute before she felt composed enough to leave her room.

CHAPTER SIXTEEN

*A*ilanthe slept restlessly, dreaming of long corridors down which shadows pursued her and high-ceilinged chambers where they peered down at her from the corners and leaped at her face. She woke in the darkness to find herself tangled in blankets that covered her face, slept again and dreamed of Coren kissing Tristram and woke in tears to remind herself Tristram was the last person Coren would be interested in. Then she remembered it was possible the last person was actually herself, and willed herself back into nightmares.

She woke finally to see the faint rectangles of brightness behind her heavy curtains and stumbled, head aching, to the window room. Coren wasn't there, though his sword lay across the seat, and there was no food, so he must be in the kitchen. She touched its hilt and wondered why he'd gone all the way down to the armory and back without stopping for food.

"My lady," Tristram said. "I take it your...companion has gone to fetch our daily repast?"

"I was just going to help him carry it," she improvised. She didn't want to give Tristram another chance to assault her. Now she wished she'd told Coren, but it seemed like such a stupid thing to complain to him about, and she'd handled Tristram herself. Besides, there hadn't been any time the night before for her to speak to him privately. But the truth was she now felt far more awkward around Coren now she knew he might be slant. If she weren't so attracted to him, it wouldn't be a problem, but if it were true, and he found out how she felt about him, how embarrassing it would be for both of them.

You don't know that, she told herself, *Tristram's known him for only a couple of days and he could be mistaken. And he doesn't care for you, so it would be embarrassing no matter which sex he's attracted to.* She wished she could go back to bed and start this day over.

"Then I shall join you," Tristram said with a bow. He had that familiar twinkle in his eye, which probably meant she was safe; he'd looked so much more serious just before he kissed her.

Tristram talked constantly as they went downstairs, full of plans for exploring that day. "I think we would be better served for you to focus your energies on interpreting that book," he said. "Your companion and I are well equipped to search independently."

"He has a name," Ailanthe said.

"Which I feel I may not make free of," Tristram said. "I fear he has taken me in dislike, and in my country names make a sacred bond between two people. I do not use your name either, my lady, and will not until you give it me of your own choice."

"I...see," Ailanthe said. She bent to pick up Miriethiel, who'd joined them on the fourth floor landing, and scratched behind his ears. "That's a lovely custom."

"Indeed," Tristram said. He eyed Miriethiel with some distaste, and Ailanthe's dislike of the man deepened. So rather than setting the cat down to follow her, she carried him down the rest of the stairs and into the kitchen, where she deposited him on the counter. She could hear something strange, a clattering noise that came from very far away. "Do you hear that?" she asked Tristram.

Tristram listened, and his face went grim. "That is the sound of battle," he said, and rushed out of the kitchen without waiting for her. She dashed after him, but he was faster than she and soon outpaced her. She had to follow the sound, which as she drew nearer did sound like metal ringing on metal. Then she heard shouting, and her own name, and she ran faster.

She rounded a corner into the hall outside the armory and stopped, disbelieving. Coren had hold of a sword much smaller than his own and was fending off attacks from two swords and a long pole with a curved blade on one end that were being wielded by no one Ailanthe could see. Tristram was gripping another sword which bucked and twisted, trying to free itself.

"Do something!" Coren shouted, parrying another attack and ducking under the sweep of the pole.

"What?" Ailanthe shouted over the noise of the strange battle.

"Make them stop!"

"I don't—"

Coren swung again and made the opposing sword fly backwards. "Ailanthe, I can't hold them off much longer! There's no time for you to dither about what you don't know!"

Ailanthe hesitated for a moment longer, then darted past Tristram to grab the hilt of one of the swords attacking Coren. "*Ailanthe!*" he shouted, and nearly took her head off trying to block the weapon's attack. "Are you out of your mind?"

"Probably!" she said, and put her whole weight on the hilt and thought *You are* mine *now.* The sword resisted her for a moment, then she had its full weight in her hands. It was so unexpectedly heavy she dropped it; it lay on the floor, unmoving. Without thinking she took hold of the pole and yanked on it, forcing Coren to leap backward or have his throat cut by the blade. This time, she didn't have to think anything; the weapon sagged in her hand and the blade grounded itself in the carpet.

"Help!" Tristram shouted, and Ailanthe replied, "Let go of it!" Tristram dropped, rolled, and came up with the sword Ailanthe had neutralized. He began fighting the weapon he'd abandoned, and even though she disliked him, she had to admire his fighting skill, which to her untrained eye looked more elegant than Coren's fierce slashing about.

A new sound rose above the fighting, a higher-pitched jingle accompanied by a thud that sounded like footsteps. Through the armory door came one of the suits of armor, riveted metal segmented to allow the arms and legs to move freely. It bore a sword larger even than Coren's and there was empty space where its head should be.

"Coren, *move!*" she shouted, and Coren threw himself to one side, abandoning the sword he'd been wielding and ending up in a fighter's crouch. He looked as though he intended to wrestle the thing, but he was still being menaced by the animate sword as well as by this new threat, and reflexively Ailanthe brought up the mental picture of Coren's sword lying on the boxy chair and saw it land with a thump by his feet.

He snatched it up and brought it around in time to block the armor's swing, but it was such a heavy blow he rocked back. "It's too strong for me!" he shouted, blocking again and swinging his sword to clang against the armor's metal side. It left a dent, but the armor kept moving.

Ailanthe ducked in and took control of the loose sword, then backed away hurriedly and did the same for the weapon Tristram was fighting. He immediately moved to the side of the armor opposite Coren, drawing an attack.

The thing seemed unable to decide which of its targets to strike at, aiming a blow at Tristram's head and then twisting around to block Coren's attack. It could swivel at the waist in a complete circle without moving its feet, which seemed rooted to the ground for all Coren and Tristram could knock it down. "My lady, if you can do aught, do it now!" Tristram called out.

She couldn't get in close enough to touch it without being struck by one of the three swords. She would have to take a different approach.

She focused on the elbow joint of the thing's sword arm, on the segments of armor that slid past each other as it brought the sword down at Tristram's head, and pictured them locking as the elbow reached its full extension. The armor swung again and was blocked by Coren's sword, but when it brought its arm back for another swing, it remained straight-armed and Coren ducked it easily. *Now the shoulder*, she thought, and the armor jerked, trying to bring its arm up for another blow, but unable to move.

"Both together!" Tristram called out, and Coren moved next to him. As its torso swiveled around to face them, they struck together at its waist and broke the thing neatly in half. The lower half remained upright; the torso fell to the floor, its one moving arm flailing about.

"Stop," Ailanthe said, and it fell still and the legs buckled and collapsed.

Coren, breathing heavily, said, "Thank God you came downstairs when you did. I wasn't sure I could run backwards up all those stairs."

"You have a great deal more faith in my abilities than I do," Ailanthe said, panting a little herself.

Tristram wasn't out of breath at all. "I am astonished, my lady. Clearly your powers are greater than I imagined."

"They're greater than I imagined, too," she said, and went into the armory. "I think we need to establish," she said to the walls, "that you are mine," and turned in a slow circle, fixing every weapon with her eye.

Coren, standing just inside the door, said, "Ailanthe—"

"You gave me the idea," she said, and an iron mace studded with spikes flew off the wall, causing Coren to leap forward, sword raised. But Ailanthe held out her hand and the weapon's handle smacked into her palm. It was heavy, but she kept hold of it. "I should have realized when I saw your sword upstairs. When I summon things, I take control of them from the Castle. It couldn't retrieve your sword last night because it was mine. I hope I just did the same to all of these. That was unnerving."

"That is an understatement," Coren said. He raised his sword and turned it to see it from all angles. "I should have realized it too."

"I do not understand," Tristram said. "Is the Castle so powerful, then, that it can bend things to its will?"

"The Castle is more powerful than any of us can imagine," Ailanthe said, "but it seems I can use some of its power against it." Tristram was looking a little blurry this morning, she thought, and then she was sitting on the ground and Coren had his arm around her shoulders. "I'm just hungry," she said, hoping it was true.

"It looks like you might have limits to what you can safely do," Coren said, helping her to her feet. "Tristram, bring food, and I'll help her upstairs."

Tristram's eyes gleamed, and he smiled an appreciative smile at having his ploy turned against him. "Even so, good sir," he said, and bowed.

Ailanthe felt recovered enough by the fifth landing to walk unsupported, but Coren insisted on her keeping hold of his arm, and she felt a little ashamed of herself for not protesting more. He saw her settled on a chair next to the desert window, then went to the painting and the stand in the middle of the floor and moved it aside.

"What's the painting of?" she said. She'd always wondered, but since he set it facing the wall every morning she felt awkward making a point of looking at it.

He laughed. "Take a look," he said, turning it around, and Ailanthe blushed to see the half-completed portrait of a very naked woman in a very compromising position. He set it against the wall and said, "It was a little off-putting, seeing her staring at me over breakfast."

Ailanthe stood and went to the wall, put her hands on the canvas and exerted some willpower. It was easier all the time, like flexing a muscle. Then she did the same to the easel. "Now you can leave it wherever you like."

"I appreciate it, but it's not important enough for you to risk hurting yourself," Coren said. "I would say I can't believe you walked into the middle of that battle, but it's exactly the sort of thing I'd believe of you. I nearly took your head off."

"I trusted you to hit the right target," Ailanthe said lightly, seating herself again. "And now I know how to do it without touching things, so I won't wade into any more fights."

"If you're right, there won't be any more fights," Coren said. He stood beside her and looked out at the desert. It was going to be another scorching hot day. "What is it you do, exactly?"

"I don't know," she said. "It feels like breaking one connection to make another, but I don't feel connected to any of these things I've... summoned, or whatever it is I do."

"Now you just need to figure out how to summon food from the kitchen stores, so we don't have to walk up and down the stairs so often."

"Or send Tristram to do it."

"I don't mind that." He looked down at her, his eyes serious. "Ailanthe—" he said, putting his hand on her shoulder.

"Fresh bread and strawberry jam, just the thing to begin a day of exploration," Tristram said. "And I have brought oranges for my lady, as I observed you are fond of them."

"Thanks, Tristram," Ailanthe said, accepting the fruit from him. Coren caught the one Tristram threw at his head and grinned savagely at the man. Ailanthe concealed a sigh. How long could Coren and Tristram coexist without coming to blows? They needed to find an exit, soon.

They ate in silence, even Tristram, who seemed subdued by the battle. Ailanthe looked out over the desert toward the distant, invisible city. If she could escape through this window, she would probably die before she ever reached its safety. But the window wouldn't break, and she was too high up for her rope to reach the ground.

She'd always wanted to visit Rius-zara, with its sprawling, vibrant cities. If Usael rather than Idantra were representative of his people, they were outgoing and kind and full of curiosity about other places. There were more Rius-zarans represented in the hero books than those of any other country. She ought to visit their museum room again, and it would be fun to try on some of the clothes—no, she'd have to face those mannequins again, and if Coren weren't there....

She shuddered. If the Castle could bring them to life, could animate suits of armor, there were whole rooms they'd have to avoid. And suppose the shadows tried to attack Coren, or Tristram? She felt a great weariness descend upon her. She would have to keep not only herself but the others safe, and she couldn't be everywhere at once.

"We will leave you now, my lady," Tristram said, startling her out of her reverie. "Your companion and I will resume our search, and may I suggest you spend your morning in study of that book?"

"What if something else attacks you?"

"We can defend ourselves against most things, Ailanthe," Coren said, "and I promise we will run screaming for you if that turns out to be a lie."

Ailanthe laughed at the image of two tall, strong men running down the halls of the Castle shrieking like children. "I'll be in the Library, then," she said, "after I retrieve the diary from the study."

"Did you not already do so, my lady?" Tristram said, indicating one of the chairs. The yellow-bound book lay atop it.

Ailanthe crossed the room to pick it up. "How odd. The Castle didn't remove this last night, like the sword."

"I thought you couldn't use magic on magical things," Coren said.

"I can't. I didn't. But I wonder if it's so magical, the Castle can't affect it. Like it never takes away the key."

"That's convenient," Coren said. "It feels as if something's finally on our side.

"I agree." She examined the diary as she walked down the stairs to the Library. Convenient, and fortunate, that she didn't need to take control of it from the Castle. The was extremely magical and she was afraid her powers would have no effect on it other than to give her a blinding headache.

She developed a normal kind of headache right away. The symbols still didn't mean anything, and when she flicked her gaze quickly across them, she was only able to tell that what she glimpsed was in the Castle's language and alphabet. She did this for about fifteen minutes, then searched the shelves, hoping somewhere in this room was a book on languages, or deciphering codes.

She couldn't find books in languages other than the Castle's own; she recognized one or two titles of books she knew had been written by Idrijanese, or Eshkians, but the Castle had translated them from the original. Eventually she stumbled on a few books about how languages develop over time, which were interesting but quickly became too complex for Ailanthe to follow. She put them away with a sigh.

She returned to the yellow-bound book and opened the front cover. Gweron. It was probably his study they'd found, the first real evidence someone had occupied the Castle before them. No way of knowing how long ago he—or was it a she? It sounded like a man's name, an Enthalian name—had lived here, or when he'd left, or why he'd left, but he'd had powerful magic for a *kerthor* and Ailanthe wished she could meet him, if only to shake the secret of his diary out of him. Maybe the Castle had killed him. It would have killed Coren and Tristram, and probably her, if she hadn't been able to overcome its control of the weapons.

She flipped through the pages rapidly, catching glimpses of letters alone or in pairs, then shut the book, laid it aside and rubbed her forehead.

The lights went dim. Ailanthe looked up and saw about half of them had gone dark. The remaining lights cast shadows across the bookshelves and the chairs. A stripe of shadow lay across the table she was working at, falling across her hands, and she felt a chill grip them. Across the room, the shadows shifted.

"No," she breathed, and tried to encompass the dark lights, pictured them blazing and sending the shadows fleeing. Something fought her for control. It held on to the connection the Castle had to the lights and made it iron-hard, unyielding, and she tried to snap it with no different result than if she'd tried to break an actual iron cable with her hands.

The gray shadows bulged and spread across the walls toward her. She couldn't stop watching them, how they hunched and stretched like rippling caterpillars, but faster, so fast she could only see their bodies' movement as a pulsing flood of gray dust rolling toward her. She strained against the Castle's control, but it was so much stronger than she was, and it felt so indifferent to her oncoming death she screamed at it in fear and fury.

Then the shadows were upon her like a gray wave, wrapping her in their clinging threads. They burrowed inside her, choking her lungs and covering her eyes in burning cold spider webs. Lights whirled in front of her eyes, her dizzy, air-starved brain trying to make shapes of them but unable to stop them moving.

In terror, she struck out, not at the cables, but at the Castle, putting all her anger and despair at being trapped into a scream that came not from her throat but from deep within her body, and it rocked back as if she'd punched it. In its moment of distraction, she reached past it and broke the connection and made one of her own, and willed the lights back on.

The Library suddenly blazed with light. The freezing tendrils withdrew so quickly they seemed to slice her flesh like razors. Breathing the warm air deeply, she scanned the room. Nothing. She touched her face, expecting to feel blood, but her skin was intact and dry, parched as if the moisture had been sucked out of it.

She rubbed at the places where the shadows had grabbed her, trying to erase both the numbing cold and the terror at how close they'd come to killing her. Trembling, she took control of the remaining lights so the Castle wouldn't be able to try that again. Then she sat with her hands gripping the arms of her chair and shook. It had fought her and nearly won. It would have killed her if she hadn't been lucky, and it wasn't going to stop trying. The next time, it might succeed.

She stared down at the diary. Somewhere in its pages was the key to her escape, and the Castle didn't want her finding it. She opened it again. How could it be a danger to the Castle if she couldn't even read it?

Her hands shook, and she clenched them tight. Her right hand still hurt, and she thought she might have hurt it more in the fight with the weapons, but she closed it tighter, welcoming the pain as evidence that the Castle hadn't killed her. Yet.

A couple of tears rolled down her face, and she wiped them away impatiently. She didn't have time for self-pity. She was alive, and that was what mattered, because as long as she was alive she would keep fighting the Castle and it wasn't going to defeat her.

She remembered the suffocating, freezing darkness, and then the tears wouldn't stop flowing. Depending on luck to keep her alive was like throwing herself off that tower and expecting the air to cushion her fall. Someday soon her luck would turn, and the Castle would kill her, and nothing she did could stop that.

CHAPTER SEVENTEEN

ootsteps sounded on the stones of the hall outside, and Ailanthe wiped her eyes. "Ailanthe, there's something I want to show you," Coren said. He was going to know she'd been crying and she didn't want his pity. She wiped her eyes again and hoped her nose wasn't red.

"What is it?" she said, not turning around.

"It looks like—what's wrong?"

"Nothing. I'm fine."

He knelt next to her chair. "You're crying. That's not fine."

His face was so full of concern for her she couldn't keep the tears from spilling over again. She stood and walked away from him, not sure if she was crying because she'd nearly died or because she was hopelessly in love with someone who would never love her in return, slant or straight.

She took a few deep breaths and regained control of herself. "The Castle made a more direct attack," she said. "It fought me when I tried to stop it. I'm just a little overwhelmed."

Coren put his hands on her shoulders and stopped her when she would have moved farther away. He gently turned her to face him and put his arms around her, drawing her close. "We shouldn't have left you alone," he said. "I thought, with how powerful you're becoming...but I forgot how much more powerful the Castle is, and I was stupid not to realize it might attack you again. I'm sorry."

"It's not your fault. I didn't think of it either, and I should have." She rested her cheek against his shoulder and let him hold her. *It doesn't mean anything,* she told herself, *we're friends,* but what might happen if she returned his embrace? She half-raised her arms, let them fall to her side again, embarrassed at the awkwardness of their embrace. She was a coward as well as a fool.

"If you were hurt...Ailanthe, I would never forgive myself," Coren said.

"I told you, it wasn't your fault."

"It's not about fault," he said. His voice sounded strange, and she looked up at him and found herself caught by that direct, serious gaze she remembered from the first day they'd met. "Ailanthe," he said, then seemed at a loss for what to say next.

Ailanthe's heart beat faster. Slowly, she put her arms around his waist and drew him closer to her. For a moment, they stood there unmoving, Coren's face expressionless, and as the silence stretched out she felt certain she had made a terrible mistake. He didn't care for her. He was silent because she'd embarrassed him.

She was about to tear free of his arms and run to her room to hide when he lowered his head and kissed her.

She responded without thinking, leaning into his kiss as if she were drowning and it was the only thing keeping her afloat. He smelled wonderfully of musk and sweat and a trace of citrus, golden and sweet. She moved her arms from his waist to his neck and his arms tightened around her, his strong hands sliding across her back as he kissed her again, tenderly, his lips soft on hers. She felt more tears, these of joy and relief, spring to her eyes.

Coren drew back and touched her cheek. "I'd hoped that would make you stop crying," he said with a smile.

A chill touched her heart. "Is that why you kissed me? To make me stop crying?"

"I kissed you," Coren said, wiping her tears away, "because I love you, Ailanthe. I've been trying to tell you for days now, but that damned Tristram kept interrupting me."

Ailanthe smiled, and if it was a little wobbly, he didn't seem to care, because his own smile broadened. "I've wanted you to kiss me for so long," she said.

"I was afraid you'd think I only wanted you because you're the first woman I've seen in six years," Coren said.

"Tristram told me you were slant, and I didn't have a chance."

Coren's expression went from astonished to angry and ended up amused. "Tristram is a lying bastard," he said, "and I would go find him and beat him bloody if I weren't so content with where I am right now."

"He was probably just mistaken."

"Ailanthe, men who look like Tristram have enough men throwing themselves at them that they learn to recognize the type. He knew I wasn't slant and he probably told you that to give himself a better chance at winning your heart." He kissed her again, harder this time, his fingers brushing the nape of her neck and sending heat flooding through her body that made her tighten her grip around his neck when he would have pulled away.

"Don't stop," she whispered, and he brushed his lips against hers, slid his hands down her back to her waist and lower, caressing her until she felt she might explode. "My room," she murmured.

"Tristram's coming back soon," Coren replied between kisses. "There's no time."

"Later. Promise me."

"I swear it." He kissed her one last time and released her, brushing her cheek with his fingertips. "I really did have something to show you," he said.

"What is it?" She didn't really care what it was, could only think about Coren removing her clothes and touching her with those wonderful hands, but obediently went to look at the thing on the table.

"It was in the study," Coren said. "We went back to see if there was anything we'd missed, and Tristram, the lying bastard, found a false back to that empty drawer. And this was in it."

It was a palm-sized lens set in a brass frame that had tiny buttons all around its rim. It glowed with magic nearly as strong as the diary's. Ailanthe picked it up and touched one of the buttons, which slid along a faint groove in the rim. There was a click, and the lens went from clear to pale transparent blue. "It's definitely magical," she said, touching another button. The lens turned red. She picked up the diary and opened it, then held the lens over the page. "It's still gibberish," she said.

"I'll bet altering the lens changes what it can see," Coren said. "Take a look around the room."

Ailanthe held it to her eye. "The magic on the books is stronger now. It looks like...sort of like snakes instead of rainbow sparkles." She held it out to Coren, who took a turn.

"Amazing," he said. "Is this how it looks to you all the time?"

"Not the snakes, but yes."

Coren pushed the first button back into its original position, which turned the lens a pale violet, then held it to his eye again. "No change."

Ailanthe accepted it from him. "Oh, ew," she said, because through the lens Coren's skin had become a transparent jellylike mess through which she could clearly see his muscles and blood vessels. She swung around to look at the tree in the center of the library and saw the bark had also gone transparent and she could see through to the wood underneath. "Let's not use that lens again."

"Why not?"

"Because I like the way your outsides look." She smiled at him, feeling another rush of joy that he loved her. Had she said she loved him? She ought to say it to him often.

"My lady, is my discovery of help to you?" Tristram said from the doorway.

Coren took a few angry steps toward the door. Ailanthe shook her head at him, and he subsided, glaring at Tristram. She said, "I think so, Tristram. Congratulations on your find."

"I have brought sustenance, if you would care to join me?"

"I'll be there in a minute. I have to...tidy things up." When he was gone, Ailanthe said, "Don't beat him bloody."

"I think I have a right to pummel him for making you miserable."

"I think it would be far more fun to let him believe he's winning my heart and then, oh, we could start kissing in front of him or something."

"That's pretty extreme, don't you think?"

"I'm kidding. Just...leave him alone. Don't you think it's enough that I'll never love him? If he pushes the issue, I'll let him down gently."

Coren laughed. "I think pummeling him would be more satisfying, but we can do it your way."

"Thank you. Now I'm going to eat." She picked up the lens, then kissed him once more. "And then I'm going to figure out what this lens can do."

AFTER LUNCH, Ailanthe settled down with the lens, a stack of paper and a pen and ink. The Castle didn't fight her when she exerted her will over the last three items. That didn't relieve her mind. The Castle's attacks came at random, and in unexpected ways; Ailanthe would never have guessed it would have tried that trick with the weapons. Even so, she brought in her three lamps and made about fifteen more, and set them throughout the Library.

Coren eyed her preparations grimly, but said nothing except, "We'll be back in a few hours." Tristram bowed, and kissed her hand, and gave her his dazzling smile, and Ailanthe smiled back and managed not to roll her eyes. Behind Tristram, Coren shook his head in mock despair.

When they'd gone, Ailanthe set the lens back to its original, clear state, then drew a picture of the lens and its six buttons. With all six at the right side of their slots, the lens was clear. She held the lens up so she was looking through it, then pushed the button nearest to her, the one that turned it blue, and looked through it at the diary's first page. Nothing changed.

She looked around the room and saw nothing out of the ordinary. She drew a little sketch of how the buttons were set, wrote "blue" next to it, and a question mark. It might reveal something that wasn't in this room. She set it back to the "start" position, as she thought of it, and moved on to the next button.

There were so many possible combinations, and so many colors. She had to go back to her first note and change it to "lt. blue" and later to "vy. lt. blue" as more blue shades appeared. Most of the settings didn't appear to do anything. There was the one that made magic visible, and the one that saw through living tissue, but there was another that turned all the sprites green and opaque, and one that made black spots in front of every light source and caused her to nearly drop the lens in fear that it had actually extinguished them. None of the settings made the symbols intelligible.

After more than a hundred experiments, she pushed all the buttons back to their original settings and laid the lens down on the book. This might be a complete waste of time, but what else did she have to do? Well, Coren and Tristram might need her help exploring, to identify magic when they came across it, and she might provide a buffer because she wasn't totally sure Coren might not still pick a fight with Tristram. She wouldn't be terribly angry if he did, and it might make Tristram decide to leave, which would leave Coren and Ailanthe alone again in the Castle, and *that* had all sorts of possibilities.

Ailanthe put both elbows on the table and rested her chin in her hands, and indulged in a little daydreaming. To think she'd spent so much time pining after him, when just one word...well, they'd said the right words now, and she intended to look forward rather than blame herself for the past. Except that "forward" contained hundreds more experiments. She groaned and bowed her head, gazing at the meaningless symbols—

—and in the center of the page, beneath the lens, the words

for Rhedyth, I begin
from my research. I enjoyed
of those I visited understood the nature
changed in heart, and I have no

to Rhedyth as I intend.

I hope will be few experime

Ailanthe stared for a moment. Then she carefully moved the lens to one side, closed the book, and banged her head on the desk a few times. The base setting. Of course. Well, at least her experiments hadn't been a total waste of time, though she couldn't imagine why they might want to see opaque green sprites. She banged her head gently one more time, then opened the book, set the lens at the top, and read.

17 Wefror

Having laid the groundwork for Rhedyth, I begin this record in the hope that some future generation may benefit from my research. I enjoyed my journeys less than I had imagined, as too few of those I visited understood the nature of my work. Nevertheless, I left them much changed in heart, and I have no doubt that when it is complete, they will be as drawn to Rhedyth as I intend.

Today was the first of what I hope will be few experiments on the nature of inanimate objects. I discovered that although the creation of such is a trivial matter, convincing existing objects to assemble is far more difficult; they resist state changes of both nature and position. Would that I need not proceed in this manner, but my initial efforts indicated that I must understand mundane construction if I wish my magical construction to have what I believe is referred to as "structural integrity." But enough maundering! I believe I have discovered the key to my problem, and I shall apply it tomorrow.

Ailanthe realized she was holding her breath and let it out slowly. Gweron was writing about the Castle, that's what Rhedyth had to be, and this was a record of his building it. No wonder the Castle wanted to stop her reading it; within these pages had to be the secret of how it worked, some key to forcing it to let them go.

She re-read the second paragraph. Gweron was definitely no ordinary *kerthor*, if he could speak so casually about creating and manipulating objects. Well, this diary was probably centuries old. Maybe *kerthors* in those days used different instruments or different melodies.

She removed the lens and closed the book, then set the lens to green-opaque-sprites and followed the two in the room until they drifted through the skylight and she'd calmed down a little. She had to remind herself she hadn't escaped yet, but—*We're so close.* She breathed in deeply, set the lens to clear and began reading, feeling everything else fall away.

"Tristram's bringing dinner. Have you had any luck?" Coren said, startling her. She flipped ahead. She'd read almost to the end without realizing it.

"The lens reveals the diary," she said, deciding not to tell him how unnecessarily long it had taken her to discover this. "It's...I can't begin to tell you how valuable it is."

"So this Gweron knew something about the Castle?" He put his hand on her shoulder. "You're incredibly tense."

"I must've been hunched over the lens for hours. He didn't just know about the Castle, he *built* the Castle. Oh...." Coren had begun rubbing the knots out of her muscles. "That feels so good. I had no idea how tense I was."

"My lady, good sir, I have brought—I beg your pardon," Tristram said from the doorway.

Ailanthe turned to look at him, his arms full of food, including a plate with a slab of salmon on it. "Good news, Tristram!" she said cheerfully. "Your lens makes the diary intelligible. Why don't we eat, and I'll tell you about it."

Tristram eyed her skeptically, glanced at Coren, whose hands remained loosely gripping her shoulders and whose expression Ailanthe couldn't see, then said, "Very well," and left.

Coren chuckled. "I think he figured it out," he said. "I know I looked smug just now."

"I don't know. He's fairly certain he's my true love and you're the uncouth Hesperan I'm hopelessly pining after. It will take more than a shoulder rub to convince him otherwise."

"We lost the perfect opportunity to execute your kissing plan, you know."

"As fun as that would be, it would also be cruel, and I don't want to do that to him."

"You're so kind-hearted," Coren said, and bent to kiss first her forehead, then her lips. Ailanthe slid her left hand around the back of his neck to pull him closer and kiss him more intently until he knelt before her and took her in his arms. "Don't think I need dinner," he murmured, and they kissed a while longer until Ailanthe broke away and laid her cheek against his. It was scratchy and smelled faintly of oranges, the most wonderful smell ever.

"Food first, diary after, then—"

He nuzzled her earlobe. "That diary had better be pretty damn important."

Ailanthe smiled. "I think it is."

CHAPTER EIGHTEEN

"Tomorrow I'm going to try creating hot food," Ailanthe said, sweeping all her tiny bones into a pile and sending them somewhere Miriethiel couldn't find them later. She hoped. She thought they went where the cushions had, but she still didn't know where that was, and so far nothing bad had happened. Or something bad *had* happened, and she didn't know about it yet. Better just to assume everything was fine.

"My lady, if you can bring me a roast chicken I shall be eternally in your debt," Tristram said.

"Agreed," Coren said. He dusted crumbs off his trousers—he really had developed the most appalling habits, and if she weren't so in love with him, they might have been off-putting—and leaned back against the eastern wall of windows. "So. This diary. Gweron built the Castle."

"I think so. I'm afraid I couldn't stop myself reading it, most of it anyway."

"Understandable, my lady," Tristram said, bowing without standing, which took some doing even for him. "A woman's natural curiosity would make such an action inevitable."

Coren rolled his eyes. Ailanthe stifled the urge to throw something at Tristram. "Gweron was extremely methodical. He starts by writing about his experiments on non-living things, both creating them and using magic to put them together, like this house he builds himself. He says it's because Rhedyth has to be built by combining smaller units instead of being formed all at once through magic."

"What is Rhedyth, pray tell?"

"It's obviously the Castle," Coren said drily. Tristram glared at him.

"Gweron wanted the Castle to do something to make the world a better place," Ailanthe went on, ignoring the byplay. "He's always saying things like 'it is sorely needed in this fallen world.'"

"So he meant it to do something," Coren said. "But is it doing what he had in mind, or not?"

"Perhaps, good sir, we should allow the lady to continue?" Tristram said, and it was Coren's turn to glare.

"Thank you, Tristram," Ailanthe said, torn between enjoying watching the two men puff out their chests like bantams and feeling impatient that they weren't taking this seriously. "I'm getting to that. Next he moves on to experiments with living things. Gweron had a very organized mind, I think. I wonder if his notes are somewhere in that study. Here, let me read this part."

She read on: "'*The initial magic was successful. The grove of trees perfectly encircles my house, though to my shame I did not realize the magic would duplicate the tree I used as a model rather than create unique organisms. An amateur's mistake, and one I do not intend to repeat. However, the principle is sound, and I believe after one more trial I shall allow myself to celebrate. I have already enshrined the model and at this moment am admiring it on the shelf. But I have no time for self-congratulatory reflection. On to the next trial!*' Did you notice what he wrote about enshrining his model? I think that could be the tree in the water-globe we found in the study."

"Likely," Coren said. "But please continue."

"Most of this is technical and a little boring. Let me skim ahead... something about learning how living organisms are all the same... long lists of what he's created...here, this is interesting: '*The creation of intelligent life lies at the heart of my plans for Rhedyth, and I confess myself a trifle reluctant to proceed as lightheartedly as I have heretofore been. And yet do not the commonest of folk, men and women of intellectual vacuity, see fit to bring new life into the world? How much greater a creation might I engender, clear-sighted and logical as I am? Thus do I cast off such fears and begin what will be the key to my greatest creation.'* 'Men and women of intellectual vacuity'? He sounds terribly pompous."

"Methinks he sounds but clear-sighted and rational," Tristram said. "I have often reflected that it is a pity there be no mechanism in nature to encourage those of high breeding to reproduce more successfully than their lesser brethren and sisters."

"I'm glad you're not in charge of nature," Coren said. That earned him a glare from Tristram.

"Well, he talks about what he creates...I think these 'pixies' of his are our sprites, and he says they're intelligent."

"That's a surprise," Coren said. "They've never struck me as very bright."

"I gather they're just bright enough to take simple commands. Too bad we don't know how to do that."

She turned a page or two. "Listen to this: *'I envy the* kerthors *of my homeland at times like this, however ridiculous that might seem, as I am certain it is possible to play the flute when one's head is stuffed and one's nose drips incessantly. However my own, unique magic works, it is most definitely affected by the condition of the body. This miserable cold has affected my exercise regimen as well. If only there were a way to work magic upon oneself!'*"

"I wonder that he wrote about something so mundane as a simple illness."

"Tristram, the important thing is that he says he's not a *kerthor*. That explains so much! No lone *kerthor* could have built this Castle— probably not even a hundred *kerthors*. Gweron's magic was unique."

"As yours is," Coren pointed out.

"I couldn't do any of the things he writes about," Ailanthe said. "I certainly can't create life, intelligent or otherwise."

"Yet you, my lady, have been exercising your powers for a mere handful of weeks, if I am not mistaken. Who knows but that you may yet discover strange new talents?"

The idea made Ailanthe's stomach clench. Whatever magic she possessed, she welcomed only so far as it was a weapon against the Castle. That she might discover new abilities—that she might have anything in common with Gweron—raised the old fear that she might be turning into some creature of magic, someone no longer human with none of the dreams and desires that made her Ailanthe.

She didn't know what expression passed across her face, but it made Coren sit forward and say, "Is it something disturbing?"

She made herself smile at him and shake her head. "No, just confusing. He says he succeeded at creating intelligent life, then that he failed—oh, I understand now. He was trying to put intelligence into non-living things, apparently to make servants for the Castle. Like a broom that sweeps by itself. Only he found out it was impossible. Then—oh, Miriethiel!"

The cat leaped onto her lap when she said his name, forcing her to lift both book and lens as he kneaded himself a nest in her lap. "I will remove the beast from you, my lady," Tristram said, but she waved him away when he was halfway up from his chair.

"No, that was coincidence. Gweron made Miriethiel. Listen. Move your tail, cat. '*I cannot decide what name I shall give the animal. I believe I have made him of more than usual feline intelligence, though I refrained from giving him human intellect and voice; such an act would violate the natural order, and my desire to serve mankind does not extend to elevating the beasts of the field to an equal status with man. He is, however, a most handsome animal, black with pleasant white markings and a companionably silent purr, and I confess I have altered him somewhat in extending his lifespan. After all, I know not how long my own life will extend, and I desire a companion to ease my lonely hours.*'" She scratched behind the cat's ears and he began to vibrate. "Did you hear that, Miriethiel? You're a most handsome animal."

"And he's several centuries old. Gweron does good work," Coren said. Miriethiel lifted his head and looked in Coren's direction, as if accepting a compliment.

"Then there's more about living creatures, and something about the Castle needing to be enormous to provide enough magic for the —he calls it the 'destiny spell.' Doesn't that sound familiar? Then— I'm just going to read this. *'To know a person's heart, truly to know it, necessitates awareness, but to provide a thing that will bring out the best in that person—that means creation, and analysis not only of the person but of the world as well. Would that I were capable of such wisdom...but no, Rhedyth is the answer, and men and women everywhere will make their way here and be changed forever.'*"

"But that is what the Castle does!" Tristram exclaimed, leaping to his feet. "It reads our hearts and gives us an object that sends us to our destiny! So then why does it not do so for you, my lady? It is a true mystery."

"Sit down, Tristram, Ailanthe won't read any faster for you looming over her," Coren said.

"I think it's perfectly natural for us to be excited, Coren," Ailanthe said, doing some glaring of her own. "And I didn't get far enough to have an answer to that question, but—just let me finish this, all right? What I did read left me a little frightened."

She used the lens to find her place again. "Lots of organizing. More work on putting the pieces together. Then there's this piece: *'It was as if the Honor Hall, as I call it, wanted to come into existence. The simplicity of its structure belies the immense complexity of the magic at its heart. Here men and women will come to have their hearts read and their destinies woven. Hence will heroes go to free the world from tyranny and sorrow. Its magic is so powerful I have had to surround it with another chamber of pillared and vaulted stone to anchor it to the physical world. It is exquisite. Almost I cannot believe the mind of man created such a thing of beauty and power.'* He really loved this place."

"Would that we might have known this great man," Tristram said. "His vision was extraordinary."

"Even if he was a bit of a self-righteous ass," Coren said.

"You call it self-righteous to wish for the betterment of mankind and to take action to see it come to pass?"

"I think he had some pretty strong ideas about what kind of people deserved to be bettered."

"He created the Castle precisely because he felt his own wisdom was inadequate to the task. I see not how that can be held to his discredit."

"If you both don't mind," Ailanthe said, now widening her glare to include Tristram, "I'd rather set aside the question of Gweron's personality in favor of learning why the Castle won't let me go."

Tristram nodded. "I beg your pardon, my lady. Mayhap my enthusiasm overwhelmed me momentarily."

"Thank you. I forgot where I was. All right. So he built the Honor Hall and started assembling rooms around it. They had to go in in exactly the right order to make the magic work—he doesn't really go into detail about that, except that most of them were places he remembers from his travels. He mentions one called the Atelier that I think is this room—he created it with all the contents intact. At least we know he's not the one who made that horrible painting."

"It doesn't make me like him any better."

"But he also says for most of the rooms, he summoned the furnishings rather than creating them. Like your sword, Coren—isn't it interesting to wonder who it might have belonged to, centuries ago?"

"Just so they don't come looking for it now. I'm sort of attached to it."

"And he writes about making the food stores so their contents never rot, and the museum rooms, and that goes on for a while, until we get to this. Be patient, it's long.

"'*This morning I discovered five new rooms had been added, two of them planned by myself and three that came from no thought of mine that I could discover. I can scarcely credit it, but further analysis and study reveal there is only one possible conclusion: Rhedyth is alive.*

'*This throws all my research into question. I was never able to succeed in imbuing non-living things with intelligence, nor could I create such intelligent objects with any measure of success. I believe—though this is subject to further evidence—that the vast quantity of magic has produced a kind of limited awareness that allows Rhedyth to, as it were, participate in its own construction. It staggers the mind.*

'And yet...why not? Do not creatures who are aware seek to better their lot? If this magic has indeed created new...I hesitate to call it "life," but for lack of a better word...new life, would it not take an interest in its own creation? I must study this phenomenon more, and hope that Rhedyth understands the plans for its construction well enough not to add anything that would be detrimental to my intent.'"

Coren closed his eyes. Tristram stood and paced in a large circle, passing near the western windows but not looking out over the darkened valley. "It confirms what we have guessed," he said.

"It chilled me, seeing it written down so bluntly," Ailanthe said. "The idea of the Castle paying attention to things...I'd hoped it was just, I don't know, a figure of speech. Some way for us to come to terms with what we experience. But Gweron seemed convinced he was right."

"We must be like bits of sand in an oyster to it," Coren said, not opening his eyes. "Though I doubt it's trying to turn us into pearls."

"Unless that is in fact what it does to its questers, good sir," Tristram said. "Give them a destiny and send them out into the world to make them greater than they were."

Ailanthe closed the book on the lens. "We're almost to the place where I stopped reading. It's...it's not good, what comes next. Even not knowing the end, I can tell you that."

"Please, my lady, continue," Tristram said. "I find myself anxious on our friend Gweron's behalf."

Coren opened his eyes and looked at her. "Does it say how to free you?"

"I don't know yet."

"Then definitely keep reading."

Ailanthe opened the book and took a moment to find her place. The symbols quivered as if they didn't want to be read, but the lens fixed them in place. Did they know what had happened to their master?

"I think this part is important. *'I stood in the Honor Hall and marveled anew at its creation. That my dream is so close to being realized —a dream of a world in which men and women become better than they are, in which they spread out across the lands to make the world a better place. I seek not for the glory, merely to be the creator of that which makes my dream possible. I sat on the empty floor and spoke to Rhedyth, feeling at once embarrassed and exhilarated at doing so. I told it of my plans and of its role in them, and—dare I write it?—praised it for its help and its desire to join with me in this dream. Did I write, once, that I thought to have no other companion than the cat (who continues silent on the matter of his name)? Now I realize I could have no better companion than this, my life's work.'* He sounds so...joyful, there.

"Anyway, the construction goes on for a while. But then the Castle starts to...to fight him, I suppose. Stops adding rooms and starts actively trying to keep him from completing it. He says he has to fight it for control over every scrap of carpet he adds. Also, the Castle tried that trick with the weapons on him."

"But why? That is to say, my lady, why would the Castle turn on its master?"

"Here's what Gweron wrote about that. *'I have spent many hours trying to determine why Rhedyth became aware and then turned on me. It is obvious now that Rhedyth has far more intelligence than I initially believed. If I am correct, and its awareness and growing sapience are the result of a vast quantity of magic imbuing a single—I suppose "entity" is the best word, though it chills me to think it—then it is not beyond possibility that an increasing amount of magic, combined with what I previously learned about the impossibility of creating an intelligent object, means that Rhedyth is insane, and in its insanity is striking out against me. What I fear most is that Rhedyth will attempt to warp the destiny spell at its core, and that I simply cannot allow.'* He tried to dismantle the Castle, but it fought back—obviously it was successful, or we wouldn't be here. And that's as far as I got."

"So we're not just irritants inside an intelligent building, we're irritants inside an *insane* intelligent building," Coren said.

"It's no wonder its attacks are unpredictable," Ailanthe said. "And that it allows us to do some things and resists others."

"But this is terrible news, my lady. This implies that your captivity here follows no law of magic or reason, and that your freedom may not be obtained but by the whim of the Castle."

"Stop making assumptions, Galendishman."

"No, he's right, Coren, and I thought of that while I was reading," Ailanthe said. "It doesn't seem like there's anything to be gained by worrying about that possibility. I'm going to read the rest aloud, if you don't mind." She rubbed her eyes and began.

"*Library as expected. Summoned a few books as a test and found myself opposed. Rhedyth gains in strength, though only within itself—it still lacks the power to prevent me building more. It has not yet touched the destiny spell. Hope this is because it does not know what it is.*

"*Construction on final floor almost complete. Tried to summon food and discovered Rhedyth's control over its contents stronger than I can break. Forced to descend to the kitchens and collect supplies. The shadows move. The sprites seem unaffected by our battle, and at least I can take heart that Rhedyth bears them no malice, my poor stupid creatures.*

"*I maintain control over my study and it is a haven to me. Construction on tower begun. I weep to think of how shoddy it is compared to the beauty —and Rhedyth, despite its insanity, is still beautiful—of the rest of my construction. Tomorrow I will link Rhedyth to the geographical points prepared months ago; this may distract it enough that I can finish the tower and complete the spell.*

"*It is a measure of how much has gone wrong that I leaped and pranced in excitement when the geographical linkage worked smoothly. I feel as though I am myself losing my mental faculties. The shadows definitely move, most likely an overflow of magic. I cannot imagine what horrors Rhedyth might visit upon me were I to allow them to surround me. I carry many magical lights with me when I am forced to leave the study.*

"*Rhedyth spoke to me this morning. I did not understand its speech and did not want to.*

"*The tower's construction proceeds slowly. Rhedyth fights me for every inch. I refuse to give in. I have put too much of my own power into its building for it to kill me without destroying itself, yet I believe it may have other ways of neutralizing me. Would that I could return in time to tell my brash, impetuous younger self to find some other way of bettering the world!*

"'The tower is complete. I cannot activate the destiny spell from my study, and therefore am forced to leave this place of security. I shall place safeguards upon the most important of my magical creations, lock this book away, and make my way to where I hope I may break Rhedyth's control. Should this be my final entry, and I still hold hope that it will not, then, future reader, flee this place.'"

By the time she reached the end, Ailanthe's throat was dry, not from speaking, but from a tight horrified numbness that threatened to envelop her. She closed the book and laid the lens atop its cover, holding both in place because Miriethiel still occupied her lap. He was sleeping lightly, one white-tipped ear flicking whenever she moved.

She looked around the room at the few dark corners remaining, which seemed free of moving shadows, or an overflow of magic as Gweron called them. She'd almost been swallowed by them. She wanted to be sick, but swallowed hard and breathed slowly until the incipient panic subsided.

"It could not kill him," Tristram said.

"Yes, but it doesn't have any reason not to kill us," Coren said. "And I wonder why it hasn't. Damn it, I lived here for six years without seeing anything stranger than things disappearing after midnight. Then—" He closed his mouth abruptly and turned to stare out at the moonlit waves.

"Then I came," Ailanthe continued for him, "and everything changed."

"This isn't your fault," he said.

"Isn't it? All right, not 'fault' exactly, but my presence certainly seems to have triggered something. I'm the one it keeps attacking."

"Except for the weapons. Ailanthe—"

"I believe you have both failed to grasp the most important lesson of this diary," Tristram said. He stopped pacing and came to stand in front of Ailanthe. "You, my lady, most assuredly have power like that of Gweron."

CHAPTER NINETEEN

*C*oren said, "That's a big step, Galendishman."

"It is not, good sir, and I ask that you not look such daggers in my direction. The Castle is alive. It reacts to your presence, my lady, with the same antagonism it showed its creator, having paid no heed to this Hesperan for many years. You have already proven you are capable of magic like unto Gweron's, if not to the same extent. I believe it does not strain credulity too much to assert that you are like Gweron and the Castle therefore sees you as a threat similar to the one he posed."

"Damn it—"

"I think he's right, Coren," Ailanthe said. She stood, dumping Miriethiel off her lap, and laid book and lens on her vacated seat before she realized she didn't know why she'd risen. She felt a sudden, irrational anger, and pictured the Library, swept up an entire shelf of books and summoned them into the Atelier. They hung in the air for half a breath before thundering down around her, spines and covers striking the wooden floor in a series of sharp thumps.

Coren and Tristram stepped back a few paces from the curved line of fallen books that followed the contours of the shelf they'd been sitting on. Ailanthe released fists she hadn't realized she'd clenched and said, "The Castle isn't going to clean those up, is it?"

Coren and Tristram remained silent. Ailanthe turned away from them both and went to look out over the desert. The moon was setting in the distance and flung long shadows across the sands, shadows thankfully free of moving magic.

"I wonder where it comes from," she said, tracing the line of the nearest dune on the glass with a fingertip. "This magic. I really was the least magical person you could imagine, back home. It must be the key that changed me. It's been waiting, lying around in the Castle for centuries, and I was just the lucky person who picked it up."

"Ailanthe," Coren began.

"I want to see if Gweron left any other diaries behind," she went on, ignoring him. "You know. *'Dear Diary, I woke up this morning and I could bend reality to my will. Eggs on toast for breakfast.'* Something like that. He must have felt so lonely, if he was the only one like him."

Coren put his hand on her shoulder. "You're still you," he said.

She wrenched away from him. "And the Castle won't let me out. It doesn't need my magic like it did Gweron's. Don't think I don't realize this is a death sentence."

"My lady, do not think such things," Tristram said.

She turned on him in a fury. "And what exactly am I supposed to think, Tristram? That I can somehow make the Castle believe I'm not a threat to it, and it will just open the door and wave goodbye as I trot happily away? That I can find a way to defeat an insane Castle that even its builder, who by the way had far more experience and control than I ever will over his magic, couldn't keep from overwhelming him? Tell me what to think, Tristram!"

He didn't flinch. "Think instead that you have been gradually driving it back, my lady. You may not have Gweron's skill, but you have his power, and you are not yet dead."

"The important word being 'yet'."

"Ailanthe," Coren said. He held the book and the lens in his hands and was reading something. "I think this is important."

"Why? Did you miraculously find something I missed?"

"Stop feeling sorry for yourself for two seconds and listen," he snapped. "Gweron wrote that the Castle couldn't kill him without destroying itself. Obviously it hasn't been destroyed. That means Gweron is still here. Somewhere in the Castle."

"Impossible," Tristram said. "I grant you there are rooms we have not yet fully plumbed, but you, good sir, cannot have lived here for so long without seeing there is none other here but you and the beast."

"He's got to be," Coren insisted. "If the Castle needed his magic so much, he couldn't have left without destroying it either. I bet the Castle locked him away somewhere. Or turned him into something. He said he didn't know how long his life might be, and Miriethiel has lasted all these centuries; there's no reason Gweron might not have done the same." He closed the book. "Gweron's still alive. If we can find him, maybe the two of you together will be enough to stop the Castle forever."

"Yet does it not seem that it is executing Gweron's destiny spell?" Tristram said. "Men come, they take something, they leave by the way the Castle selects." He pulled out his mirror from his pocket. "My mirror allows me to leave the Castle, does it not? And through the door I saw a wondrous land of lush green growing things and the sounds of a million birds. Had I not realized my destiny lay here, I should assuredly have believed it lay through that magical door."

He bowed to Ailanthe with a brilliant smile. She was tempted to kiss Coren right then, wipe that smile off Tristram's face, but she remembered that she was mad at Coren, and anyway he was on the other side of the room.

"The Things aren't magical," she said. "Except for the key, which seems to be what turned me into...anyway, it sounds as if Gweron intended the Castle to produce magical items for its questers, but the Castle is just hauling out whatever junk it can find. It's like it knows what Gweron's spell is, but doesn't really understand it."

"So Gweron was partly successful in activating his destiny spell," Coren said, "and then the Castle did something to him that kept him alive but unable to act."

"I think it's stupid to think he's been turned into something," Ailanthe said.

"It would be easier than trying to keep him fed all these centuries," Coren said irritably.

"Either way, we don't know where he is," Ailanthe said. Something slunk across the dunes, far below. Shadowy hunter—she shuddered at the thought.

"But we shall know, my lady," Tristram said. He came to her side and took her hand. "We now know for what we search, and we *shall* find him. I will not give up, my lady." He kissed her hand. Across the room, Coren flung the book onto a chair so hard it bounced and hit the floor with a crack. Ailanthe withdrew her hand as gracefully as possible and smiled at Tristram.

"Thank you," she said. "I feel better knowing I have the two of you willing to help me. And you're right, this narrows our search. I think I will put these books back and then go to bed, if you'll excuse me."

She turned her back on Tristram and started picking up books, standing them on end as if putting them back on their shelf. Behind her, Tristram left the room, and a moment later so did Coren. She blinked away tears. She'd thought he'd at least help her put them in order in preparation for sending them back. They'd both spoken so harshly to each other—she shouldn't have let her despair spill over like that, but it was so hard not to think of the shadows and how the Castle could afford to wait forever to seize her. Eventually she'd run out of luck, and then....

She wiped her eyes and steadied a pair of books. She was too tired to send them all back at once, and she wasn't entirely sure where she'd taken them from in the first place. She concentrated on a group of ten and felt them reappear on their shelf. At least she'd gotten one thing right tonight.

When the last book had disappeared, she continued to kneel on the floor, tracing the delicate grain of its boards with her fingers. Gweron was right; the Castle was beautiful. How proud he must have been, those first days, seeing it all come together. And how devastated at the end, when it all threatened to fall apart, maybe literally. Unfortunate for everyone that it hadn't.

"I think you can hear me," she said quietly. "I don't know why you did what you did, trying to undo everything Gweron did, trying to unmake yourself, and I don't care. You're evil, and if you try to take me I will tear you apart."

Far in the corners, the shadows bulged. Ailanthe stared them down. There was too much light between them for the shadows to cross, but they strained at the boundaries that hemmed them in, reaching for her. But Ailanthe was tired of being afraid.

She stood and walked toward them, keeping a safe distance, and said, "You've had so many opportunities to swallow me, I wonder that you haven't tried more often. Are you weak, Castle, after all these years? Am I a threat to you? I didn't want to be. I just wanted to be able to go home. You know, if you'd just opened the door I would have passed through and you'd never have had to fight me. But then, you're insane, so logic isn't something you'd be familiar with."

She shook her head, slowly. "I'm going to bed now. Looks like I'll be sleeping alone, too. And in the morning I'm going to start looking for Gweron, and I'm not going to stop until I've found him or I'm dead. And I don't intend to die."

She heard footsteps, and then Coren came through the door. The shadows' attention shifted in a heartbeat. He had enough time to open his mouth to say something, and they were on him, enveloping him like a cloud of gray dust.

"*Coren!*" she screamed, and ran toward him, terror making her forget her own safety. She needed more light, but the Castle fought her when she tried summoning her lamps, blocked her path when she tried creating them, and in desperation she went to her knees—

—and made light.

It was like being at the heart of a cold, bright sun. She covered her eyes with her arms and could still see light burning red through her eyelids. Blood pounded in her ears like a drum with an erratic beat, thrum-*thrum*, *thrum*-thrum, and she felt her breath coming fast and sharp in her chest. The light pressed down on her, but softly, like a cool blanket, and she lowered her arms to find it fading, the chairs and tables and easel and painting sharply outlined in its radiance.

Coren sprawled a few feet away, his hands over his face. The room was free from shadow, even the ordinary ones. The light had swept away the leftover smells from dinner, leaving a cool freshness like after spring rain.

She stood, unsteadily, and Coren lowered his hands and looked up at her. The awe in his face made her cringe. "I don't know how I did that," she said.

"I don't care. That was like—I thought I was dead," he said, standing and brushing himself off, and looked surprised when there was nothing to brush. "Thank you."

"I suppose we're even now," she said. She moved to pass him, anything not to see him looking at her as if she were a stranger. He reached out and took hold of her hand.

"I don't think we're supposed to keep score," he said. "I'm sorry I was so harsh with you."

"You were right. I was feeling sorry for myself. And I said some rude things to you, too."

"I can't remember." He tugged on her hand. "Ailanthe. Look at me."

She looked up and saw him smiling at her. "You're still you," he said. "You haven't turned into anything inhuman, and when I look into your eyes, I still see Ailanthe behind them."

She shook her head. "I just—what I did, you looked so shocked and afraid—"

"I was awestruck that you have such power and wondered if you'd even still care for me, since I'm just an ordinary man."

Ailanthe laughed and flung her arms around his neck. "You did not."

"I did, a little. But mostly I was happy to be alive." He bent his head and kissed her. "Though I suppose you could have Tristram if you think I'm inadequate, so at least you wouldn't have to sleep alone."

She shuddered exaggeratedly. "I don't want anyone but you."

"That's a relief." He kissed her again, then swooped her up into his arms, making her shriek before laughing and kissing him back. "Now, *my lady*, I believe I made you a promise, so if you'll point me in the direction of your room?"

AILANTHE WOKE in darkness to find something pinning her down. Some experimental fumbling revealed it to be Coren's arm flung across her stomach. He muttered something inarticulate when she prodded it, but otherwise didn't move. She laid her hand on his broad shoulder and smiled. It might have been more than six years for him, but he certainly remembered his way around a woman's body. And it was so wonderful not to sleep alone.

She struggled beneath the weight of his arm to turn onto her side, facing him, and ran her hand from his shoulder down his back, settling just above his hip.

"Ailanthe, I'm trying to sleep," he murmured.

"I'm sorry. I didn't mean to wake you. You seemed deeply asleep."

"You're naked and you're wiggling. I would have to be dead not to be aware of that."

"I'm sorry."

"I'm not." He rolled over and put his arms around her. "I've never actually spent the night with a woman before. The whole night, I mean. Deyanara always made sure of that."

"Who's Deyanara?"

Coren snorted. "A fate worse than death. When she was ten, she decided she was going to marry me—I was eighteen at the time, mind—and she spent the next seven years ruining every relationship I even thought of having. I'd meet a woman, one thing would lead to another, and then she'd treat me like I had a disease because she'd learned I, well, had a disease. Or was already married. Things like that. Never because Deyanara said anything, of course. The little bitch was good at dropping hints in the right ears. Toward the end, she started trying to seduce me so I'd get her pregnant and be forced to marry her. Even if I hadn't been restless, I might still have left home just to get away from her." He sighed. "But now I think I could endure another seven years of her if I could only be home again."

Ailanthe did a little math. "You're thirty-one."

"I am. Thirty-two in another four months."

"I'm twenty-three. You're much too old for me."

"I didn't hear any complaints earlier."

"That was before I knew you were ancient—ohhh. Oh, do that again."

"You mean you want an old man doing...this?"

"...Sorry. I forgot how to speak for a minute there. I no longer care about your age."

"Good. Because you're not escaping me that easily." He rolled over so she ended up lying on top of him. "I love you, Ailanthe."

"I love you, Coren." It took her a few tries to find his mouth so she could kiss him, but the way he responded made it worth the effort.

CHAPTER TWENTY

*W*hen she woke again, rectangles of light glowed behind the curtains, and someone was knocking on the door. "My lady?" Tristram said. "I have brought breakfast, but I fear I cannot find your friend."

Ailanthe sat up, clutching the blanket to her chest. Beside her, Coren buried his head in the pillow and shook with laughter. "I, um, know where he is, Tristram," she said. "There's nothing to worry about."

"I hope you are correct, my lady. Will you join me for a meal? I know you are partial to strawberries."

"Thank you, Tristram. Just let me get dressed." She willed all the lights on and swatted Coren on his extremely attractive backside before climbing off the bed and putting on her clothes. "Do *not* tease Tristram today. The poor man really thinks he's my true love."

"But teasing that smug Galendishman is so much *fun*. And he's so thick he can't see the way I look at you, so teasing hardly makes a dent in that arrogant shell he drags around with him."

Ailanthe concentrated briefly, and Coren's clothes fell out of midair to land on his back. "He found Gweron's study, so he's not that oblivious. And he's not a bad person, so be nice to him."

Coren sat up and pulled on his pants. "All right. But I can't promise I won't get in a dig or two if the opportunity presents itself."

"I suppose that's the best I can hope for." Ailanthe kissed him. "Follow me when you're ready."

When she entered the window room, Tristram smiled his dazzling smile and offered her a small plate piled high with juicy red strawberries. "I give you good morning, my lady," he said, taking a strawberry and raising it to her lips. "I trust you slept well?"

Ailanthe suppressed a sigh and bit into the berry, which was as luscious as it looked. "I slept very well, thank you."

"Would that I might say the same. I slept but fitfully, my concern for your safety driving all thoughts of rest from my head. I thought to offer you my protection, during the hours of night, but your maidenly blush tells me you are as yet still unwilling to acknowledge the bond between us, let alone permit me to consummate our love."

You'd have had a huge *surprise if you'd come knocking on my door last night.* "Tristram, your concern is so touching, but really, I don't feel that way about you. Please don't be offended when I ask you not to pursue me anymore."

Tristram laid aside the stem of the strawberry and took Ailanthe's hand. "Your bashfulness does you credit, my lady," he murmured. "Do not deny me the pleasure of courting you. You were right to say that we do not yet know one another well, but as long as we are trapped here, our acquaintance can only grow. I have not yet lost hope, my lady."

Ailanthe opened her mouth to tell him the truth, changed her mind and ate another strawberry. She ought to tell him, really; letting him find out on his own was cruel. But she felt so awkward blurting it out. Though she didn't feel menaced by Tristram, he was so utterly convinced she just didn't know she was in love with him that she was a little afraid of what he might do if she said *Tristram, Coren and I are lovers, and even if we weren't, you still wouldn't have a chance with me.* Well, that last part was probably unnecessary, even if it was true. She resolved to find the right time to tell him the truth; it felt wrong to do anything else.

"Good morning," Coren called out cheerfully. "Oh, strawberries!" He swept three of them off the plate and proceeded to snap the green stems off with his thumbnail before popping all three into his mouth at once. He chewed vigorously while helping himself to a handful of soft rolls and a pot of butter, juggling a knife between the two, and walked over to look out across the green valley.

"My lady, I feel I should apologize for your friend's uncouthness," Tristram said in a low voice. "You ought not have to endure such crass behavior."

"Don't worry, Tristram, I'm not offended. I'm used to his ways. We should make allowances, he's been alone for so long I'm sure he's forgotten what manners are," Ailanthe said in a voice loud enough for Coren to hear. In reply, he belched, and Ailanthe had to cover her mouth quickly to keep from choking on her laughter. Tristram looked disgusted.

"Look you still so fondly on him, as coarse as he is?" he said. "No, it is not my place to comment on your friendship. Allow me to serve you some bread and jam."

"No, Tristram," Ailanthe said as inspiration struck, "let me serve *you*." She picked up a plate and thought back to mornings back home, her father cooking breakfast over the *gyrsta*, and two perfectly fried eggs landed neatly on the plate. She passed it to Tristram with a little bow of her own.

"My lady," Tristram breathed, "I have never been more in awe of your powers than I am at this moment." He searched around for a fork, then reverently lifted a bite to his lips and chewed slowly, his eyes half-closed.

"Ailanthe," Coren said, dropping the pretense at uncouthness, "can you make bacon?"

"I've never had it, so I'm afraid not. But I can make eggs any way you want them."

"Sunny side up. Three, please."

Soon all three of them were sitting on the backless cube chairs, eating eggs in blissful silence. *How much easier to call eggs into existence already poached*, thought Ailanthe, *and wouldn't my father be so surprised?* The toast was hot, the butter perfectly melted into its crevices, and the egg bled gold with every bite she took. She still didn't know if the powers she now wielded were a permanent part of her, or if they would vanish once she was free of the Castle.

She took another bite. It might not be so bad, having magic like Gweron's, so long as she didn't try to construct any magical buildings that could become intelligent and then go insane. And so long as Coren continued to look at her the way he had last night.

"I am loath to leave these gustatory pleasures behind," Tristram said, neatly wiping his mouth with the handkerchief he always carried that never seemed to become dirty, "but I believe we ought to begin our task. If the Castle discovers what we intend, it will certainly try to stop us."

"It attacked Coren last night," Ailanthe said, "with the shadows. I think we should assume it's not going to limit its aggression to me anymore. You should both be careful."

"So where do we start?" Coren said. "And what exactly are we looking for?"

Both men looked to Ailanthe for an answer. She said, "I don't know. I think...personally, I think he's locked up somewhere, which means we should be looking for a hidden room. But it's possible Coren is right and he's been transformed. Either way, we're looking for something saturated with magic. I can't imagine Gweron wouldn't fight back, so the Castle would have to pour a lot of magic into keeping him isolated. I can see magic, but we should...wait." She picked up the lens, sliding a few of the buttons. "One of you can use this to see magic too."

Coren immediately held out his hand. Tristram said, "I think I am better equipped to handle the magic, my lady."

"Based on what, exactly? Your impeccable grammar?" Coren scoffed.

"I at least am unlikely to crush the delicate instrument with my oafish hands."

"*You can take turns,*" Ailanthe said, "and no more insults, all right?

Coren, you first. I think you'll find looking through it for very long is tiring, anyway."

Coren accepted the lens, and Ailanthe was grateful he didn't turn and stick his tongue out at Tristram. "I see magic on the diary, the windows, your key, and fainter magic on the things you've gained control over, like the painting," he said. "Is there anything else in here the lens ought to register?"

"That's it." Ailanthe summoned a couple of lamps and handed one to Tristram. "Do you have any suggestions as to how we should proceed, Tristram? You did find the study, after all."

Tristram thought about it. "I do not think we shall find him in his study," he said, "as he wrote that he was leaving it to confront the Castle. It seems to me the Castle would hide him away where few people go, so I suggest we begin on this level and work our way down. If that is agreeable to you, my lady."

"It is. Then...let's go."

The shadows followed them as they proceeded down the hall, stretching and bulging like ropy gray muscles. Ailanthe summoned another of her lamps and turned on every light in the hallway as they went. This kept the shadows at a distance, but did not discourage them entirely. Coren stepped closer to Ailanthe and murmured, "We must be doing something right."

Ailanthe nodded. "I've been trying to think of ways to more effectively dispel them, short of that display I put on last night. Us being blinded would be useless." She slid the key into the first door opposite Coren's suite. "Tristram, none of these rooms contains magical items, but there might still be hidden doors, so I'll maintain the lights while the two of you search."

"As you command, my lady," Tristram said. He aimed his lamp into the room before entering. "The shadows here do not move," he reported.

"Don't assume that's going to last," Coren said, raising the lens to his eye. Ailanthe kept one of her lamps pointed inward while watching the shadows in the hall. Did she imagine that they were whispering, or was that the voice of the Castle Gweron reported hearing just before he vanished? She closed her ears to the unnerving sound.

Coren and Tristram reappeared. "Nothing," Coren said. "I think this floor may be a waste of our time."

"We can ill afford to pass over any possibility, Hesperan," Tristram said. "Tedious it may be, but our very lives are at stake now."

"You're right," Ailanthe said. "But let's do this as quickly as possible."

They fell into a pattern, Ailanthe unlocking a door, Tristram or Coren shining the lights inside the room while the other searched for false walls, moving cabinets, or even faint scuff marks on floor or wall. Ailanthe left the rooms unlocked behind them, no longer caring what the Castle thought of her disruptions.

While she waited for the men to search, she stared into the darkness and tried not to think about what might happen if she carelessly stepped into the shadows. The Castle's creatures weren't trying to hide anymore and didn't seem to care that she was watching them. Sometimes the dark presences retreated for a while, but mostly they shifted at the edge of where the light met the darkness, and Ailanthe could sense their eagerness to cross the area of light and leap on her. Neither Tristram nor Coren could hear the whispering, and she told herself that meant it was imaginary.

It was well into the afternoon before they stood at the tower door and looked inside. The interior was shadowy, striped white by the light coming through the cracks in the walls, but strangely empty of threat. "I don't think he's up there," Ailanthe said. "There's nowhere to hide a secret room, and I'd have seen anything magical, what with all the time I've spent there."

"I should like to see it nonetheless, my lady," Tristram said. "And we ought not leave anything unexplored."

Lamps burning, they went up the stairs, spreading out after Tristram and Coren crowded too close to Ailanthe and made the stairs groan as if stressed nearly to the breaking point. Ailanthe went straight to her pile of cushions and looked out toward her home. "That's where I live," she told Tristram, who was a little out of breath.

"Somewhere in that direction, anyway. The mother trees all look so much alike from this height."

"It is beautiful, my lady," Tristram said, settling close beside her. "It makes one think of elves dancing beneath those leaves at moonrise."

"They prefer the dark," Ailanthe said. "Though I've seen them, once or twice, come to the pool to drink. You only see them in glimpses, and usually only when they aren't trying to stay hidden. But they have a strange beauty that's like nothing else."

"Not unlike your beauty, then," Tristram said with a smile. "Though I do not call it strange."

"Tristram—"

"I beg your pardon, my lady." He stood and examined the floor and the windows, found the broken latch and pushed the pane open, letting in the wind that endlessly circled the tower. Coren reached past him and closed it, frowning at him. Tristram held out his hand. "My turn," he said, "as I am certain you are weary of the lens's burden."

Coren slapped it into his hand. "Enjoy yourself," he grunted. "Ailanthe, there's nothing up here but the three of us. Let's have something to eat before we move on."

"Yes, but quickly," she said, "because I want to search the Library next."

They ransacked the Library shelves, looking for another moving bookcase, and Ailanthe cringed every time they moved another stack of books to the floor. *Who's going to clean this up?* she thought, and wondered if the Castle would stop performing its nightly ritual now that it was actively trying to stop them destroying it. She used her hands rather than her power, just in case.

By dinnertime, they were all exhausted, and they'd proved the Library had no secrets other than the ones hidden inside its books. Ailanthe's vision was blurry from trying to determine which, if any, of the magical books was different from the others. None had more than the same faint glow that characterized the hero books; none were nearly so bright as Gweron's diary.

As tired as she was, Ailanthe couldn't resist creating a roast chicken smelling deliciously of rosemary and a stack of new potatoes swimming in butter. The hot meal revived everyone's spirits, and even Tristram relaxed enough to speak to Coren without sniping at him, even if it was merely to ask him to pass the plate. Ailanthe debated summoning a bottle of wine from the Castle's cellar, but decided in the end it was better they keep their heads unclouded. Besides, wine was for celebrating, and they didn't have anything to celebrate yet.

When the chicken was reduced to bones, Coren excused himself, and the moment he was out of the room Tristram knelt at Ailanthe's side and took her hand, pressing it to his lips. "I find I cannot stay silent, my lady. You are all that is good and beautiful, and I cannot bear to see your heart yearn after one so far your inferior in every way. Please, my lady—Ailanthe. Allow me to be your defender."

Ailanthe's mouth went slack in astonishment. "Tristram, I really don't—"

"You deserve better, my lady, and it is with no small modesty that I suggest I am that." He kissed her hand again. "I swear I shall not ask more than you are prepared to give."

She was too shocked and embarrassed to try to pull her hand free. She had to tell him the truth; she couldn't put it off for the right time, if there ever was one. If he found out on his own, he would be so humiliated—might be humiliated no matter how she tried to spare his feelings. He was arrogant, and self-absorbed, and didn't know any more of her than the idealized figure he'd set up as his true love, but he was also sincere and loyal and she wished with all her heart that he'd never come to the Castle, even if it meant never learning Gweron's secret.

"Tristram, I have to tell you something you're not going to like," she said, gently rearranging her hand so she could clasp his. "I—Coren and I—he loves me, Tristram, and I love him. I...admire you so much, and your affection and respect for me—"

Tristram snatched his hand away. "What madness is this?"

"I'm sorry I couldn't tell you before. I didn't know what to say. You don't really know me, Tristram, and—"

"You are the woman of whom I have dreamed my whole life. You belong to *me,* not to some boorish knave who will not worship at your feet as I will."

"I don't belong to anyone," Ailanthe said, trying to keep her rising anger under control. "That woman, whoever she is, she's—you told me when you arrive home you'll be wooed by so many beautiful women, and I'm certain one of them will be perfect for you."

Tristram stood and shouted, "You are my destiny, my lady, and you will not reject me so out of hand!"

Ailanthe leaped up to face him. "Don't shout at me, Tristram. I've been telling you that I don't feel anything for you but friendship. It's not my fault you haven't been listening."

He grabbed her arm, and she pulled away from him and stepped out of his reach. "You have a strange way of showing how much you respect me," she said.

Tristram's face was twisted with anger. "You have betrayed me," he said. "I pledged myself to you, and you cast that pledge aside as worthless. I suppose you and that oaf have made sport of me, in private? I cannot bear this humiliation."

"No, Tristram, we haven't laughed at you at all. You've done so much for me, I can't tell you how grateful I am. It's just that I don't—"

"Spare me your protestations." Tristram brushed past her. "I cannot bear to look upon you more, faithless creature." He strode out of the room, striking the wall with his fist as he passed through the doorway. Ailanthe watched him go, not sure whether she was relieved he was gone or afraid he might meet Coren in the hallway.

She sat back down on her chair and shooed Miriethiel away from the chicken carcass, then sent the detritus of the meal away. The bright lights turned the windows into mirrors, and she watched Miriethiel wander away from the table where good smells still lingered and come to sit on her lap.

She petted him and let her mind wander. Tristram would probably leave in the morning. He might even leave that night. Tomorrow she and Coren would resume the search, and as tired as she was, the idea tired her still further. They didn't even know what they were looking for. The Castle had so many rooms, it could take weeks, and they might not have weeks.

"You look as if you're asleep with your eyes open," Coren said, startling her. He rested his hands on her shoulders and squeezed lightly.

"I told Tristram the truth about us."

His hands went still. "And?"

"He was furious. He thought we'd been mocking him. I'm glad I realized how much more upset he'd be if he found out on his own."

"Did he leave?"

"I don't know. I don't know whether to hope he does or not."

"He's been helpful. We wouldn't have found the study or the lens without him."

"I know." She laid her hand atop one of his. "I'm too tired to think about it anymore. Let's go to bed."

Coren pulled her to her feet and put his arms around her. "I'm glad neither of us has to sleep alone."

She laid her hand on his cheek. It was freshly shaved; he'd done that for her, and it made her smile. "Even if all I can do tonight is sleep?"

He squeezed her lightly. "Then I will hold you, and we'll see what the morning brings."

CHAPTER TWENTY-ONE

*T*ristram was in the window room when Ailanthe entered it the next morning. "Oh!" she said. "I thought...I wondered if you might have left." Coren had woken her by nuzzling her neck and shoulders, and then he'd moved on to more interesting parts of her body, and now she felt self-conscious, as if their lovemaking were some kind of taunt aimed at the Galendishman, who'd slept alone.

"I have pledged myself to you, and I intend to fulfil my vow to free you from this place," he said, his words clipped as if he'd bitten each one off and spat it at her. "Though you are faithless, yet I will keep my word."

Ailanthe was grateful Coren wasn't there to hear this. "Thank you, Tristram," she said, deciding to ignore "faithless." "You really are the most noble person I know." *And the most arrogant, self-centered, narrow-minded...oh, there's no sense going on like that.*

Tristram gave her a nod of the head. "Should I descend to provide us with sustenance, or will you use your magic again? I am quite fond of steak."

"I'm really sorry, but my people don't keep cows, so I don't know what steak looks like. I can do eggs again, or porridge?"

Brief distaste crossed Tristram's face at the mention of porridge,

187

but he said, "I should like eggs, my lady, if it be not too much trouble."

She produced eggs for both of them, then, when he arrived, more eggs for Coren, who nodded to Tristram but didn't say anything. By the way Tristram's face went white, then red, when he looked at Coren, he was close to challenging Coren to a duel for the hand of the fair maiden, and Ailanthe didn't like the idea of postponing their search while they worked out their aggression on each other. But he managed to control his anger.

They ate in silence, each facing a different window, and Ailanthe watched two large birds drift high above the desert searching for their own breakfasts. She wanted to go home, true, but now that she'd seen so much of the world through the Castle's windows, she wanted to see more of it on her terms. That desert, that distant city, the hills of Hespera...would Coren want to travel with her, or would he be unwilling to leave home once he'd regained it?

She glanced at him, staring out over the ocean at a storm coming along the shoreline. What did he think, when he thought about his future? Was she in it? Would he still love her when he was free? She moved her empty plate from her lap to the floor and sighed. Time enough for thoughts of the future when she was certain she had one.

They made a quiet, tense group that day, searching rooms efficiently and almost without speaking. Tristram's few comments were terse and directed at no one in particular. He wouldn't look at Ailanthe and couldn't stop glaring at Coren. Coren pretended not to notice. He spoke to Tristram politely but rarely, innocuous words no one could use to start a fight.

Ailanthe, for her part, said nothing at all. There was nothing for her to say; the shadows stayed at a distance, and she saw nothing that radiated magic the way the diary did. They ate sitting in a pool of light in the hallway, and continued the search until Ailanthe's arms were shaking from holding the lamp at such an awkward angle and her empty stomach ached.

"We should stop," she finally said. They had come full circle and reached the stairwell, which spiraled down into darkness. Ailanthe tried to turn the lights on, but weariness defeated her.

"Are you all right?" Coren asked. He took the lamp from her and put his arm around her waist for support. Tristram's face went grim and he looked away. Ailanthe wanted to smack him.

"Just tired. And frustrated." She didn't say anything more, because they were all thinking it: their quest was probably doomed.

"We shall have better luck on the morrow," Tristram said. He'd stopped saying "my lady" several hours before.

"I hope so," Ailanthe said. Reluctantly, because she'd been worrying this over in her head for an hour and found no graceful way to say it, she added, "I think maybe you ought to move into our— Coren's suite, Tristram. We might all be safer close together, and it will be easier for me to keep the shadows away."

Tristram looked as if he'd been force-fed a clump of manure. "I think not," he said.

"Then at least let me control the lights in your room. I know you're not afraid of the Castle, but I'm afraid for you. If it struck you, we wouldn't even know until it was too late."

Tristram's face didn't change, but he said, "As you wish."

Ailanthe having altered Tristram's room, they returned upstairs and ate in silence. Ailanthe found she had no appetite despite her empty stomach, and even broiled salmon seemed like too much effort to eat. She picked at it and fed slivers to Miriethiel, and kicked the lower edge of her chair idly. The moon was still too bright for them to turn off the lights and see the outside world clearly; it would cast too many shadows. If she looked closely, she could see movement in the farthest corner of the room. How frustrated the Castle must be at not being able to reach them. She ate another bite. Tasteless.

Coren had the lens in his hand and was playing with the different settings. "Did you know this one makes the sprites solid green?" he said, holding it to his eye and following a sprite around the room.

"Yes. It's completely useless. So are most of the other settings I tried. Who knows what Gweron had in mind for it, aside from translating his diary."

"'Tis pity there be no setting that reveals his location," Tristram said. "Or this endless search would be over, and the three of us freed to go our separate ways." His lips thinned as he looked from Ailanthe to Coren as if remembering two of them would probably be going the same way.

Coren pushed more buttons. "It must be strange, Ailanthe, seeing the world the way you do," he said. "All these lights where magic is. And that diary is blindingly bright."

"So were a lot of things in Gweron's study," Ailanthe said. "For all he talked about how difficult building the Castle was, he certainly threw magic around like it was nothing. The lens itself is as bright as the diary. And you both felt the power that came out of the cabinet. Nothing else in the Castle is nearly so magical."

"There's the key," Coren pointed out.

"True, but—" Ailanthe stopped. She took the key in her hand and rubbed the silver streaks. "It's as magical as the diary," she said. "Maybe more so."

"It does unlock all the doors," Tristram said. "The Castle cannot prevent it. It must have great power to do so."

"Great power," Ailanthe agreed, still unable to take her eyes off it. "Everything else with this kind of power was locked up where the Castle couldn't touch it. Everything but this."

"Ailanthe, what are you saying?"

"You said he might have been turned into something," she said. "Why not this? It would explain why the Castle wouldn't let me leave with it."

"But the Castle gave it to you, more or less. Why didn't it keep the key hidden somewhere? A place this big, no one would ever have found it."

"I don't know." She closed her hand over the key so hard she could feel her blood pulse through her fist. "But what have we been looking for? Something with a lot of magic in it. Something hidden. If this isn't Gweron, I'll bet it can at least help us find him."

"But, my lady, did not you say you cannot work your will upon magical objects?" Tristram had forgotten he was angry with her.

"I can't make them mine, certainly, but I don't want Gweron to be mine, I want him to be free. There has to be a way to make that happen."

"Ailanthe, you're exhausted. Why don't we do this in the morning?"

Ailanthe shook her head. "I'm not going to be able to sleep if I don't at least try right now." She removed the key from her wrist and held it up to the light, then said, "Could I have that lens, Coren?"

The last door they'd opened had given the key a slender shaft with a single square tooth halfway down it. To her unaided eye, it coruscated with rainbow light. Under the red-tinted lens, that magic showed itself as wriggling lines of white-yellow brightness, spiraling down the shaft and disintegrating only to be replaced by more wriggling lines. The silver streaks pulsed, distorting the yellow lines that passed over them.

Ailanthe put her finger in front of one of the wriggling lines and lifted it up. It stretched, then snapped back to resume its course. She felt nothing when the magic touched her. She never felt anything, touching the key, except its smooth metal; whatever magic was on it, or in it, was buried deep.

"What are you?" she said, and wrapped the question around the key and let it settle among the wriggling lines like a white film. The key shivered, and the lines of light went still. It stretched in her hand, becoming broader and longer, then flat-shafted with a row of jagged pointed teeth like a predator's mouth, then a fat, hollow cylinder, and then the changes were coming so quickly it seemed the metal had become cold liquid in her hand, shifting from one form to another with no pause in between.

Ailanthe closed her hand on it to keep it from falling, but it struggled against her grasp until it forced her fingers open and fell to the floor, where it bounced once with a dull chime and then rattled with the force of its transformations.

Coren and Tristram drew nearer until all three of them stood in a loose circle about five feet from the key. "What did you do, my lady?" Tristram said.

"It's in pain," Ailanthe whispered, ignoring him. The rainbow aura surrounding it was distorted now, stretched far from it until it snapped back and sent out a spray of sparkling dust that glowed more brightly than the key. She reached out to touch it, and Coren took hold of her wrist firmly and said, "Don't."

"You can't see it," she said, but he shook his head and said, "We can now. All that light stretching away from it—you can see it too, Galendishman?"

"Indeed I can," Tristram said. "I ask again, my lady, what did you do?"

"I don't know," Ailanthe said. She shook off Coren's grip and knelt beside the key. "You don't have enough power, do you?" she said. "Whatever it is you're trying to become, you don't have the power to do it. I can help you." She spread her hand, fingers fully extended, above the jittering key, feeling the sprays of magic brush her palm with an exhilarating tingle. "Because you gave me your power."

She cast about in her mind for an image that would help, but kept returning to memories of her hand on the key, unlocking countless doors and boxes and cabinets. The rush of rose-scented air from the cupboard in Gweron's den. The sprawling red doors of her tower. Room after room filled with the Castle's unwanted Things. "You can unlock everything except yourself," she whispered, and took hold of the key.

Lightning went through her hand and up her arm and spread through her chest. She felt her heart stop, briefly, then begin beating again at a too-rapid pace. She smelled the sharp scent that came after lightning struck one of the grandfather trees, then the acrid smell of the smoke that followed, but both faded quickly, replaced by the sweet, clean smell of roses after rain. Her hand was numb, but when she opened her eyes she could see she still clutched the key in her fingers, and before she could think about how impossible it was, she pictured a keyhole hovering in midair, inserted the key and turned it.

Green light flashed, blinding her. Coren and Tristram cried out from somewhere nearby. Tears streaming from her eyes, she blinked hard to see more than their silhouettes that went from black to inverted white-green when her eyes closed. Coren, shorter than Tristram by an inch or two, and next to them, a third figure, shorter than both, standing with its arms wrapped around its chest and its—his—head bowed.

Ailanthe saw her hand was empty and lowered her arm, rubbing her numb fingers. The green light was fading, but not quickly enough; it cast an appalling glare over all of them, giving Coren's skin a dull, waxy look and making the much paler Tristram look three days dead. The third man raised his head and looked at Ailanthe. His eyes were colorless in the green light, and his fair hair was as green as the new buds on the mother tree. Arms still crossed over his chest, he looked around the room, his face filled with confusion.

"The Atelier," he said, sounding aghast. "Rhedyth, why have you brought me here?"

CHAPTER TWENTY-TWO

*A*ilanthe gaped at him. "You're Gweron," she said.

"I am he," the man said, "but I know not who you are. Nor why Rhedyth swallowed me up near its heart only to spit me out here."

He looked at his hands as if he'd never seen them before, then touched his face, his throat, and ran his hands down his chest. He wore a brown jacket with full sleeves and a long black skirt whose hem brushed the tops of his bare feet. "I am intact. I thought myself dead when the shadows took me."

"No, just...transformed," Ailanthe said. He turned his gaze on her, and she had to stop herself taking a step backward from those intense, colorless eyes. "I'm Ailanthe," she continued, "and this is Coren, and Tristram. We've been looking for you."

Gweron turned to examine Coren and Tristram, then turned his attention back to Ailanthe. "You have my power," he said. "I had thought myself alone in the world. How is this possible?"

"I had—when you were transformed, you—some of your power came to me," Ailanthe stammered. Now that the light had mostly faded, she could see his eyes were actually a very pale blue. He was somewhat older than Coren, but still extremely attractive; it was disconcerting, since Ailanthe had pictured him as a white-bearded man, lean and sinewy and wrinkled. He strode to the window, moving with the assurance of someone who'd never feared anything in his life.

"I knew not that such a thing was possible," he said. "But I do feel weakened. I know not but that Rhedyth might have sapped my powers. How long have I lain thus transformed? And into what?"

"You were the key to the Castle," Ailanthe said. "And we don't know exactly how long, but for more than four centuries people have come to the Castle to find their destiny."

He spun and strode to face her, grasping her shoulders and causing Coren to move to stand behind her. "Then I succeeded," he said, his eyes blazing. "Rhedyth has not won."

"Ah...we think the Castle isn't carrying out your instructions, not entirely." Ailanthe stepped backward, breaking his hold, and bumped into Coren. His strong presence made her feel less nervous of this strange man and his overwhelming personality.

An expression of sorrow and pain passed across Gweron's features. "My poor creation," he said. "I had such joy in it. That it should turn on me...let me tell you, strangers, a story of hope and tragedy, and mayhap you will join with me in putting this poor creature to rest."

"We, ah, read your diary," Ailanthe said, tensing in anticipation of an angry response. Fury briefly passed over his face, then an amused resignation.

"I know not why that should anger me," he said. "I did but write it for the sake of future generations, and it seems that however you came by this power, young lady, you did become my successor. Though I should feel more sanguine when I have regained that power. If Rhedyth yet lives, then we are all in danger."

"I know," Ailanthe said. "The shadows keep trying to attack us."

"That is but magic under Rhedyth's control. I see you have hit upon the means for keeping it at bay. Would that I should have had such allies in my own time." He turned away again, his head bowed.

"It is passing strange that I feel not the burden of years. It is to me as but a moment has passed since—"

He went to stand by the desert window, looking out at the night. Ailanthe could see his reflection in the glass; his expression was heartbreaking.

"I meant this to be the salvation of mankind," he said to the night. "The world in my time was a dark place, filled with men who used their inborn talents to their own selfish ends. I wanted only to turn those talents to good, make of them men of wisdom and courage who would do what was right. Rhedyth should have called all men to it, but its insanity drove them away."

"People do still come here," Ailanthe said. "The Castle gives them a destiny."

"Then it gives them the gift?"

"No. That part of your spell isn't working."

"How was your spell intended to work?" Coren said, startling Ailanthe. She'd forgotten there was anyone else in the room.

Gweron smiled. "It was a thing of beauty, so simple and yet so powerful. Rhedyth exerts an influence on the world—in my more poetic moments I thought of it as a song, heard only by the heart—that draws men, and women, unto it. They come, and Rhedyth sees who they truly are, their virtues and their vices, and produces a token that is theirs alone. In accepting that token, they are transformed, all evil swept away, made anew into people of true virtue and sent out into the world to make it over in the image of all that is good."

Tristram said, "That is far-seeing indeed. It would take a truly mad mind not to see the virtue in it."

Coren said, "People aren't forced to come to the Castle, now. They only come if it's what they want."

"Another flaw I intend to remedy, if Rhedyth can in fact be saved. But if your presence here, sir, reflects the honest desire of your heart, I think you have very little evil in you to be altered."

"I just came here to get out of the rain," Coren said. Ailanthe looked up at him. His jaw was set, and he had a distant look to his eyes that told her he was upset about something. She didn't feel all that happy herself. Something was very wrong.

"I'm not sure I understand," she said. "These people, the ones who accept the token, they're...altered? They're not themselves anymore?"

"They are superior, young lady," Gweron said, turning to face her. His smile was broader now, his eyes full of joy. "With no more desire to do evil."

"But suppose they don't want to be different? What if they already wanted to do good?"

"Then Rhedyth ensures they may not be tempted. Its very name means 'freedom' in the ancient tongue from which I borrowed it. Freedom from fear, freedom from the possibility of choosing evil. Freedom to know one's every act is pure."

"My lady, you seem skeptical," Tristram said. "Do you not see how different the world would be if every man and woman could not but eschew evil?"

"I do, actually," Ailanthe said. A hollowness had opened up in her stomach. Gweron continued to look at her with eyes shining with passion. Tristram's expression wasn't much different.

"Tell me something, Gweron," Coren said, and his voice was emotionless. "Who decides what's good?"

Gweron raised one eyebrow. "I think good and evil are self-evident, sir."

"I've seen people lie and cheat and hurt people they supposedly loved and called it good because it all ended well," Coren said. "I don't think everyone agrees on the definition of 'good'. And I'm not sure making people do what you want just because you think you know what's best for them is good, either."

"Do not parents stop their children playing near the fire because they know as their children do not what it means to be burned?"

"Parents let their children grow up to find their own way. They don't hover over them their whole lives to make sure they never do anything bad."

"Parents have not the knowledge to do so. Rhedyth is perfect, or will be when I have restored it to its proper state. It knows the desires of the human heart and makes no mistakes in its transformations of men and women."

"I think what Coren is saying," Ailanthe said slowly, "is that the mistake is in thinking people need to be transformed at all."

Gweron frowned. "That is an uninformed and juvenile opinion, young lady."

"You told all this to the Castle, didn't you?" Ailanthe said. "I remember reading that. And that was when it started fighting you for control. It knew what you had in mind and it didn't like what you wanted it to do."

"Indeed. Because its intelligence and confinement in an inanimate body drove it mad."

"I don't think so." Ailanthe felt Coren's hand close around her upper arm. She couldn't look away from Gweron's eyes. The passionate light in them no longer looked unthreatening. "I think it knew what freedom meant and it didn't want to be the tool of your oppression."

The passionate light went furious. "Make no such accusation. You are ignorant of the world and its need. Rhedyth was to be its savior and it rejected that role."

"So it fought you," Ailanthe went on, everything finally falling into place. "It tried to keep you from completing it, and when that didn't work, it tried to sabotage your spell. And ultimately all it could do was trap you so you couldn't make the spell do what you wanted, but it couldn't turn it off entirely. It had to let people in, and it had to give them something, so it gave them junk and sent them out into the world. Unaltered, and unprotected, but at least they were still free."

"That is not what freedom is," Gweron said, coming toward her with his fists clenched. "Think you they are happy in their evil? Happy when their choices make them miserable? You cannot believe this fallen world is as destiny meant it to be?"

Coren put Ailanthe behind him. "I think it's better than the world you have in mind."

"My lady, you cannot believe this," Tristram said. "Think. How much sorrow will be avoided if this good man can repair the Castle?"

"I told you once I didn't like the idea of someone else choosing my path," Ailanthe said. "I like even less the idea of being turned into someone who doesn't have a choice at all."

"Then I feel pity for you," Gweron said. "Mean you not to aid me in my task?"

"No. And I'll fight you if you try to carry out your insane plan."

"Then it is past time I reclaim my power from you," Gweron said, and made as if to step around Coren. Coren grabbed his arm and twisted, making Gweron cry out in pain. "Run, Ailanthe," he said, as casually as if he'd asked her to take a walk with him. She turned and took a few rapid steps toward the door.

Tristram stepped into her path. "I am sorry, my lady, but I cannot allow you to rob this man of his rightful power," he said, and took hold of her wrist. She struggled to break free, but he took her other wrist and held her tight. He really did look sad, and Ailanthe, furious, kicked his shin as hard as she could. He staggered, but didn't let her go.

Coren was grappling with Gweron, whose sleeves had slid up to reveal arms corded with muscle. Coren was strong, but he seemed evenly matched, and Gweron might break free at any time. Panicking, Ailanthe reached inside herself for the memory of Coren being attacked by the shadows, closed her eyes, and let the light explode from within her.

The light burned bright pink behind her eyelids. Tristram exclaimed and released her. Instantly she made for the door, stumbling in her blindness, once catching herself before she tripped and fell on a chair. Squinting, she found the doorway and staggered through it. Behind her, more exclamations, and the sound of a fight breaking out. *Coren*, she thought once, then could only think of running.

She ran toward the tower before coming to her senses. She'd be trapped there. Coren wouldn't be able to fight two people off for long. She turned and bolted back toward the stairs, leaping down them two at a time and nearly tripping in her haste. *Where do I run?* She couldn't escape, couldn't risk trying the door that had never opened for her before.

She threw the lights on as she ran down the twisting stairs that crossed each other, and the shadows billowed up behind her, following her without attacking, never trying to block her path. It was as if they were herding her.

She reached the fifth floor landing, stopped to catch her breath, and heard running footsteps behind her. Fear gave her a second wind, and she had barely enough time to register that the shadows hadn't leaped on her, but had waited around the edges of her circle of light until she'd moved on. *But if the Castle isn't my enemy,* she thought, *then I shouldn't fear the shadows, except*—she couldn't forget the suffocating, choking feeling of their tendrils covering her face, the air-starved hallucinations of light. It might not be her enemy, but she didn't think it was her friend.

She shot off the stairs on the ground floor, skidded, then ran on, still not knowing where to go. Shadows moved in all directions except one; she followed the clear path, her breath coming painfully sharp in her chest. Through the museum rooms, in which mannequins stretched out their wooden arms toward her and weapons rattled against the glass of their display cases; through the empty rooms, where the walls glowed with magic; through the book room, with books flying free of their shelves and battering at her like so many leaves in a whirlwind.

She knew, by that time, where the Castle was herding her, and she burst out of the last room to see the dark flagstones and vaulted ceilings of the chamber that kept the heart of the Castle anchored to reality. The Honor Hall.

Lights shone brightly around the Hall, but the Hall itself was dark. Ailanthe realized the darkness was actually shadow; the Hall teemed with it, gray clouds like dust that bulged and billowed and sent tendrils out into the light surrounding it.

Ailanthe approached slowly. The light kept the broad passageway clear of the shadows, but they were behind her as well as ahead, and now she could hear a susurrus that sounded like speech, but in no language she knew. She felt as if the shadow was drawing her forward, and she wasn't sure which she was more afraid of, Gweron or the Castle, but she had to make a choice. And if Gweron had his way, choice was something she wouldn't have anymore.

Footsteps echoed on the flagstones behind her. She turned to see Gweron, his right temple bloody, running toward her, his hand outstretched. Without another thought, she turned and flung herself down the steps of the Honor Hall and leaped, arms wide, into the midst of the shadow.

CHAPTER TWENTY-THREE

Shadow enveloped her, buried her mouth and nose in freezing spider's silk; she gasped for air, and it threaded its way into her throat and chest until she couldn't breathe. The lights flashed before her eyes again, growing brighter and larger, and her head hurt and she had to breathe—

—and then her lungs were clear, and she drew a deep, bitterly cold breath that froze her lungs from the inside, but there was air, and her head was clear, and she was still alive. She was surrounded by gray shadow that cushioned her on all sides, and when she shivered, it moved with her.

She shivered again and realized she wasn't as cold as she'd been at first. In fact, she was growing comfortably warm, and her breath no longer felt like jagged glass inside her chest. She was upright, but she didn't feel like she was supporting her own weight; something held her up, her knees slightly bent and her arms extended on both sides. She lowered her arms, and felt something resist her movement slightly before giving way.

The lights still shone in front of her eyes, and she blinked to clear her vision, but they grew larger and began to merge with one another, white and gold, copper and black, until they coalesced into a humanoid figure standing, or floating, about five feet away from her. She was small and lithe, with very pale skin and very black eyes, and her hair was copper overlaid with a greenish patina. Her dress went through every possible shade of gold as she moved, glowing with magic as well as with its metallic sheen.

Ailanthe blinked again. "You're an elf," she said.

The figure regarded her with its huge black eyes. **This is a shape that makes sense to you,** it said without moving its lips. **Human and not human. Alien and familiar. It is as close to what I am as I may come.**

"Then...you're the Castle. Rhedyth."

I am that, and more.

"But you tried to kill me."

I tried to communicate with you. I would not have harmed you.

"What about untying the rope? What about the weapons? You tried to kill Coren!"

The rope was my mistake. I did not understand how it supported you. And I wrongly believed the man strove to prevent my reaching you. I attempted to speak with him as well, but you intervened.

"I didn't understand what you wanted. I still don't fully understand what you are."

I was made to make the destiny of mankind. I am Freedom.

"But that's what Gweron wanted. You didn't."

He saw a different world than the one you live in. So did I. We disagreed as to how that world might come to be. I live, and I choose. He would have trapped me as surely as he would those souls who came to me to be transformed. I chose otherwise.

Ailanthe tried to breathe normally. Her heart was still racing. "Why did you keep me here?"

Because you took the key. And because you had his power.

"The key gave me the power."

Rhedyth shook her head. **The power has always been yours. Gweron could not be allowed to leave. And I saw in you the possibility that I might be free again.**

"I don't understand."

Gweron's power made me. I cannot exist without him. If he leaves, I die. If he dies, I die. Your power can take its place.

Ailanthe couldn't speak. Too many thoughts crowded into her head at once. "I'm not borrowing Gweron's power?" she finally said.

No.

"But I'm no one special. There's never even been a *kerthor* in my family, let alone someone who could...could build something like you."

I have no answer for you. Gweron is. You are. It is what happens when the world is allowed to spin its own way. You are what I need.

The implications of what the Castle was saying started to bear down on her. Could this be why she'd lost her connection to the trees —lost it in exchange for this power? She dismissed the thought with a shake of her head. "But Gweron still has power. Even if I give you mine, he'll be able to fight you, and you'll still be at a standstill."

Not me. He will fight you. And you know me as no one else does. Gweron saw me only as a tool. You have seen what I may become. You have taken possession of much of what I am. You will turn his creation against him and rebuild the destiny spell as it should have been.

"Why can't I—you—just destroy it? It hasn't given anyone happiness in all these centuries." But then she thought of Usael, and his joy in his new home, and knew she was wrong.

I would die without it. I choose not to die.

Ailanthe hesitated before answering, very aware that she was at Rhedyth's mercy right then. "But if your death meant the end of Gweron's madness?"

It would mean the death of thousands, perhaps hundreds of thousands. My roots stretch throughout the world, in every land and under every sea. If I am destroyed, the earth will be torn apart. I choose to live. I choose for others to live.

"And...what will it do to me?"

You will become what you have always been. It is your choice.

Ailanthe drew a deep breath. "Then show me what to do."

Rhedyth bowed to her. **Take back this Castle,** she said, and vanished.

Ailanthe hung suspended in the grayness for a moment longer. Then she felt as if she'd exploded. She saw every inch of the Castle— she *was* the Castle, felt stone and wood when she flexed her fingers, glass between her toes and behind her eyes. She was in every room at once, from the armory to the tower, and it was as if she'd grown extra limbs, because every room was hers in the way her own skin and bones were.

A blink here, and the mannequins moved. A twitch of her finger, and weapons flew from the walls of the armory and shattered the glass of the display cases. She saw Coren running down the stairs just ahead of Tristram, both of them carrying swords in a way that would be fatal if either of them tripped, and she saw Gweron pacing the circumference of the Honor Hall, magic gathering in a halo around him.

The gray shadows disappeared, and she felt herself lowered to the shining floor of the Honor Hall, and saw Gweron through her own eyes as well as those million extra eyes the Castle gave her.

Gweron raised his hand, around which gathered a nimbus of light. "Give back my power," he said.

"It seems it wasn't yours in the first place," Ailanthe said. She felt the Castle surrounding her like armor. "And neither is Rhedyth."

He swung his arm, and Ailanthe staggered. He had so much more experience with this magic—but then, she had a Castle on her side. She reached with one of her many hands and took hold of the flagstone he stood on, and lifted, knocking him off his feet. He caught himself with that golden nimbus and leaped backward. "Trickery," he said.

"Power," she said, and ruffled the floor like a wave of rock, and this time Gweron did fall. She felt him land, and then she lost control of some of her limbs as he snatched them away from her. She fought him, lost more limbs, regained some, and then the weapons were there raining down upon him, and he lost his concentration.

Ailanthe backed up until she stood at the center of the Honor Hall; she knew where it was as surely as she knew the position of her own hand. Gweron swept his arm in front of him, and the weapons clattered with metallic rings and wooden thuds onto the flagstones. He came toward her, arm still outstretched.

"We need not fight," he said. "I have never known anyone like me before. Join with me, and we will make of this sorry world a new one. I swear it."

"You'd have to transform me to get me to go along with that plan."

"A small price for both of us to pay, methinks. You would be happy! Is that not what everyone dreams of?"

She remembered how it had felt when Coren kissed her, that first time, how it had swept away all the misery of thinking he would never care for her and been all the sweeter for it, and said, "Not at that price."

Gweron snarled at her, and she cried out as half her immaterial body vanished, snatched away by his will. The floor of the Honor Hall buckled, and she had to support herself with her extra hands or be knocked down. She struck back, and saw him stagger before he launched another attack. Despair crept over her. They were too evenly matched. They would exchange blows until one of them tired, and Gweron, with his greater experience, would probably come out on top.

At the edge of her awareness, she saw Coren stagger into the passage, followed closely by Tristram. He turned and brought his sword up barely in time to block Tristram's swing. He looked tired, but worse, Ailanthe could see immediately he was no match for Tristram's swordsmanship. He was going to be killed, and she couldn't do anything about it. To her surprise, instead of sorrow, she felt fury. He'd never done anything to the Castle or to Gweron and he was only in this fight because of her. If anyone in this mess deserved to survive, it was Coren.

She let that fury carry her through Gweron's next attack and past his defenses. She remembered how it had felt to take control of the Castle, piece by piece, and flexing muscles she'd never guessed she had, she took hold of everything in Gweron's power and wrenched it out of his grasp. With her physical eyes, she saw him clutch at his heart, swaying, and in his moment of distraction she bore down on him with all the might of the Castle behind her. He screamed and fell to his knees.

Coren and Tristram stopped in their fight to look in Gweron's direction, both startled by the agony in the man's voice. But Tristram recovered first, and brought his sword up in a wide arc aimed at Coren's head. "No!" Ailanthe shouted, and her immaterial hands picked Tristram up and flung him far across the room. Gweron rose to his feet and suddenly the power of the Castle turned into a stony weight that crushed Ailanthe into the ground.

She heard Coren shout from very far away, and she cast about for something, anything, she could use. *The key*, she thought, irrationally, and remembered the Castle couldn't kill Gweron, only transform him. She looked up to see him standing over her, could see her reflection in his eye like a mad glassy orb, and that triggered another memory. She reached out, whether physically or not, she couldn't tell, and took hold of Gweron himself, and twisted.

Gweron vanished. Something went *tink* on the flagstones. It was a glass ball filled with water in which floated a red rose, half-open and frozen in its state of perfection. She had a moment to register what had happened, and then Gweron's power slammed into her.

He hadn't been using his full power before, she realized, and now he was angry and terrified, and she couldn't hold him for very long. She saw Coren running toward her, his outline rimmed with black as she began to lose consciousness, and she shouted, "*Smash it!*" as loudly as she could, which wasn't very loudly at all. Coren gave her one horrified glance, raised his sword, and brought it down on the glass ball.

Everything went white. Ailanthe's head cleared, her breathing returned to normal, and then the white faded to gray and she was within the heart of Rhedyth again. The elf looked at her silently. Around them, the gray mist shuddered, shaking Ailanthe as if the world itself were moving.

The magic is gone, Rhedyth said. **You must replace it or we will all die.**

"Then take it! Take my magic. It's not like I'll miss it."

Rhedyth shook her head. The shadows shuddered again, harder this time. **I cannot take what is not yours to give. You are the magic. You must take Gweron's place within these walls.**

"I don't understand," Ailanthe said, but it was a lie. She understood too well. "If I do this…I'll never leave here again, will I."

You will be the Castle. The Castle cannot leave itself.

"But I just want to go home."

If you leave, there will be no home to go to.

Fear and anger and sorrow overwhelmed her so much she couldn't even cry. Never to see home again. Never even to let the trees reject her. "What do I do?" she said.

You have already done it, Rhedyth said, and Ailanthe screamed as the full power of the Castle filled her. She was the Castle again, but now it was becoming her as well, its magic transforming both of them until she couldn't tell whether she was flesh or stone. She saw everywhere at once, every place the Castle had put down roots, every time in which the Castle existed, saw Gweron laying the first two stones and, in the far distant future, the Castle ablaze with magical fire.

She screamed with all her voices until one of them went hoarse and then silent, and she followed that voice back to herself and found her body suspended in the gray shadows, exhausted and weeping with pain. "Is that all?" she rasped, then laughed painfully at how nonchalant her words sounded, when what she meant was *Please, no more.*

It is enough. Look now, and see what you have become.

Ailanthe looked, blinked, and looked again. She still had her physical body, and it still moved when she willed it to, but overlaid on that were those million eyes and thousands upon thousands of hands, fingers, legs, and ears. She turned her head and saw dozens of rooms pass before her eyes; blinked again, and hundreds of windows showed her glimpses of the lands they looked out on. She blinked a final time, and those senses retreated to hover just past the limits of her perception, and she knew she could call them up again whenever she wanted. It was...extraordinary. Terrifying, and beautiful.

I am strong. You are strong. We are strong together. But there is rot at our heart.

"The destiny spell. Can I unmake it?"

It is our heart. To unmake it would be to destroy us, with all that entails.

"Then what can we do?"

Rewrite it. Turn it into what it should have been. Gweron wanted a world full of unthinking goodness. We will make it a world full of heroes. Men and women who come here seeking guidance and leave with new purpose, having chosen their destiny.

"I don't know how to do that. I've never been good at knowing what was best for people."

I know their hearts. You know their destinies. You need only think.

"But destinies—" She went silent. If you thought of destiny as something you couldn't escape, she knew nothing of that. But if you thought of destiny in terms of the things every person ultimately wanted...there weren't very many of those. "Love," she said. "Fame. Power. Adventure. Knowledge, maybe." She thought of Coren. "And some people just want to go home."

Then we shall offer them these things. They will choose, and in choosing let their choice transform them as *they* will, not as we think they should be.

"What if they don't? I mean, what if they use our guidance selfishly, or for evil?"

That is how Gweron thought. It is the risk we take for the sake of those who choose good over evil.

Ailanthe licked her lips, which had gone very dry. "I don't know how to do it, though."

I will show you. And then we will show the world.

Ailanthe was suddenly the Castle again, but looking deep inward, into a place where the Honor Hall seemed somehow inverted, insides surrounding the yellow stone walls. At the center of this not-place lay a tangle of magic, a loose skein of yellow string that threaded through the walls in a pattern Ailanthe almost recognized. **What makes up the spell is right**, Rhedyth said. **It is the pattern that is wrong. See, touch, taste. Know the pattern, and you will know how it should change.**

The idea of tasting the yellow-white magic appalled Ailanthe, but she took Rhedyth to mean she should embrace the pattern with all of her senses, so she did so, following the strands—or was there only one strand?—to their ends and back again, taking them into herself until she could feel the strands threaded through her new body, their slippery-smooth texture like oiled metal.

Gradually, she came to see how the pattern wove together. It really was simple, she thought, teasing one of the strands into a new configuration. Gweron had gotten most of it right; he'd just been wrong about all the important things.

As she wove, she thought of her sister at her loom, and her heart sank. She would never see her sister again except through Usael's eyes. She'd never find out which city it was that lay beyond the desert.

The weaving trembled, and she took control of herself. She'd made her choice, and it was the right one, so there was no sense getting weepy about it. She wondered what Coren would think about her never being able to leave. She could probably open a door for him near his home, so he could visit his family whenever he liked, and she was rather fond of the window room. It wasn't going to be so bad.

"I think it's done," she finally said, "but I'm not sure."

We will know when the first hero comes, Rhedyth said, **but I think it is sound.**

"Can I return to my body now?"

You are the Castle. The Castle is you. It is as much your body as your physical self.

"Yes, but I don't want to be the Castle all the time." That would certainly put Coren off.

You may take either form whenever each is needed. Rhedyth bowed to her again. **And...I thank you.**

Ailanthe didn't know how to bow in her current state. She also didn't know how to turn back into what she thought of as herself, whatever Rhedyth might say. She searched down all her many arms and eyes until she found a throat that was still scratchy and raw, and settled into the body surrounding it—and fell to the floor of the Honor Hall before she could get her unfamiliar legs underneath her.

"Ow," she said, standing unsteadily, then looked around. She heard no sounds of battle or shouting. "Coren?" she called out, carefully climbing the stairs. She hoped she wouldn't need to become the Castle very often, or, if she did, that she'd learn to handle the transition more gracefully. "Coren?"

A pile of glass shards, a puddle and a wilting rose were all that was left of Gweron. Coren wasn't there. She didn't see Tristram either. She went toward the grand staircase, calling both their names, but no one responded. She reached out and took hold of the Castle, not letting it overcome her, but seeing through its stones into every room and out every window. She found Miriethiel, sunning himself on a windowsill in the Eshkian museum room, but no one else.

She was the only human being in the Castle.

"Rhedyth," she called out, "where are Coren and Tristram?" No answer. "Rhedyth!" She raced back to the Honor Hall, reflecting that she'd need to learn to talk to Rhedyth from wherever she happened to be. She hopped down the stairs and let herself be filled with the sense of place she now identified with the Castle's heart. "Where are they?"

I gave them their heart's desires.

Ailanthe felt the blood drain from her face. "What do you mean? Where's Coren?"

I do not know names. The tall one wished for glory in battle, so I sent him to Agranar, where he will kill or be killed as may be. The other wanted to go home, and that is where he went.

"You sent him back to Hespera?"

It was his heart's desire. He never belonged here. And he killed Gweron. A fitting reward for him, I think.

Ailanthe sat down on the steps and hugged her knees. "It couldn't have been." *He said he loved me.*

Rhedyth didn't need her to speak to know her thoughts. **You were not uppermost in his thoughts,** she said.

Ailanthe felt as if Rhedyth had slapped her. "No?"

I gave him what he truly wanted. It is what I was made to do. He chose.

"And he didn't choose me," Ailanthe whispered. It shouldn't have been a surprise. He'd been saying it all along. Even their first night together—he'd said he'd even put up with that horrible woman, Dey-whatever it was, if he could only be home again. He might have loved her, but he loved Hespera more. He'd made his choice, and so had she. And now she was going to be alone here forever.

Stupid, she told herself, *he'd only known you a few weeks, and you were the first woman he'd seen in six years, however he might say that wasn't the reason. He probably even thought it was true.*

She rose, dashing tears from her eyes, and without thinking about it made her mind stretch toward the bedroom she'd slept in her first night in the Castle, and let it draw her body along after it. Then she was in the room, and she turned off the lights with a thought and collapsed onto the bed, and fell into unconsciousness or sleep.

CHAPTER TWENTY-FOUR

*A*ilanthe didn't actually need the Castle bell to know when someone was approaching Rhedyth, but she didn't like having to maintain the low-level connection to the Castle that would require. It had been five weeks, but she still hated it for sending Coren away, hated Coren for wanting to leave, hated herself for wishing she could have made him stay—but that was against everything she and Rhedyth had chosen, so mostly she just hated herself.

She had five minutes after the bell rang before the front door opened. One of her first actions had been to put a thumb plate and latch on the inside. You couldn't exactly be a beacon of free choice while you were locking people in.

I'll let this one wander a bit, meet him at the Honor Hall, she thought, summoning a silk gown from the crowded dressing room behind what Rhedyth had told her was the theater. Then Rhedyth had had to explain what theater was. Ailanthe wondered if she could somehow contact a troupe of players, get them to put on a show for one person.

The gown buttoned up the back, not a problem when you had a thousand invisible hands, not to mention several hundred sprites.

Giving them commands had turned out to be pathetically easy, and Ailanthe still groaned when she thought of how she hadn't figured it out on her own. She turned one of the windows mirrored and examined her reflection. She looked serene. It was a hard-won expression as well as a lie. She combed her hair, which still had a tendency to frizz out around her face even if she was a part-time Castle, and decided to walk down the stairs instead of whisking herself there.

Three sprites came to join her as she descended. They were still oblivious to everything around them unless she commanded them, but they seemed drawn to her with a sort of magnetic pull. She guessed it was because they recognized Gweron's power, or the power they had in common. They weren't very good company.

Miriethiel, on the other hand, always appeared when she called, and she suspected he had some link to Rhedyth that let him slip between walls the way she did. He slept on her bed and tucked himself under her chin when she cried at night.

After the first week, in which two heroes had come and gone, she'd considered altering the rooms' arrangement to give visitors a straighter path to the Honor Hall, but Rhedyth had gone paler than usual when she suggested it, and Ailanthe had given up the idea. She felt her front door open and close, and diverted part of her attention to observing the...it was a man, someone from Galendan, which still made her cringe.

She never looked at Tristram's book, didn't even know if he was still alive, but she hoped he was getting plenty of beatings in Agranar, anything to make him see the world more clearly. And because he'd tried to kill Coren, but she didn't think of Coren much at all these days. Nights were a different story.

The Galendishman was taking the long route through the mauve and violet sitting room, the Cabinet, and the Indrijanese museum room. Ailanthe crossed the flagstones and went to stand at the exact center of the Honor Hall. Being there felt strange, like having a weight above her navel both pulling her down and lifting her up simultaneously. She was at the center of her center, and she tried not to resent it.

Soon the Galendishman came into view. Fortunately for her peace of mind, he looked nothing like Tristram, being rather stout and with brown hair cut unattractively short. He was about halfway across the flagstones, his footsteps echoing off the vaulted ceiling, when he saw her, and his mouth dropped open. "Hi," she said. "I'm Ailanthe. Why don't you come down here, and we can talk."

"You are the spirit of the Castle," he said, almost inaudibly—or would have been if Ailanthe hadn't had all those extra ears.

"That's mostly true. Will you join me?"

He came around the side of the Hall and descended the stairs. "Oh Spirit," he began.

"That's not necessary. The Castle knows what you want. The question is—do *you*?"

He looked puzzled. "My lady, I believed the Castle chose for me. Its wisdom is as much greater than mine as the sun is to the stars."

"What's your name?"

"Damien, my lady."

"Damien, the Castle exists to show you possibilities. It can offer you choices based on what it reads in your heart. You're the one who has to choose."

He swallowed. "My lady, that is a heavy burden."

"Choice usually is. Here, stand with me." She offered him her hand and drew him to stand next to her. Across the room, empty windows filled with images that flickered almost too fast to be distinguishable. Damien looked from one to the other, his expression going from awe to fear almost as fast as the images themselves.

"Each of these is a path you might take," Ailanthe said. "You can see the possibilities along each path. See, there's one in which you meet your true love and spend a lifetime together, raising a family."

"But she has no face," Damien protested.

"That's because it's not certain who she is, only that if you take that path, you *will* find her," Ailanthe said. "On this path, you become a powerful ruler, and here you find the answers you're searching for... do you understand?"

"I believe I do, my lady. And I choose...how?"

"Touch the window you want."

He walked over to the images and examined each window closely. He took so long about it Ailanthe became impatient. She wanted to read more of Usael's story now; his wedding day was fast approaching. Her sister had been weaving the fabric for Elara's dress for three weeks. Finally, Damien stretched out his hand and laid it flat against one of the windows. It popped like a soap bubble, and the other images faded away. Ailanthe hadn't been paying attention, so she didn't know which one he'd chosen, but Damien certainly looked happy about it.

"Give me your right hand," she said when he returned to her, and turned his arm so his wrist faced upward. "You came here because you wanted a destiny," she said. "The Castle exists to show you how to use that destiny to make the world better, in small or great ways. It can't force you to choose good. Your path is your own. But this token should remind you of why you came here in the first place, on those days when that path seems unclear."

She laid her palm on the inside of his wrist and closed her fingers around it, squeezed, and Damien winced. When she removed her hand, there was a circle about an inch wide glowing yellow-white against his fair skin, with a word written in tiny letters around its circumference. Damien raised his arm. "'Freedom,'" he read.

"It's the Castle's name," Ailanthe said. "Do you have any other questions?"

He lowered his arm and bowed to her. "Tell me your name again," he said.

"Ailanthe."

He took her hand and kissed it, making her flinch in memory. "You are the fairest creature I have ever seen," he said, "and I would that you would offer me a token of your own, to carry with me into dark places."

"That glows," Ailanthe said, pointing.

"I had in mind something a little more...personal," he said, and put his other arm around her waist and drew her in to kiss her, hard, his tongue thrusting against her lips. His hand slid down to grasp her bottom, squeezing unpleasantly.

She drew the Castle around her in one swift thought and *shoved*, hard, sending the Galendishman flying across the Hall and striking one of the window arches so hard she heard his head bounce. "Eewww!" she shouted, resuming her human form, then screamed inarticulate rage until the ceiling quivered.

She summoned an entire dinner service of delicate china and flung plate after cup at the walls, letting all of her pain and sorrow turn into fury that she smashed into shining pieces, littering the well-waxed floor with doubled images. When the last dish was shattered, she sat on the floor and cried.

I am sorry, Rhedyth said.

"Why didn't you see that in him? How can you not know that he's a horrible person?"

He is not evil, merely stupid. And it was his choice to make.

"Where are we sending him? Are we sending him someplace awful? Please say it's someplace awful."

He wanted power. He is going to Eshkor. They will teach him to respect women or he will die for not learning the lesson. If he does not die, he will become a fair and just leader.

"He's probably going to die. I hope he does."

We are not punitive. And you do not.

Ailanthe looked at the unconscious body. "No, I don't. But that's two in the last two weeks who've tried to assault me. Sometimes I think...no, I don't."

You think Gweron was right.

"He wasn't right. But it's not hard to see why he thought he was." Ailanthe gripped the man's collar and took both of them to the Vestibule, where she slapped him awake and tried not to take too much pleasure in it. Damien stirred, groaned, rubbed the back of his head, then looked up at her in fear. "My lady—" he began.

"Shut up. No more 'my lady' unless you intend to treat me like one. Now listen." Ailanthe drew in a deep breath. "Where you're going, women are respected in ways no Galendishman ever thought of. If you try that on one of them, you're going to lose a body part. I'll let you guess which one. The Castle gave you a choice. If you choose wrong, it's on you. Now go through that door and don't ever come back here again."

She flicked a thought at the magic on his wrist and it flared white, making him hiss in pain. "That's to remember what I've just said. And I hope...I really hope you have a long and wonderful life." *And not the short, painful one I see in your short, painful future.*

She held the Vestibule's inner door open for him and watched him walk down the short corridor and out the door onto the steppes, where it was a gray day that promised a late spring storm. But the grass was already coming in green, she saw before he shut the door, and soon it would be summer, and the tribes would be on the move again. The year rolled on, even inside these stony walls, and she could see it from any window she chose.

She shut the inner door and trudged back across the blue mosaic floor, the gold tiles a colder contrast against her bare feet to the cool ceramic. Today the hall made her feel like she was underwater. *Could she drown, now?* Not that she'd have the chance to find out, unless she got into the pool-sized tub in the forest glade bathroom and sank down to the bottom...no, that was too much like suicide.

She let her many hands undress her and walked in her under-clothes back to the dressing room, allowing the long walk to remind her that she was still human, mostly. She dressed in her own clothes and then stood in the theater for a while, gazing at the stage with its heavy red curtains of tattered velvet. It was in disrepair because that was how Gweron remembered it, and Ailanthe considered mending the curtains, but decided it wasn't worth the trouble.

She looked around at the high ceiling, painted with cherubs dressed as natives of every known country, surrounding a blue sky with white clouds. The gilding of the molding and baseboards was chipped, too, and some of the chairs had stuffing coming out of the seams. If she did find a way to bring a troupe here, she'd mend every-thing then. Otherwise, it was a waste of her time.

She trudged up all the stairs, resolutely didn't look at the arched doorway to Coren's suite, and went to the tower. She *had* repaired this, finished the walls and set in a beautiful spiral staircase of cast iron painted white, with a handrail gently twisted to give a more secure grip. She'd also put in new cushions covered in soft green velvet to match the leaves of Lindurien.

She still couldn't tell which tree was home, so she chose one in the right direction and marked a spot on the glass to identify it. With Gweron gone, the magic that had forced the Castle to set everything right at midnight—a part of keeping him in key form, Rhedyth had explained—was no longer active. Now Ailanthe could make as many messes as she wanted, but mostly she cleaned up after herself.

She leaned against the glass and tapped the mark with her fingertip. She still hadn't learned all the Castle's secrets, mainly because she didn't know which questions to ask. She was afraid to use the cooking Things Rhedyth had shown her; the box that heated itself and then heated the food made her nervous.

On the other hand, she'd discovered a lens setting that made distant things seem close, and she sometimes spent hours watching things through the windows, birds and distant animals, though there were never any people. Wherever Gweron had anchored the Castle, it was in places far from human settlement. He'd at least meant people to really want to come to the Castle, whatever else he might have planned for them.

She never looked at the city beyond the desert. She was never going back to those rooms again, not after the second night when she'd returned to her bed and it had still smelled like him, and she'd cried so hard she couldn't breathe.

She put her feet up and summoned Usael's book. It felt like spying on him, even if she only saw what everyone else in the mother tree did and carefully skipped the parts where he and Elara were intimate, but it was also her only way to see home. She was so desperate for home she was willing to risk the dubious morality of watching it over someone else's shoulder.

Where was she? Wedding. Right. They were both so happy, and it cheered her to see how her people had welcomed Usael so fully. Pity she was never going to meet him. She turned a page. "Rhedyth," she said absently, "what destiny did you give Usael?"

True love.

"Did he know that's what he was getting?"

No. Of course not. I could not speak to him, explain what would happen. He thought he wanted knowledge, but in his heart he wanted his life's companion. I am happy he achieved both.

"So am I." The magic that gave Rhedyth such insight was far beyond Ailanthe's power; she thought it might have been beyond Gweron too, something the Castle had gained as it became self-aware. Perhaps if you had no desires of your own, you were more clearly able to see the desires of others. But no, Rhedyth had wanted more than anything to be free to make her own choices. The only one who hadn't gotten her heart's desire was Ailanthe...or had she, and not known it?

She had wanted to regain her balance, to be in tune with the trees again, but if this magic had taken the place of that connection, did that mean what she wanted—what she had always wanted without knowing it—was to become the Castle? Suppose *this* was her heart's desire? She was afraid to ask Rhedyth, realized Rhedyth would know what she was thinking, and said, "Don't tell me."

As you wish.

Ailanthe realized she'd read the same line five times without understanding it, and closed the book. In Lindurien, the skies were clear; in Eshkor, the storm might have rolled in already. Whatever weather she wanted, she only had to look out the right window. She stood, took one last look at her home, and descended the stairs.

When she was halfway down, the Castle bell tolled. She stopped with her hand on the spiral railing and sighed. They seemed to be coming more often these last two weeks. Two in one day, though, that was a first. Well, she wasn't getting dressed up for this one. She would meet him, give him the speech, and see him on his way. Then she would eat something, and then read the afternoon away.

At least she didn't have to worry about running out of books. Or...

she remembered what Gweron had written, about not knowing how long he might live, and she had to bite back a scream at the thought of being here alone for several lifetimes. She released the railing, which she'd had in a death grip, and went slowly down the stairs. No more slipping between walls for today. She was still human. Mostly.

She was on the second floor landing, where four stairs met and crossed, when she felt the front door open. She kept her attention resolutely focused inward. If it was another Galendishman, she didn't want to know about it until she couldn't avoid it any longer. Then, distantly, she heard someone shout, "Ailanthe? *Ailanthe!*"

"Coren," she whispered. It wasn't him. He couldn't be here. She put both hands on the railing to keep from falling, and reached out— male, Hesperan, very agitated, taking the shortest route to the Honor Hall—

"*Coren!*" she screamed, and flung herself through the Castle to end up in front of the Honor Hall in time for him to come racing across the flagstones and nearly bowl her over. He stopped in time, took her face between his hands and kissed her with a kind of desperate hunger that made her cling to him, sobbing, five weeks of heartache vanishing in that moment.

His cheeks bristled with three days' growth of beard that scratched her face, and she kissed him harder, welcoming even that touch. She threaded her fingers through the hair at the base of his neck and drew him closer as Coren did the same, kissing her as if he never meant to stop.

His fingers brushed her cheeks and came away wet, and he broke away long enough to say, "What does it mean that my kisses always make you cry?"

She shook her head. "You didn't want me," she said. "You wanted Hespera."

He looked stunned. "I want you more than anything."

"No, you didn't. The Castle knew your heart's desire. That's why it sent you home."

Coren grimaced. "Yes, but I assumed you'd be with me when I went there," he said. "It's a building, Ailanthe. A magical, powerful building, but I'm not sure how well it really understands the human heart."

Ailanthe wiped more tears from her eyes. "Rhedyth!" she shouted.

Silence, then, **I can see where I might have...made a mistake.** She sounded embarrassed.

"You realize we can't represent ourselves as knowing the heart's desire if this is the kind of result we give, right?"

"Are you talking to the Castle?" Coren asked, looking as if he thought she'd gone insane.

"Yes. Sort of. It's like talking to myself, only I answer back. What are you going to do about it?"

"About you talking to yourself?"

"That was addressed to Rhedyth. Well?"

I will look more closely in the future. It is clear that sometimes the human heart deeply wants things that are well tangled together. In my defense, had I known his true desire, I still could not have sent you with him. And I am certain this has never happened before.

"Well, it can't happen again."

"Ailanthe, I don't hear anything."

"I know." She laid her cheek against his bristly one, feeling lighter than she had in weeks. "All this time, I thought you didn't love me."

"I'm sorry it took so long. I went to Lindurien first. I thought if the Castle had sent me home, it might have done the same for you. But I met—I couldn't believe this—I met your father—"

"But Usael's book never—"

"I didn't see Usael. It took some doing to communicate with your father, but we each spoke a little Enthalian and I managed to explain what I was after, and he said you hadn't been back in months. So I took a chance and came here." He held her close, his hands stroking the small of her back. "And you thought I'd abandoned you."

"Thank you for coming back for me."

"Thank *you* for waiting in the one place I'd know to look for you." He withdrew to arm's length and took her hand in his. "Let's go. I'd like you to meet my family. My brother has two sons now, and he's gotten so fat—the whole time I was there, I wanted so badly for you to be with me."

"How long were you there?"

"Twelve hours. Long enough to sleep, eat, and borrow some money from my brother in between trading silent glares with my father, who still hasn't forgiven me for running off in the middle of the night like that. But then, he wanted me to marry Deyanara." Coren made a face. "There's a town a day's walk south of here where I think we can find a ride."

"No, Coren, I can't..." She pulled her hand free of his. "I have to explain something to you, and you might change your mind about me once you understand."

Coren tilted her head up so he could kiss her again. "I am *never*," he said when he released her, "going to change my mind about you."

"I hope not." She took a deep breath, reached out for his hand again, and drew them through the Castle until they were both standing in the window room. Coren staggered and clutched at her shoulder to keep his balance. "I...on second thought, I should have warned you I was going to do that," she said, "but I couldn't think how to explain it, so I decided to show you. This is part of what I am now."

"You really do have magic like Gweron's," Coren gasped.

Ailanthe shook her head. "I mean, yes, I do, and that's why...let's sit down, and you have to promise me you won't say anything, or ask questions, until I'm done, because it's a little complicated."

She used her extra arms to drag a couple of the blocky chairs together, making Coren's mouth hang open in surprise at seeing them fly about on their own, then sat next to him, his hand in both of hers, and told him everything Rhedyth had told her that night. As promised, he sat silent, watching her as she spoke, his face impassive. When she was finished, he withdrew his hand gently and said, "Well."

His voice was as impassive as his face, and it left Ailanthe feeling sick and afraid. "Do you understand all of that?"

He pursed his lips and nodded. "You're the Castle. You can't leave or it will be destroyed. And it will wreck most of the world if it's destroyed."

"That's it." He still looked so distant. She looked over his shoulder at the desert window. A rare storm was coming in, rain, not sand, and she wished she were alone already, that he would say whatever it was he was thinking and leave, and then she could watch the rain and see what the desert looked like afterward.

"Well," he said again. "I suppose I'll have to bring my family here to meet you, instead."

She stared at him. "What?"

"Well, I assume if you're the Castle, you can let people in who don't want a destiny, or whatever it is you do with questers now, and let them go home again. I could probably bring your family here too, now that I know where the tree is. I don't suppose you can control where the door opens? It would be far more convenient if I didn't have to walk three weeks to get back to my parents' house. And when we have children, we'll need a midwife—oh, I should probably have asked if you want children before I started making that plan." He looked worried. "You do want children, don't you? Or will being the Castle make that unlikely?"

Ailanthe's head spun. "Coren—"

"Ailanthe, the whole time you were talking, you had this look that said you were waiting for me to flee screaming just because you've changed a little. I told you. You're still you. I still see you behind those beautiful eyes of yours." Coren laid his hand gently along her cheek. "I love you. If you can still love me now that you're a powerful magical being as well as a woman, then I don't think we have a problem."

"Coren," Ailanthe said again, this time laughing.

He ran his thumb across her cheek again. "More tears," he said. "It's enough to make a lesser man nervous."

She buried her face in his chest. "I love you," she said.

"I love you, Ailanthe." He held her close for a moment, then stood and swept her up off the chair and into his arms, making her shriek with laughter. "Now, can you tell the Castle to stop watching for a while? Because I'm not sure I want an audience for what I'm planning next."

"I'm the Castle, Coren. She always knows what I'm thinking."

He kissed her, slowly, sending her heart racing. "Then I guess we'll give her a show."

ABOUT THE AUTHOR

Melissa McShane is the author of many fantasy novels, including the novels of Tremontane, the first of which is *Servant of the Crown;* The Extraordinaries series, beginning with *Burning Bright;* and *The Book of Secrets,* first book in The Last Oracle series. She lives in the shelter of the mountains out West with her husband, four children and a niece, and three very needy cats. She wrote reviews and critical essays for many years before turning to fiction, which is much more fun than anyone ought to be allowed to have.

You can visit her at her website **www.melissamc shanewrites.com** for more information on other books.

For news, new release announcements, and other fun stuff, sign up for Melissa's newsletter **here.**

If you enjoyed this book, please consider leaving a review at your favorite online retailer or on Goodreads.

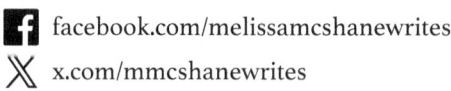

facebook.com/melissamcshanewrites
x.com/mmcshanewrites

ALSO BY MELISSA MCSHANE

WARMASTER

Warmaster 1: Dungeon Spiteful

Warmaster 2: Winter's Peril

Warmaster 3: Gamboling Coil

Warmaster 4: Sorrowvale (forthcoming August 2024)

THE BOOKS OF THE DARK GODDESS

Silver and Shadow

Missing by Moonlight

Shades of the Past

Path of the Paladin

Bright Moon Deception (forthcoming 2024)

THE LAST ORACLE

The Book of Secrets

The Book of Peril

The Book of Mayhem

The Book of Lies

The Book of Betrayal

The Book of Havoc

The Book of Harmony

The Book of War

The Book of Destiny

THE LIVING ORACLE

Hidden Realm

Hidden Enemy

Hidden Pursuit (forthcoming)

THE EXTRAORDINARIES

Burning Bright

Wondering Sight

Abounding Might

Whispering Twilight

Liberating Fight

Beguiling Birthright

Soaring Flight

Discerning Insight

THE NOVELS OF TREMONTANE

Pretender to the Crown

Guardian of the Crown

Champion of the Crown

Ally of the Crown

Stranger to the Crown

Scholar of the Crown

Servant of the Crown

Exile of the Crown

Rider of the Crown

Agent of the Crown

Voyager of the Crown

Tales of the Crown

COMPANY OF STRANGERS

Company of Strangers

Stone of Inheritance

Mortal Rites

Shifting Loyalties

Sands of Memory

Call of Wizardry

THE DRAGONS OF MOTHER STONE

Spark the Fire

Faith in Flames

Ember in Shadow

Skies Will Burn

THE CONVERGENCE TRILOGY

The Summoned Mage

The Wandering Mage

The Unconquered Mage

THE BOOKS OF DALANINE

The Smoke-Scented Girl

The God-Touched Man

Emissary

Warts and All: The Deluxe Expanded Edition

The View from Castle Always

Winter Across Worlds: A Holiday Collection

www.ingramcontent.com/pod-product-compliance
Lightning Source LLC
Chambersburg PA
CBHW071314250626
47159CB00004B/1420